# UNFORGIVABLE ACTS

## LAURA SNIDER

Severn River
PUBLISHING

Severn River Publishing
www.SevernRiverPublishing.com

ISBN: 978-1-64875-177-6 (Paperback)
ISBN: 978-1-64875-178-3 (Hardcover)

# ALSO BY LAURA SNIDER

**Ashley Montgomery Legal Thrillers**

Unsympathetic Victims

Undetermined Death

Unforgivable Acts

Unsolicited Contact

Never miss a new release! Sign up to receive exclusive updates from author Laura Snider.

**SevernRiverPublishing.com/Laura-Snider**

*For my mother, Madonna Mergenmeier.*

*My world is surrounded by inspirational women, but you were the first.*

*Thank you for being you.*

# PROLOGUE

The air was heavy. Thick with humidity and laced with electricity. A storm was coming. She could feel it all around her, gathering strength. Heavy clouds billowed in from the west, blanketing the sky. Rolling in over the treetops, swallowing the early morning sun, bringing respite from the already intense summer heat. Rain, long awaited, would soon come tumbling from the darkened sky, but she paid little attention to the shift in weather.

Her gaze was trained on the Chevy Silverado trundling down the winding gravel drive. It was blood-red with rust cresting over all four wheel wells. The truck moved quickly, but the driver handled the vehicle with the grace and ease of someone intimately familiar with the curvy driveway. It was close enough now for her to see the driver's face through the bug-stained windshield. His sharp cheekbones and stubbled jawline were all too familiar to her. A dream of a man that later turned into a nightmare.

The vehicle bounced around the final curve, kicking up dust. She pursed her lips and pushed her body back, shrinking farther into the heavy foliage surrounding the ten-acre wooded lot. Twigs scratched at her arms and ripped at her clothes. She stopped when the jagged points of her spine pressed against the rough bark of a wide tree. She glanced to her left to see a poison oak plant curving around the tree trunk, but she didn't shrink away. A rash was the least of her worries.

The truck came to a stop near a large red barn. It was the main structure on the property. Aside from the barn, there was one small outbuilding. It stood almost directly behind the barn, and everyone called it "the shed." Both structures were sturdy but in need of a paint job. Red flakes peeled away from the wood in long strips, curling under the humidity and heat of the summer. A rotting exterior to match the wicked deeds that occurred within.

The driver's side door creaked open, catching her attention. The driver rose so he was standing on the truck's running board. "Frank," the woman hissed through gritted teeth. His gaze swung past her without stopping, and hate flowed through her. She wanted to kill him, but she couldn't. At least not yet.

When Frank had looked all around him, he nodded as though satisfied that he was alone, and he hopped down, his cowboy boots crunching in the gravel. He walked toward the bed of the truck, and her eyes followed his familiar gait. Step, shuffle, step, shuffle, always favoring his right leg. It was an ancient injury, a wound from the old days. Back before he started using the shake-and-bake method of cooking. When it was dangerous to be anywhere near an active lab. When one tiny spark or the incorrect amount of pressure could cause the air within an entire building to explode, raining fireballs of glass and chemicals.

The tailgate dropped with a heavy thud, and Frank leaned

forward, gripping several two-liter bottles, clasping them in his hands carefully, almost affectionately. The woman shuffled where she stood, shifting her weight from one foot to the other, waking her joints, readying herself. The bottles were not the reason that she'd come. But they were so close. Not more than fifty paces away. And she hadn't used in what felt like forever, thanks to her legal troubles.

She was really trying to be good this time. The judge had told her to "abstain from mood-altering substances," and that's what she had been doing. She was tired of letting everyone down, including her attorney, Ashley Montgomery. But now that she was in the presence of it—the drug that had dragged her to the ground—she felt that familiar need, the want. It raged through her body with the kind of power that drowned out all other thoughts. One hit was all she needed to take the edge off. Just one.

But no, she couldn't think like that. Dope was how he controlled her. How he had taken everything precious from her. And she was allowing him to control her even now, when he didn't even know she was there. She brought her hand up and smacked herself in the head, trying to rattle the desire out of her thoughts.

*Focus, focus, focus, you fool*, she told herself. One wrong move here, and she'd be dead.

Frank carried the bottles toward the barn, setting one on the ground while he lifted the heavy steel bar that rested across the barn door. Frank's barn did not look like a barn on the inside, but that bar outside the door, the one meant to keep animals inside, had never been modified. He'd furnished the inside of the building like a home and added additional indoor locks to keep others out, but that bar across the door— that was used when he wanted to keep someone inside.

The barn door creaked as Frank pushed it open, grunting

under the weight of the heavy wooden doors. In his distraction, she saw her window of opportunity. She needed to catch him off guard. If she didn't, he could easily overpower her, and her plan would die before she had barely begun to put it into motion. She popped up from the darkness, sprinting with everything she had, her skinny legs pumping, taking her nearer and nearer to the barn.

Even though she had thought it out, she now realized that her "plan" had more than a few faults. It was a decision driven by desperation rather than preparation. She hadn't considered the crackle of fallen leaves under her feet, or the heavy silence created by acres upon acres of trees. She had no weapons, no way to defend herself if things went south. And most of the time, when it came to Frank, south was the only direction any woman traveled.

She hadn't made it more than five steps before Frank whirled and his eerie green gaze settled on her. His eyes had always fascinated and frightened her. They were unlike any others she'd ever seen. Mossy and murky like a Louisiana bog. When he saw her, his expression twisted from one of bewilderment to irritation, and finally landed on rage.

"I don't remember callin' a whore," he growled.

Looking back on that moment, she would wish that she had a retort. That she'd said, *Good, because I am no whore*, but the words did not come to mind. Nothing did. Not while under the stress of the situation. The uncertainty of what would come next. But then, to her complete and utter relief, he grabbed the two-liter bottles and darted inside the barn, slamming the door behind him. She could have laughed out loud. He thought she was there to steal his product.

She had just made it up to the twin barn doors when she heard the telltale *click* of a lock sliding into place. But Frank would not get away that easily. He had unwittingly gone right where she wanted him. Where he was trapped. She balled her hand into a fist and pounded on the outside of the door so hard that paint chips wedged their way into her skin.

"Go away," Frank said. He was so close. She could tell by his voice. It came from just on the other side of the double doors. Feet away, maybe even inches.

She was out of breath, panting from the exertion, but she forced a few words out. "Where are they, Frank?"

"Who?" Frank said. Here, he laughed. It was more of a chuckle, really, but it made her blind with rage.

"You know exactly *who*. The girls. Where the hell are the girls, Frank?"

"What girls?"

So, this was how it was going to go. She should have known he'd play dumb. Pretend like she'd imagined it all. If she were high, he would have been able to convince her that there were never any girls. That she was having a bad trip. That's what he had done in the past. But she knew better now. She had discovered the devil lurking beneath his thin layer of skin. And now she was here for the truth. The whole truth. He wouldn't talk his way out of it this time.

"You know what I mean, Frank. Just tell me where they are, and I'll leave you alone."

"Git outta here, ya crazy bitch."

That word—*bitch*—and the way he said it, like she was a rabid dog, set her off. If he wasn't going to play nice, then neither was she. She cast her gaze around, looking for something she could use as leverage. Her gaze settled on that heavy metal bar. The one that he had used against so many women in the past. She almost chuckled at the poetic justice that would come with *her* locking *him* in for once. She approached the bar and lifted it, straining under its weight. But after a few moments, she was able to raise it high enough and release it, allowing gravity to do the rest. It moved slowly at first, then gathered speed as it fell, landing with a heavy *bang* that shook the entire barn.

"What the hell was that?"

The woman didn't answer.

"Come on, sweetie. We can work this out."

Now she was *sweetie*. But he only used that word when he knew she had him by the balls. This time was no different. He was finally realizing how dumb it was to bar all the windows, especially since this door, the door she'd just locked from the outside, was the only exit.

*Arrogance*, she thought. That was the thing with men, especially those that had wielded so much power over others for so many years. They forgot that they were human, that they were mortal like everybody else.

"Where are the girls, Frank?"

"I told you—"

She cut him off. "I'm not messing around anymore. Where are the fucking girls? When I find them, I'll let you out."

Frank was silent for a long moment, then he grumbled something under his breath.

She placed a hand up to her ear. "I didn't catch that."

"The shed," Frank shouted.

She should have guessed. Why hadn't she gone there first? Maybe because she had hoped—no, prayed—that he wasn't locking them inside that tiny building without any running water or air conditioning. Not in this heat. But deep down, hadn't she guessed? Frank was his own special kind of monster. It would be inconsistent with his personality if he'd treated them any better than he might a dog. And there was a reason Frank didn't have a dog, not even one for guarding. He couldn't—or wouldn't—keep it alive.

"Very good. Now, I'll just step away to go check it out, and then I *might* be back to release you.

"You *might?*" Frank said.

For once, the woman was thankful that Frank's property was in a cell phone dead zone. Even if he had his phone with him, it was useless. She felt certain the lack of cell service was one of the reasons he had chosen this very property. That, and all the trees. It offered seclusion far past anything else in the area.

She smiled, but it was humorless and sardonic. A reaction to the thought that she was using all his hard preparation, his attempts to keep his unforgivable acts hidden, against him. It made her feel powerful, like she mattered. Thanks to his efforts, he couldn't call for help or retaliate. He was completely dependent on *her*.

But that wasn't why she had come. His torment, while fun, was secondary to her main goal. She jogged over to the shed. It, too, was locked from the outside, but with a traditional lock. The key hung on a metal peg on the side of the small outbuilding. She grasped it and jammed it into the lock. Rust caked the outer edges of it, causing the key to catch. She jimmied it as she twisted. The entire door shook. She heard movement inside. The creaking and shifting of a mattress. The woman froze.

"Hello?" asked a croaky voice. "Water?" The voice coming from inside was undoubtedly female, but her words were slow.

"Yes. Just hold on," the woman said. "How many of you are in there?"

"I am alone."

*One girl*, the woman thought. Where were all the rest? She

twisted the key hard, and the lock sprang open. The scent of sweat, excrement, and body odor filled her nostrils, and she had to fight the urge to gag. A girl, no older than fifteen, sat hunched on a dirty mattress. Sores covered parts of her face and arms, and her hands shook, unable to remain still. She was coming down from a high, at the very bottom and near a crash.

"We need to get you out of here. Can you stand?"

"I think so." The girl started to rise to her feet, and then she seemed to come to her senses, her gaze focusing hard on the woman. "Who are you? Where is Frank?"

"Frank is gone."

"Do you have dope? I just need one hit?"

Oh, how the woman understood those two questions. She also felt those two desires burning through her veins, begging, needing just one more high and promising that she'd never need it again. Until the next time.

"Follow me." She motioned to the girl, purposefully skirting her questions.

Surprisingly, or maybe not so surprisingly, the girl followed without complaint. The woman led the girl through a path cut into the underbrush. It wasn't well-worn, but it could be seen by those who knew where to look. They made their way up to the road where a black SUV was waiting. A man sat behind the steering wheel, a ball cap drawn low across his brow, obscuring his features. The woman motioned toward the car.

"Get in."

"He will take me to Frank?" the girl asked hopefully. She had an accent, but she hadn't said enough for the woman to place it.

At first, the woman considered a version of the truth, telling the girl that they were going somewhere better, but decided against it. She was too tired and too pissed off to form a coherent fairy story that would be more enticing to this girl than Frank's version of Disney World.

"Yeah, sure."

As soon as the woman said those two words, the girl pulled open the back door to the SUV and hopped inside. *Trusting*, the woman thought. *Too trusting*. But maybe "trust" was the wrong word. "Need" fit the circumstances far better. Because this girl was not making voluntary choices anymore. Her addiction was to the point that she'd probably take out her own eye if Frank asked her to.

A moment later, the man rolled down his window. "You getting in?"

The woman shook her head. "I've got one last thing to do."

The man chewed his lip. "That isn't part of the plan."

"Screw the plan."

"You'll have to find your own way home."

"It won't be the first time and probably won't be the last."

"Suit yourself," the man said, before putting the vehicle in gear and speeding off.

The woman pulled a Zippo lighter out of her pocket, thumbing it open. A flame shot to life, dancing in the slight wind. A smile spread across the woman's face. *This is my chance to get the truth*, she thought, before jogging back down the path toward Frank's barn.

But when she reached the clearing, she realized that she wasn't alone outside the barn. Someone else had arrived, and they were at the barn door, talking to Frank, jiggling the heavy beam that barred Frank's exit.

*Shit*, the woman thought. *Frank is going to get out and then....* She shuddered at the thought of what he might do to her. Rip her fingernails off one by one before slitting her throat? Tie her up and douse her in gasoline before setting her on fire?

He was capable of anything. She cursed her dumb luck. She should have left when she had the chance. Because Frank would catch her if she was on foot. It was a long way back to town. But she wasn't left with any other choice. She had to run.

# 1

## ASHLEY MONTGOMERY

A siren blared. Distant at first, but the sound steadily grew louder. Ashley sat up, listening intently, gauging its location. It was coming from the east side of town, where Brine's only fire station was located.

*Fire truck*, she thought.

It could be law enforcement, but both the police department and sheriff's office were located at the center of the small town, in the courthouse square a block away from the Public Defender's Office. If the sound had come from there, it would have started loud, then tapered off.

Ashley turned back to the stack of files on her desk. As the only public defender in a town of six thousand people, she had to stay on task. Time was always of the essence. The tabs for the light-brown legal files all faced her. They weren't in alphabetical order or arranged in any coherent way other than that they were all files needing Ashley's attention. Each file contained criminal charges for a different female defendant, but all were charged with meth-related offenses.

It wasn't only possession charges, though. There were other charges peppered in there, like thefts, assaults, forgeries, burglaries, and criminal mischief cases. These crimes came about because meth made people desperate and unpredictable. Ashley had never seen another drug like it, aside from maybe heroin and opioids.

It altered the user's brain in an irrevocable way, changing the way they thought, removing everything that mattered from their lives and replacing it with meth. Addictive on the very first try, especially if the person ingested it intravenously. Which seemed to be the desired method lately because it avoided the erosion of their teeth, a condition commonly called meth mouth.

Ashley sighed and turned to the top file. It was a new arrest for a local woman named Erica Elsberry. She'd been picked up at eight o'clock that morning. The charge was simple possession of methamphetamine, but it was her third offense, which made it a felony in Iowa. Erica and Ashley had a tumultuous past, but it saddened Ashley to see what had become of the woman.

Erica had grown up in Brine. She was in Ashley's high school class. A mean girl that had once been popular and beautiful. But that was then, back before life had beat her down. Back before her best friend was murdered and her son was sexually assaulted the very next year. When those tragedies had happened, Erica had taken her anger out on Ashley because Ashley had represented the men that had killed her friend and stolen her son's innocence. Erica had even arranged a protest against Ashley that had turned violent. Ashley had been furious with Erica at the time, but that was ancient history.

Now, Erica needed her, and Ashley would be there to guide her through the criminal justice system as she had done for so many defendants before her. She wasn't there to coddle her clients, but she was on their side. Often, she was the only support system they had left. Erica had once been surrounded by throngs of friends, but she was now alone. All those people that had claimed to "have her back" had disappeared shortly after Erica's very first arrest.

Even Erica's eight-year-old son was gone. He had been removed from her custody by the government months earlier and placed into foster care. It turned out that a single mother high on meth tended to have a very hard time caring for a child. Erica had several aunts, uncles, and cousins that still lived in Brine, but they'd all disowned her. When so-called friends and family saw her out and about, they walked past her without even offering a "hello." Ashley was all Erica had left.

Ashley discarded the thoughts of the past and flipped to the second page of Erica's file. It was the order of initial appearance. The hearing where the judge appointed Ashley as Erica's attorney and set her bond. The file stamp indicated that hearing had occurred that morning, at nine o'clock. *She must have seen the magistrate before she was booked and processed*, Ashley thought. Law enforcement must have taken her straight to court. There was no other way for Erica to have already seen the judge. Ashley eyes traveled to the bottom of the page where bond was listed as $5,000, cash only.

*Shit*, Ashley thought, *Erica is never going to be able to come up with that kind of money*. But she supposed that was the purpose of setting such a high bond. Ashley never could understand why judges and prosecutors insisted on incarcerating users. They weren't violent. At least they weren't any more violent than drinkers. And like alcoholics, Erica had an addiction. A substance abuse disorder.

Locking Erica up cured nothing; it solved no problems. They weren't providing her treatment in jail. There was no funding for that. They were merely housing her until they got

their conviction and released her back into society. The lead
prosecutor in Brine, Charles Hanson, claimed that incarceration "broke the cycle of usage," but he was wrong. It wasn't
breaking any cycles. It was a *part* of the cycle. The last portion
before it was set to repeat.

Ashley closed the file and set it at the top right corner of
the desk. It was the start of a pile dedicated to jail inmates.
They were the clients that needed the most attention. The
most handholding. And she understood that it was necessary.
She had been incarcerated in that windowless jail in the not-
too-distant past. The helplessness she had felt while behind
bars—the way her mind seemed to curl in upon itself—was
something she would never forget. Erica had never been kind
to Ashley, but Ashley wouldn't abandon any client in that, or
any other, jail. That was the purpose of this new pile, to
remind herself that she needed to see these clients as soon as
possible.

The next file was an indictment for Morgan Stanman for
burglary in the third degree. It was a serious charge, but it was
nonviolent. The allegation was that Morgan had stolen some
tools from an unoccupied, unattached garage. The homeowner had been away for the weekend, and he hadn't bothered to lock the garage. Ashley suspected that he rarely used
the tools that Morgan had allegedly taken, and he only
noticed that they were missing because he had an outdoor
camera that recorded Morgan entering in the middle of the
night. When he saw that, he searched the building, top to
bottom, noting a long list of missing items.

It annoyed Ashley because the conviction meant little to
the homeowner, the "victim," but it could result in a long term
of incarceration for Morgan. The charge was a felony, and on
its face, it seemed like a property crime. Which it was, but
there was more to it than that. Morgan's motivation had been

meth driven. Addictions were expensive. And dealers weren't handing the stuff out for free.

Ashley sighed heavily. She was tired of seeing lives destroyed by methamphetamine. It was a problem every-where, but it had wreaked havoc on small-town America. In the Midwest particularly it had grown into a bona fide epidemic. It was cheap, highly addictive, and relatively easy to make. All factors that made it ideal for the small-town drug trade.

She flipped Morgan's file open.

The indictment had Morgan's name and case number in the caption as well as her recent mug shot. In her picture, Morgan's head was tilted down, but she stared directly at the camera. Her dusty blond hair was shorn crudely at shoulder length in an almost comical way. It was uneven and jagged, like Morgan had cut it herself with a set of dull scissors. But the way it draped over Morgan's face, hiding both sides from the edge of her eyes to the tips of her ears, created an almost haunting effect. Like Morgan was a lioness, peeking out from behind the long, African grass, watching her prey.

This wasn't Morgan's first arrest, or her first mug shot, and it wouldn't be her last. But the picture that Ashley stared at now was vastly different than those in the early days. In this image, Morgan wasn't smiling as she used to in the early photos. Her once sparkling green eyes had grown dull and rimmed in red. Purple bags hung beneath her eyes, so dark that they almost looked black. Sharp cheekbones jutted out of sunken-in, crater-like cheeks and sallow skin stretched taut over a barely concealed skeleton.

It was hard to believe that this woman had ever been beau-tiful. But she had been. If Ashley were to pull Morgan's file from five years earlier, the face staring out would be vastly different. A vivacious woman in her mid-twenties with a sparkle in her eye and mischief in the soft pout of her full lips. But that was what meth did to a person. It was like a leech that survived not on blood but on the essence of life.

A second siren, followed by a third and a fourth, pulled Ashley out of her thoughts. She closed Morgan's file and set it in the upper left corner of her desk, the designated pile for clients out on bond. Four additional file folders sat in front of her. All female, all new arrests. She had intended to go through those files as well, but the sound of this second round of sirens had originated nearby. Meaning they had come from the police or sheriff's department.

Something was happening. Judging by the quick escalation in the number of emergency responders, it was big. Ashley didn't ignore big happenings. They almost always ended up as a file on her desk. And they weren't the nonviolent-type crimes like those currently sitting on her desk. The cases that garnered this kind of emergency response usually turned into the major violent felonies. The ones that consumed all of Ashley's free time.

She quickly rose from her seat, stepping over several stacks of files lying across her floor, and headed down the hall toward the front of the building. She passed two offices that were meant for more attorneys, but they remained empty. There was no budget for additional staff. She continued down the long hall, stopping at the last office just before the reception area. As she neared the office, the familiar chatter of radio traffic filled the air. She didn't understand the police codes and barely discernable jargon, but her friend and the office investigator did.

"Katie," Ashley said, rapping her knuckles on the open doorframe.

"What is it, boss?" Katie asked. She said *boss* in a teasing, affectionate way.

Ashley had hired Katie seven months earlier, but their friendship had begun long before that. When she'd made the hiring decision, Ashley had spent a good deal of time agonizing over it, wondering if it would alter the nature of their friendship. It put Ashley in a position of power over Katie, and that could change the dynamics of any relationship. After all, that was one of the things that had led to the demise of Katie and Detective George Thomanson's friendship. But so far, nothing had changed between Ashley and Katie, and Ashley was hell-bent on keeping it that way.

"Did something happen?" Ashley asked. Judging by the way Katie was staring at the radio like a young boy listening to *The Lone Ranger* back in the days before television, the answer was yes, and in a big way.

Ashley entered the small office and dropped into one of the two chairs across from Katie's desk. The chairs were lumpy and uncomfortable and the desk worn, but it was the best Ashley could do on a shoestring budget. She couldn't even afford to pay Katie. Her investigator's salary had come from private donations—raised using a crowdfunding website and from the assistance of a Des Moines reporter—rather than proper funding.

"Sounds like it," Katie said, without looking away from the scanner.

"What's going on?"

They kept close tabs on police scanners. It had been Katie's idea to do it. As a former Brine police officer, Katie knew the local cops were chattier over the radio than the larger—and savvier—police departments. She also under-stood the lingo. Originally, Ashley had doubted they would get much information from listening to scanners, but she had been wrong.

The scanner had turned into a valuable tool in Katie and

Ashley's limited arsenal. It was a treasure trove of early case details. For the first time, they now had access to information at the same time as the prosecutor. It evened the playing field. And with the discrepancy in budget and resources between the prosecutor's office and the public defender, Ashley would gladly take any advantage she could get.

"Sounds like a fire down at Frank Vinny's place," Katie said.

"The barn?" It was a knee-jerk reaction, an automatic response rather than a true question. Frank didn't own any other property. It had to be the barn.

Frank's "barn" looked like a traditional barn structure from the outside, but it had been modified on the inside. Ashley had never been near the structure, but she'd gathered tidbits of information from her clients over the years. Most people said that it looked like a home on the inside, but there was something sinister about it. They never could quite put a finger on what bothered them about it, but so many clients had made the same observation that Ashley couldn't discount it.

Maybe it was the fact that the barn was built deep in a wooded area. A small clearing smack-dab in the middle of acres upon acres of heavy foliage. It offered complete seclusion where anything could happen. She didn't know the types of things that went on in that barn, but she had her suspicions. Suspicions that she never hoped to validate.

"Yup," Katie said. "The barn."

Ashley groaned. "He probably set a fire while cooking meth."

It wouldn't be the first time Frank's business literally went up in flames. Nor would it be the first time that Frank had been involved in the criminal world. His crimes were all meth related, but that didn't mean they were nonviolent.

He was a manufacturer, not a user, and he had to protect his business. On the streets, "protection" was synonymous with violence. Which was something Frank must have done well because he'd managed to be the only manufacturer in Brine County. Anyone who wanted meth got it from him. That didn't sound like much on its face, but meth was easy to manufacture. In other counties, there were lots of small-time dealers in addition to the larger manufacturers. That was not the case in Brine. Frank manufactured, sold, and delivered. All dope deals started and ended with him.

Fear was the only way for Frank to have such a stronghold on the meth market. And Ashley had seen glimpses of that side of Frank. She had once represented him for cutting the fingers off a guy named Sean Markle. Sean later changed his story, claiming that he'd slipped while slicing a tomato. Apparently, he'd enjoyed the pain enough to slice off two more of his fingers.

Both Sean and Frank were habitual criminals, so the prosecutor didn't care about the case all that much. He gave Frank a week in jail and let him out, believing Sean would even the score once Frank was out on the street. But the prosecutor had been wrong. Sean disappeared within a week. Nobody knew what happened to him, but Ashley suspected he was dead.

"It hasn't rained in forever. It wouldn't take much for that whole place to go up."

A thunderstorm had passed a couple of hours earlier, but it was a fast-moving storm that provided very little rain. What little precipitation that did happen to fall didn't even begin to soften the edges of the deep drought that had been plaguing the region.

"True," Katie agreed. Her eyes still did not leave the scanner.

"It sucks for him, but maybe this time he will learn his

lesson. That barn wasn't worth much anyway. He'll build it back in no time."

Frank had been caught manufacturing methamphetamine more times than Ashley cared to remember. But with Ashley as his attorney, he'd been able to skirt by with simple possession charges with no significant periods of incarceration. With each arrest, Ashley had tried to persuade Frank to find a new profession. There were times that she thought she'd gotten through to him. That he would change his ways once released. But then he would get out of jail and he would continue with business as usual down at the barn. Clearly the court's intervention hadn't done anything to deter him from manufacturing. Maybe a chemical fire would.

"Is Sir George at the scene?" Ashley asked.

When she referred to Detective George Thomanson, she often gave him nicknames. This time she had chosen a royal-sounding name, but other times she called him "Georgie" or "Georgie Porgy." It drove him nuts, but Ashley found his irritation to be hilarious. She didn't have a lot of humor in her life, so she had to get her laughs somewhere.

A chuckle burst from Katie's lips. "Sir George," she repeated. "He thinks he's a knight in shining armor, for sure. Whether he saves anyone other than himself is still up for debate, but yeah, it sounds like he's there."

George Thomanson was the only detective employed by Brine's small police department. He and Katie had once been friends—back when they worked side by side—but that relationship had fallen apart when George had treated her as an underling and then used information about Katie's past to save his job at the expense of hers during a bout of budget cuts. As a result, Katie encouraged Ashley's nicknames and seemed to revel in George's irritation almost more than Ashley did.

"Well," Ashley said, rising to her feet. "I think you should go down there and check it out."

"Are you sure? Maybe it was an accident?"

Ashley thought for a moment, mulling over the possibility, but dismissed it. "Yeah. I'm sure. If it involves Frank, it's going to end up with our office somehow. Frank rarely does legal things. I have to assume he was up to some kind of mischief, so we might as well get a jump on the investigation."

"Okay," Katie said uncertainly.

Ashley knew what Katie was thinking. She didn't want to talk to George.

"You don't need to interview anyone or anything. Just pop down there for a few minutes to take some pictures. See what you can find. You don't even have to let the officers see you. In fact, it would probably be better that they didn't."

The foliage surrounding Frank's property would make pictures impossible unless Katie snuck onto the land itself. It was too early to know what they were looking for, but pictures couldn't hurt. They could refer to them later—after Frank had been arrested and charged for whatever nonsense he had caused this time—and hopefully find ways to poke holes in the State's case.

Katie took one last look at the radio, then stood and stretched. She reached over and grabbed her keys, placing them in her pocket. "Whatever you say, boss," she said, a smile creeping into the corners of her lips. "You know I'm always eager to get out from behind a desk."

That was the truth. Katie had always worked best in the field. It was the reason why Ashley was sending her to check out the scene. Katie would see things, find evidence that no other officers would. Or so she hoped.

# 2

## KATIE MICKEY

It was early June, seven months since Katie had started working *with* Ashley Montgomery at the Public Defender's Office. She accentuated the *with* when she thought of her employment because Ashley made a point to make everyone in the office feel like they were on equal footing. Working together for a common goal. There were only three of them, but Ashley made sure both staff members knew their worth.

Sure, Ashley had expectations—higher than most—but she never hovered over Katie. When she had an assignment, she'd give Katie the cold, hard facts, then step away, allowing Katie to approach the investigation in her own way and at her own pace. It was a refreshing change of speed after George Thomanson's hovering at the police department.

She'd enjoyed the past seven months, but she'd grown restless lately. Nothing larger than the run-of-the-mill burglary had occurred. Every day was beginning to feel the same. But it sounded like something big was happening down at Frank Vinny's barn, and Ashley had asked her to check it out. Katie slung her camera bag over her shoulder, eager to get out in the field.

"Do you want to come along?" Katie asked as she joined Ashley in the hallway outside her office.

Ashley held up a stack of files. "No. I've got to go visit a few people in jail. You know how they get."

Katie nodded. It was one of the first things Katie had learned when she started working for Ashley. Clients in jail were needy. They were stuck behind bars with little else to do than worry about their case. They demanded Ashley's immediate attention, and if they didn't get it, they'd grow unruly and difficult to control. The relationship between attorney and client was as delicate as a seedling that had just burst through the soil. Any harsh condition or misstep could destroy it.

"But keep me posted," Ashley said, "and if you see Frank, make sure he knows to keep his mouth shut."

"I will, but it seems like he should know that by now."

"He should, but he won't. You know Frank. He thinks he can talk his way out of anything."

Katie did know Frank, but she'd never worked with him from this side of the law before. She wondered if he would believe her when she said that she worked for Ashley now. It wasn't all that long ago that she and Ashley were on opposite sides of the law, fighting like vipers.

"If I see him, I'll tell him," Katie said before heading toward the back of the office.

The exit at the back of the building spilled directly into the parking lot. The lot was owned by the city of Brine and required a parking pass, but Katie was too cheap to pay for one. It was thirty dollars a month, which didn't sound like much, but it added up and Katie was already struggling to make ends meet. Instead, she parked a couple of blocks away on the side street of a residential neighborhood.

The air was hot and sticky after the brief rain shower earlier that morning. Summer weather in Iowa could be tricky. Sometimes rains lasted all day, dumping buckets of water through the night and continuing the entire next day. Other times storms moved in unexpectedly, blowing sixty-mile-per-hour straight winds, crackling with lightning. But those storms were over and gone as quickly as they had come. The weather that morning had rolled in, strong and fierce, before breaking and allowing the sun through, shining as though nothing had happened.

Farmers had been complaining about the drought for months now, but farmers constantly complained about the weather. It was always too *something*. Cold, hot, dry, whatever. So, Katie hadn't paid much attention. At least not until lately when she started noticing the change in the soil. It cracked and split open, creating tiny fissures through the land. Dust seemed to hover in the air, catching in her throat, forcing her to cough. The formerly green grass had grown brittle, crunching underfoot.

When she neared her Impala, she unlocked it with her key fob. Then she opened the door and hopped inside, jamming her key into the ignition and cranking up the air. She reached over and gently placed her camera bag on the passenger seat and turned on her in-car police scanner, eager for more news about the fire.

Katie pulled out of her parking spot and headed south of town on highway 159. She knew where she was going from her patrol days. After six years driving these roads, she knew them inside and out. But even if she didn't, she could simply follow the black cloud of smoke. It billowed into the air, wafting up from a centralized location, like the cloud that followed a fireworks display.

The smoke continued to thicken as she drew closer to the scene. The voices of firefighters filled the car, shouting orders to one another through the scanner. It made her nostalgic for the days when she felt like she was part of a team. Ashley was an excellent boss and a true friend, but they didn't work side by side. They each had their own roles that they performed individually. When Katie was an officer, she was one part of a pack, like a pod of orcas, but now she felt more like a lone shark. And anyone who watched Shark Week knew that even a great white shark was no match for a pod of orcas.

That was why she was eagerly awaiting the creation of the Mental Health Response Team, or MEHR team for short. It was the city council's pet project, headed by councilman Forest Parker. He'd been the voice behind defunding the Brine Police Department, which had made him her enemy up until she lost her job and he'd selected her as the proposed lead to the MEHR team, which was slated to replace the police department.

Just then, Katie's phone began to buzz in her pocket, pulling her out of her thoughts. She glanced at the screen before answering. It read *Tom Archie*. Tom was a friend of Katie's and Ashley's former boyfriend. He, too, would be part of the eventual MEHR team.

Katie picked up and pressed the speaker phone button. "Hey, Tom. What's up?"

"I just wanted to know if we are still on for drinks tonight. I've arranged for Forest and Rachel to be there, too."

Tom had been taking classes at Drake University in Des Moines, but he was home for the summer interning for Forest. Tom was majoring in psychology, and he intended to move back to Brine as soon as the MEHR team was up and running to join as a member and finish his degree through online classes. Rachel was the victim of a crime seven months earlier, but she'd been charged with a criminal offense. After her acquittal, she moved in with Ashley and was also expected to become a member of the MEHR team.

"It sounds like our after-work drinks has turned into an official meeting," Katie said dryly. Tom always did this. He'd plan something that sounded laidback and fun but then turn it into the opposite.

"No, no, no, it'll be completely casual."

"Riiight," Katie said. She was not convinced.

"You could bring Ashley along," Tom said after a short pause. "She's not on the team."

He said it as though he'd just come up with the idea, but Katie knew better. Tom was a good guy—always available to lend a helping hand—but he also seemed to feel that his altruism gave him the constant moral high ground. Like he knew what was best for everyone else.

"I'll propose it to her, but I doubt she'll accept."

"Why?"

Katie sighed heavily. "Because she's busy and she's still upset with you."

Ashley had officially ended the relationship with Tom, but it had been Tom's fault. He'd been untruthful with Ashley about a female roommate. Lying and pretending that he lived alone until Ashley showed up one day to discover his deceit. He hadn't physically cheated on her, but lying to her face on a regular basis was nearly as bad. Ashley had been heartbroken when she'd found out the truth, which was why she still struggled to forgive him.

"But it's been seven months. How long is it going to take?"

"It'll take as long as it takes. You can't rush these things."

"But—"

Katie cut him off. "I'd love to discuss this further, but I've got a fire to investigate." She had just pulled off to the side of the road in front of Frank's property. "I'll let Ashley know that we are meeting up tonight, and she can do with it what she wants."

"Okay."

"See you later," Katie said, hanging up and getting out of the car.

A mixture of reluctance and excitement warred within her as she turned to look at the treetops. Her eyes locked on the giant column of smoke twisting into the sky, black as night and blotting out the intensity of the sun. The hairs along Katie's arms stood. The scene looked like something out of a horror movie.

She used the back of her hand to swipe at the sweat beading along her brow. Then she used the ponytail holder she kept around her wrist to tie back her long, red hair, pulling it off her already perspiring neck. The temperature had been unseasonably warm for June, but the fire made things worse. It was so intense. Katie could feel its heat pressing against the front half of her body even though she was still a quarter mile away.

George's police cruiser was parked at the top of the gravel drive, lights whirring, but there were no other law enforcement vehicles in the area. With budget cuts, she suspected that George was the only officer on scene. There would be countless firefighters, but there simply were not enough officers unless the sheriff's department decided to help out, and that was doubtful.

The sheriff had always refused to respond to complaints out at Frank's property. He claimed he was related to Frank, but Katie wasn't sure if that was even true. If it was, Frank was a distant relation, at best, but the sheriff had always used it as an excuse to get his whole department out of dealing with Frank, so she didn't see why that would change now.

Katie scanned the trees as she approached Frank's property. She needed to find another entry other than the driveway. She couldn't just come down the driveway like a first responder. Everyone down by that property knew Katie and considered her the enemy now that she had taken a job working with Ashley. There was no way that they would let her get anywhere near the fire. She had to come up with a different plan. When she was almost to the gravel drive, she noticed a small break in the trees where the foliage had been disturbed. It was a path. Overgrown, but still visible upon close inspection.

There was something ominous about it—the way the branches twisted around one another, casting deep shadows —but Katie didn't have many options. It was either this path or the driveway. The path it was. Before going into the foliage, she popped her camera lens off. She took several photographs of the path, then prepared to enter. As she came closer, she tried to focus on snapping as many pictures as possible. It distracted her from the unsettling feeling taking root in her gut. Something bad had happened in these woods, and she wasn't sure if the danger had yet passed.

# 3

## ASHLEY

After Katie left, Ashley continued working on paperwork for a while, but she gave up after thirty minutes. Her mind wasn't in it. Katie was out there *doing* something, and she was wasting her time on paperwork. Yeah, it was important, but it could wait until later. Her time would be better spent at the jail.

She pushed her chair back from her heavily scratched but sturdy desk. It was the same one that had been there when she joined the office fifteen years earlier, and it would stay for the foreseeable future. She barely had the funds to make payroll, and people were always more important than things.

After grabbing her keys, she walked down the long hallway that led to the front of the office. She passed the two empty offices and Katie's office—the scanner still blaring with sounds from the fire at Frank's barn—before entering into the reception area. A tall, thin, dark-haired girl sat at a desk, typing at a computer. Her back was to Ashley, her long, thick hair hanging over the back of her chair.

"How's it going, Elena?"

Elena jumped and spun, her hand coming up to press against her heaving chest. "You scared me."

"What are you working on?"

"The draft of that motion for a new trial for the Gibbons case."

Elena was barely nineteen years old, and she had no formal legal training, but she'd been working for Ashley for a year now and she'd proven to be a quick learner. She was probably far more intelligent than most new lawyers. Lately, Ashley had taken to giving her more and more responsibility, just to see what her limits were. Of course, Ashley would always review Elena's work before officially filing it, but so far, she'd found only a few small mistakes.

"I should have it finished in the next half hour, if you want to review it before the end of the day," Elena said.

"I'm heading to the jail to go visit a few clients. I'll look at it when I get back."

"I don't know if you remember, but I plan to leave early today. My mother is sick, and I need to go with her to the doctor."

Ashley didn't remember, but she nodded anyway. Elena's mother had been sick for a while now. She'd had multiple doctor appointments, but they couldn't seem to figure out what was wrong with her. Elena's presence was required for all appointments because she was the only person in her family that was bilingual. Her mother and father spoke Spanish. They could speak some broken English, but they would not be able to understand complicated medical jargon. Ashley hardly understood it herself, and English was her only language.

"Take all the time you need," Ashley said. "That motion can wait until tomorrow. We have several days before the deadline to file."

"Thank you," Elena said, hopping up. "I'll leave now, then."

Elena acted like Ashley was doing her a favor, but she had

no idea just how much Ashley needed her. She was invaluable as an employee, and Ashley would do anything to keep her. Katie would be leaving in a year or two to join the MEHR team, which had always been the plan, but it meant that she would need Elena more than ever when the time came.

"I'll see you in the morning," Ashley said, pulling the front door open. "And lock the door behind you when you leave," she called over her shoulder before stepping out into the oppressive summer heat.

The jail sat next to the courthouse, kitty-corner to the Public Defender's Office, and Ashley turned to look at her home away from home before heading in that direction. A sign reading "Public Defender" was affixed to the front of the office, but the intense Iowa winds had blown it loose. It sat off-kilter, slightly tilted to the right. Ashley reached out and straightened it before taking off across the street.

Kylie, the jail administrator, was behind the front window when Ashley arrived. She was seated at a desktop computer, typing.

"Hey, Ashley," Kylie said without looking up. She pressed a couple of keys on the keyboard, shuffled several papers in front of her, then stood, giving Ashley her full attention.

Kylie was in her mid-twenties with curly black hair that she had tied back away from her face with a bandana. With broad shoulders and sharp, knowing eyes, Kylie came off to most as intimidating. But not to Ashley. She'd known Kylie for far too long to see her as anything other than the kind-hearted softie within. "Who do you need to see today?"

"Erica Elsberry."

"She just came in an hour or so ago. I don't know if the guys are done processing her in. Let me check." Kylie moved to the desktop computer and punched several buttons. She studied the screen for a few moments before turning back to

Ashley. "It's your lucky day. She just made it through booking. Come on around."

A buzzer sounded, and Ashley gripped the heavy iron door that led into the bowels of the jail. She'd done this countless times before, but the slamming of the door behind her and the click of the lock sliding into place never seemed to get easier. At least not since she'd been wrongly accused and incarcerated for the murders of two former clients a few years earlier.

Kylie led Ashley down the familiar hallway and stopped at the first meeting room. There were several of them, but this was the room that Ashley liked the best. Kylie said something into an intercom, and the door unlocked. When Kylie pulled it open, Ashley took several deep, calming breaths before striding inside.

"I'll bring Erica through the other door in a couple minutes."

Each meeting room had two doors, one for the attorney that opened out into the less secure area of the jail, and another for the client. The room was small and unpartitioned. There were partitioned meeting rooms on the other side of the jail, but Ashley never used them. She didn't want any barriers between herself and her clients, real or imagined. Two blue plastic chairs sat on either side of a desk older and even more beat up than the one in Ashley's office.

Ashley dropped into her seat and waited for Kylie to bring Erica in. She removed a stack of papers and a highlighter from her laptop bag and settled into some paperwork. Sometimes, if Kylie got delayed for one reason or another, it could take as long as thirty minutes to bring Ashley's client. Fortunately, there was no such delay, and Kylie ushered Erica into the room in less than five minutes.

Erica shuffled inside wearing a jail-issued jumpsuit. It was dark green and hung from her gaunt frame, looking more like a trash bag than clothing.

"Have a seat," Ashley said, nodding to the chair across from her. She slipped the paperwork she'd brought back into her bag, leaving only Erica's file in front of her.

Erica pulled the chair back, its legs making a *thwump, thwump, thwump* noise against the floor, and she dropped into it, keeping her eyes downcast. Ashley didn't blame her. She had to be ashamed. She'd once held a certain amount of power in their small town, even over Ashley, and now, well, she'd given everything up for meth.

"You're here for criminal trespass and possession of methamphetamine." Ashley started every new-client meeting by reciting their charges. She didn't waste time on niceties. She had lots of clients, all of which needed her undivided attention.

"With drugs, you know there's a three-strike rule. A third conviction automatically makes it a felony, no matter how much meth you allegedly had on you."

"All I had was residue. It wasn't even enough to get high. They scraped it out of a baggie they found in my pocket. I didn't even know that it was there."

Ashley looked up from her file. "It doesn't matter, Erica."

Erica's eyes widened, but Ashley had little sympathy. She'd warned Erica on at least three prior occasions that a third strike was inevitable unless she cleaned up her act. Every time, Erica had been eager to promise Ashley that it was the last time. She'd never use again. But two weeks later, there she was, sitting in jail making the same hollow promises as before.

"I don't understand." Erica's hands shook, and she fidgeted with the sleeve of her jumpsuit.

Ashley crossed her arms, exasperated. "Yes, you do." She stared at Erica for a long moment, studying her appearance.

She had never been beautiful, but she'd at least been attractive before the meth. To men, especially. Her voluptuous figure had a way of turning heads, even when she was quite young. But not anymore. She'd grown as skinny as a rail, her cheeks dipping into her face like craters.

"But it wasn't even mine. It was Frank's."

"Speaking of Frank," Ashley said. She skirted past the content of Erica's last remark and focused on Frank for two reasons. One, Erica sounded like a petulant child, and two, because it didn't matter who *owned* the meth. All that mattered was who had possession of it. It was in Erica's jacket, so she had won the unwelcome prize of arrest. "You were arrested in the field right outside his property—"

"I wasn't trespassing," Erica interrupted. "I have gone through that field a million times before to get to Frank's property. It's the quickest way to get there from town. It's never been a problem, so I don't see why it is now."

"It's a problem because the property owner says it's a problem. He's put up 'no trespassing' signs everywhere. There's one literally every twenty feet. You had to see them. If you didn't, we should get your eyes checked."

"I still don't see why it's a problem."

"Moving on," Ashley said. She saw no point in continuing to go back and forth with Erica. Her understanding of the problem didn't matter. The property owner had made it clear that he didn't want anyone on his property, and she'd been there. That was all the State needed to get past her seizure and search incident to arrest, and thus, the discovery of the methamphetamine.

"It sounds like you were near Frank's place." The field she was found in was a large fifty-acre property, but it abutted the highway, and the deputy had listed the mile marker in his report. Mile marker 1135. Frank's property started somewhere in the middle of mile marker 1136.

"Yeah. I was on my way to Frank's."

"Why?"

Erica sighed heavily. "You know why."

Ashley leaned back and tapped Erica's file with the end of her pen. "I have my suspicions, but I don't *know* anything."

"I needed some dope, okay. I was going to buy some."

*With what money?* Ashley wondered, but she kept that question to herself. Erica didn't have a job. She hadn't had one for over a year now. The only money she had coming in was from public assistance, which was not free cash. She'd have to trade her food stamps for money. That, or steal other people's things and pawn them. There was one other option, selling herself, but Ashley didn't even want to think about that. No option was legal, so it was better that Ashley, as her defense attorney, never learned the truth.

"Do you know what's going on down at Frank's place?"

"A fire."

"A fire," Ashley repeated, quirking her eyebrow. "How do you know that? Were you there?" Ashley had always suspected the fire occurred while Frank was cooking. If that was the case, Erica could have easily been there when it happened.

"No, I wasn't there. I heard about it is all. One of the jailers was talking about it. He said he heard about it from a dispatcher."

Erica wouldn't make eye contact with Ashley, which could mean that she was lying. But what was the lie? Had she been there to start the fire, or was she lying about how she'd learned about it? Ashley would guess it was the latter, but she never quite knew with Erica. In this case, she didn't want to know. At least not yet. A day might come that she would need to pin Erica down to the truth, or at least some version of the truth that a jury might believe, but today was not that day. "Where is Frank?"

Erica scoffed. "I thought he was at his place, obviously, because I was going there to buy the dope. I don't know where else he'd be."

"You didn't see him when you were in that field?"

"What? Hiding among the beans?"

Erica was treating the question like it was ridiculous, but it wouldn't be the first time that one of Ashley's clients hid from law enforcement in a crop field. Corn was better at concealing a person, but beans were pretty tall this time of year. If Frank had lain down in them, the cops would have had a difficult time finding him.

"Yes. In the beans," Ashley said, crossing her arms.

"No. I didn't see him."

Ashley studied Erica. She twisted and squirmed in her seat, unable to meet Ashley's gaze. Ashley made it a habit to appear as though she believed her clients, but she was having a hard time doing that today. By her fidgeting, it seemed as though Erica knew a hell of a lot more than she was letting on, and it was making Ashley nervous.

Not for Erica, but for Katie. Ashley had sent Katie out into Frank's woods to take pictures. By herself. And Frank wasn't a good person. He'd always made Ashley nervous. There was something nefarious about him, lurking beneath his seemingly cordial exterior. If backed in a corner, what would he do? With his only home burning to the ground and surrounded by cops, he would not only be backed in a corner, but he'd be furious.

# 4

## KATIE

The foliage on the path was thick, grasping at Katie's clothes as she struggled forward. Brambles caught in her hair, and twigs slapped at her ankles. Every few steps, she'd stop and take a few pictures, documenting the path and its surroundings. It might not be important, but it was too early to tell.

Sweat dropped down her back, soaking her T-shirt—a Goodwill purchase, black with the words *No Fear* written across the front—so it stuck to her skin. The heat was overpowering, yet she continued stumbling her way toward the fire. Trees hung across the path, blocking most of the sunlight but also blocking any breeze, making the air stagnant and thick with smoke.

Katie guessed that the fire was not yet under control, judging by the way the heat continued ratcheting up. Her instincts screamed for her to run, but she forced herself to keep moving forward. If the fire leapt from the barn into the trees, she would be in real danger. Nobody would come to her rescue. The only person who knew that Katie was stalking around in Frank's woods was Ashley, and she was in the middle of a client meeting. Neither George nor the firefighters knew she was there, and that was by design.

But she'd come this far already. All she could do was continue on, snapping pictures as she went. Her camera was an old Nikon. A gift from her father on her sixteenth birthday. Back before he was arrested and incarcerated for embezzling money from his clients. It had been state-of-the-art back then, but as with all technology, it was outdated by today's standards. She would have liked to have something newer, but she was well accustomed to the difference between wants and needs.

It hadn't always been that way, she'd been a spoiled child, but she'd received a crash-course education in money management when the government seized all her parents' assets and her mother ran off with a man she'd been having an affair with. At the tender age of sixteen, Katie was on her own. She could have alerted child services, gone into foster care, but people weren't keen on fostering the teenage daughter of a felon. She would have ended up in a group home rather than with a family, and that sort of institution sounded a lot like a prison to Katie.

She shook her head, dislodging the unpleasant thoughts of her past from her mind, and focused on the present, which was unpleasant in its own right. The smoke was growing thicker, making her eyes water and her throat scratchy. It would be best for her to take her pictures and get out of there before things grew any worse. She aimed her camera at the forest floor directly to the right of the path, ready to press the shutter button, but stopped short. *What is that*, she thought, lowering the viewfinder from her eye. Something was lying on the forest floor, flashing bright in the dappled sunlight trickling through the trees.

Katie removed a pair of gloves from her camera bag and

snapped them on. She was no longer a law enforcement officer, so she needed to be careful with evidence. Leaving her
fingerprints on it meant something wholly different now. And
tampering with it was a crime. She could not remove this
object from the scene, and she should not leave any fingerprints, so the best she could do was document well with
pictures.

She leaned closer, studying the object. It looked like a gold
bracelet, possibly expensive. She took several photographs of
it where it lay, then she picked it up and examined it, taking
photographs from every angle. It was a solid gold bangle with
a light pink trimming on both sides and some sort of design
stamped into the gold.

At first glance, it felt familiar to Katie, but she couldn't
place where she had seen this bracelet before. Maybe it was
common—something everyone was wearing and found in all
the fashion magazines—and that feeling of recognition meant
nothing. Or perhaps she had seen it on a specific person. But
with all the smoke and suffocating heat, she simply could not
remember. She'd think about it later when she was out of
danger.

Her photographs providing reference, Katie set the
bracelet down exactly where she had found it. She continued
along the path, trudging forward until she finally reached a
clearing where everything seemed to be ablaze. Grappling
with her camera, she brought the viewfinder back up to her
eye and snapped picture after picture, capturing the chaos of
the moment. Firefighters ran in all directions, some spraying
the fire, others trying to dig away dead underbrush to prevent
the fire from spreading to the dry woods.

There were two main structures on the property that Katie
could see. A barn and a large shed at the back of the barn.
Flames burst from the roofs of both buildings. Katie zoomed

in, snapping pictures of both structures, trying to document every inch. It was unlikely that the firefighters were going to be able to save either building, so these photographs might prove to be invaluable at trial.

She focused on the doors and windows of both buildings, zooming in and pressing the shutter button over and over again, trying to capture every inch of the buildings from her vantage point. It would've been nice to get pictures from the back and other side as well, but this was the best she could do. Nobody was going to allow her to get any closer, and honestly, she didn't want to.

George was standing a safe distance from the fire, about halfway up along the gravel driveway. He was alone, and he looked bored, picking at his nails, glancing up every so often. He should've been busy taking photographs like Katie, but he was never one for extra work. Like Katie, he was assuming it was a meth fire, and the evidence of that would be in the chemicals inside the building, not outside.

If that was the case, where was Frank? She'd expected him to be sitting next to George, possibly in handcuffs, answering questions. She scanned the scene again, this time more desperately, looking from one face to the next. None of them were Frank. A heavy sense of uneasiness settled in her chest. She couldn't help looking over her shoulder every few minutes. Was he behind her? What would he do if he found her out here?

They hadn't had a good relationship, she and Frank. She'd arrested him far too many times for that. The last time, he'd called her a "fucking cunt" that "nobody wanted, not even if she was a whore," and she'd shoved him in the back of her police cruiser with a little too much force, "accidentally" banging his head against the roof.

*It's probably time to leave*, she thought. She couldn't shake the feeling that she was being watched, and she had gotten all the pictures she needed. The environment was not healthy anyway. The heat had grown even more intense, and the smoke was catching in her throat. She was just turning to head back up the path and return to the office when one of the firefighters shouted, "Someone's in here. Call an ambulance!"

# 5

## ASHLEY

Ashley ended her meeting with Erica prematurely, leaving the detailed questions about the fire at Frank's unasked. She was due to be in court for an unrelated sentencing hearing in fifteen minutes.

On her way over to the courthouse, she pulled out her phone and clicked on Katie's name, jotting out a quick text. *You be safe out there*, she typed, sending the message as she ascended the front steps to the courthouse doors. She was worried about Katie out there all alone, possibly with Frank lurking around. If he'd been in custody, she would have heard from him by now. Ashley was always his first call whenever shit hit the fan, and her phone had been silent.

She rushed up the grand staircase that led to the District Associate Court Courtroom with seven minutes to spare. She'd expected to see her client perched on one of the benches in the hallway, waiting for her, but Aubrey Miller was nowhere to be seen.

"Shit," Ashley hissed quietly. "I told her to be early."

Ashley opened the courtroom door and glanced inside, just to make sure Aubrey wasn't waiting for her in there. The door was windowless and heavy, so she opened it gingerly in case court was in session, but that wasn't necessary. It was deserted. As she was closing the door, she heard a noise on the staircase, and she turned just in time to see Aubrey running toward her, taking two steps at a time.

"There you are," Ashley said as Aubrey rushed toward her, her chest heaving. "I thought I told you to dress like you're going to church."

"I don't go to church."

Aubrey was a good five years younger than Ashley, but she didn't look it. Drugs had destroyed her skin, and apparently fried her brain as well, because she was wearing a T-shirt and jeans.

"It was a metaphor, and you know it. Here." Ashley fished around in her laptop bag and pulled out a button-up short-sleeved shirt. It was a fake silk material that shimmered in the florescent lights.

"That's ugly," Aubrey said with a grunt.

"I don't care. Put it on." Ashley held the shirt out to her client and Aubrey reluctantly accepted it, pinching it between her thumb and index finger, holding it away from her like it was radioactive. Ashley glanced at her watch again. "Put it on."

"Seriously?" Aubrey asked, scrunching up her nose.

"We've got two minutes before your sentencing hearing is supposed to start. We don't have time for this nonsense. You remember that I am arguing for probation and the county attorney is arguing for prison, right?"

"Yes," Aubrey said with a reluctant nod.

"Then you need to look nicer than a street urchin. It shouldn't matter, but looks do count."

Aubrey grudgingly slid her arms into the sleeves and buttoned it up.

Ashley didn't think it looked all that bad. She'd bought it

earlier that day at a secondhand store in Brine's dying down-town district because she'd suspected that Aubrey would ignore her dress code advice. "Now, let's get in there before the judge starts without us." Ashley shoved the door open and lead her client down the aisle between rows of empty benches.

On some occasions, all these pew-like benches were filled with spectators, but that was only when there was a high-profile case. Often, the courtroom was like this—empty aside from the parties. Meaning the judge, attorneys, and defendant. Charles Hanson, the Brine County Attorney, was already seated at the prosecution table, looking smug.

"Where'd you come from?" Ashley asked Charles as she removed her computer from her bag and placed it on the table in front of her. Aubrey stood awkwardly beside the table, but she sat when Ashley gestured to the seat next to her. "You didn't pass me in the hallway, and I just looked in here a few minutes ago."

"Oh, I was back in chambers," Charles said, picking at his fingernails. "I needed to discuss something with the judge."

"I hope you weren't discussing *this* case," Ashley said, her tone accusing. Attorneys were not supposed to speak with the judge outside the presence of the other attorney. In legalese, they called it an "ex parte" communication. It was against the rules, but it wasn't uncommon in small towns where the attorneys had unfettered access to judge's chambers.

Charles looked up at Ashley, his eyes flashing with rage. "No. That would be unethical."

Ashley rolled her eyes, thinking, *You didn't think it was unethical when you did it yesterday.*

"It's really none of your business, but if you must know, I was discussing the open spot on the bench. Judge Rudolph is retiring."

"Yeah, and it's about time."

Judges in Iowa were forced to retire at the age of seventy-two, but Ashley had been ready for Judge Rudolph to retire for years. He was based out of Webster County, which was four counties away from Brine, but the judges in the district rotated every month. That meant that Brine had to suffer through Judge Rudolph's nonsense two months out of every year. It didn't sound like a lot, but it felt like *forever*.

Judge Rudolph wasn't a bad person, he just didn't understand the meth epidemic. He took the Nancy Reagan approach to addiction and firmly believed in "Just say no." That was all well and good when you were raised by decent parents in a well-adjusted home, but that wasn't the case with Ashley's clients. They came from horrible backgrounds and were introduced to drugs at a very young age. That "Just say no" ship had usually sailed before they were even teenagers.

"I'm hoping to replace him," Charles continued. "Judge Ahrenson is the lead of the Judicial Nominating Committee this time, and I'm hoping to get his support."

"Great," Ashley said with unmitigated sarcasm. The only person that would be worse than Judge Rudolph would be Charles Hanson.

"Is everyone ready to proceed?" A small woman had come into the courtroom from a door beside the judge's bench, interrupting their conversation. It was Judge Ahrenson's court reporter. Ashley released a breath she hadn't realized she'd been holding. If she had to spend any more time thinking about Charles Hanson's chances of ascending to the bench, she might vomit.

"Yes, Margaret," Ashley said. "Sorry. I didn't realize the judge was ready for us."

Margaret had been Judge Ahrenson's court reporter for as long as Ashley could remember. She was kind, but she wasn't gentle. Part of her job was to keep Judge Ahrenson's schedule, and she kept the attorneys on task. The judge made the decisions, but Margaret held a certain amount of power. She was at his side and in his ear at all times. He valued her opinion.

"I'll let him know. We'll be in shortly," Margaret said, before turning on her heel and marching back into chambers.

"Stand up when the judge gets here," Ashley said, leaning close and whispering to Aubrey. "Make sure to address him as 'Your Honor,' if you address him at all."

The judge would give her a right to speak at sentencing. It was called the right to allocution, but Ashley hoped that Aubrey wouldn't say anything. Her clients almost always made things worse for themselves when they did. Aubrey nodded just as Margaret and Judge Ahrenson entered the courtroom.

"All rise," Margaret said. She was carrying her sleek black stenotype machine. "The Honorable Judge Ahrenson presiding." Margaret sat in the seat in front of the judge's bench, placing her machine in front of her.

The judge followed behind her, wearing the traditional black robe. He was a slim man of average height with thinning gray hair and eyes that were crystal blue and sharp as an ice pick. His robe billowed off his wiry frame as he walked briskly.

"You may be seated," Judge Ahrenson said as he lowered himself into his chair at the bench. He waited as Ashley, Aubrey, and Charles Hanson all followed suit. "We are convened today in State of Iowa versus Aubrey Miller, Brine County Case Number AGCR019381. Are the parties ready to proceed?"

"Yes, Your Honor," Charles said.

Judge Ahrenson's cool gaze shifted, settling on Ashley.

"Yes, Your Honor," Ashley said.

"Ms. Miller has entered a guilty plea to possession of methamphetamine, second offense, an aggravated misdemeanor. Today is the date set for sentencing. I see no motion in arrest of judgment or other pending motions, so we will proceed. Mr. Hanson, I'll hear your recommendation first."

Charles cleared his throat and rose to his feet. "Thank you, Your Honor. As you know, this is Ms. Miller's second offense. She was most recently arrested and convicted of the same thing six months ago. Last time, she received probation, and here we are again. Obviously, probation did not work. She's been out on pretrial release, but I see no substance abuse evaluation has been completed or filed with the court."

All drug offenders were ordered to complete a substance abuse evaluation prior to sentencing. Ashley always told her clients to comply with the court's orders and to complete treatment before their plea or sentencing, but they rarely listened. Methamphetamine was an all-consuming drug. Her clients couldn't seem to find the will to detach themselves from its grips while at liberty. Aubrey was no exception.

"She has no job."

That was another suggestion that Ashley often made to her clients, but they rarely took her seriously. Again, Aubrey had not followed this request. Not that she would make much of an employee anyway with her raging meth addiction. If she could bother to show up at work, she'd probably be high and get fired anyway.

"She isn't in school. Which, to me, indicates that she has no intention of becoming a productive member of society. It is for those reasons, Your Honor, that the State is requesting that Aubrey Miller receive the maximum sentence of two years in prison."

Ashley could feel Aubrey go rigid beside her. She was scared, and she had reason to be, but what did she expect? She hadn't followed a single one of Ashley's recommendations.

"Thank you, Mr. Hanson," Judge Ahrenson said as Charles

lowered his substantial bulk into his seat. He'd gained a good thirty pounds in the last year.

Ashley would be lying if she said she didn't quietly appreciate how everything seemed to get harder for Charles with his increase in weight. His breathing was heavier, and she overheard him complaining about pain in his knees on multiple occasions.

"Ms. Montgomery," Judge Ahrenson turned to Ashley, "I'll hear your recommendation now."

Ashley rose to her feet. "Thank you, Your Honor. Ms. Miller has pled guilty and taken accountability for her involvement in this crime. She is young, in her thirties. She has an addiction. She is here for possessing methamphetamine, a drug that everyone knows is difficult to shake. No, she has not gotten into treatment, but that is just another symptom of her all-consuming addiction. What she needs is treatment, not incarceration. For those reasons, the defense is requesting that the court order Ms. Miller to a suspended sentence with probation to the Department of Correctional Services."

The Department of Correctional Services was just a fancy name for probation. They provided all kinds of supervision services, including pretrial release, probation, and parole. Ashley's request seemed like a longshot since Aubrey had already been sentenced to probation and that had clearly failed, but Ashley still hoped for the best. It didn't help that meth had become an epidemic in Brine County over the last few years, and Ashley had made this same argument to Judge Ahrenson more times than she could count.

"Thank you, Ashley," the judge said. "Would your client like to make a statement before I render judgment?"

Ashley glanced over to Aubrey. Thankfully, her client shook her head.

"No, Your Honor."

"Very well. I've listened to the arguments of the parties. I've considered the defendant's age, criminal history, and the parties' recommendations. I note that the State is at one end of the spectrum, while the defense is at the opposite end. I am going to fall somewhere in the middle. I am going to order Ms. Miller to serve one year in the county jail with all but thirty days suspended. She'll be placed on probation to the Department of Correctional Services for two years."

"What does that mean?" Aubrey whispered to Ashley.

"It means you'll go to jail for thirty days, and then you'll be on probation like last time," Ashley whispered back. "If you screw up on probation, you'll face the remainder of your one-year sentence in jail."

Judge Ahrenson had launched into a speech about the evils of methamphetamine. It was something all parties in the courtroom had heard enough times that they could probably recite it from heart, so nobody was listening.

"I'd rather go to prison," Aubrey whined.

"Well, it's too late for that. And, quite frankly, the judge does not care what you *want*."

Prison was far easier time than jail because there were other things to do other than sit and twiddle your thumbs. If a prisoner was well behaved, she could hold a job and spend a good deal of time out in the yard. Jail had no such privileges.

"I don't want to share a cell with Erica Elsberry for a full month. She's self-absorbed, and she's always talking. I'm not going to get any sleep."

Ashley shrugged. "I'll get you some earplugs." Aubrey looked incensed, and Ashley didn't blame her. "Look, I'm not happy about this either, but it's a final sentence."

As though Judge Ahrenson had heard her, he said, "That will be the final judgment of the court. The court is in recess."

He had finished with his meth lecture, and court was over. A jailer would arrive soon, and Aubrey would be led from the courtroom to start her thirty days in jail.

It was all pretty frustrating. Ashley couldn't help feeling dejected. The judge probably felt like he was splitting the baby between the recommendations—and he was—but it did little to help Aubrey. She wouldn't receive substance abuse treatment while in jail.

In thirty days, she'd come out the same as before, only more desperate for a fix. It wouldn't be long before she'd be right back in the same seat, but the next time would be a felony charge. Aubrey would likely be in and out of jails and prisons for the rest of her life. That was the hamster wheel called the criminal justice system. Once you were caught up in its spokes, there was usually only one way out—and that was death.

# 6

## KATIE

The ambulance arrived faster than Katie had expected. It must have been coming back from a trip to the Brine County Medical Center, which was out in the country and closer to Frank's barn, because all Brine ambulances were housed at the fire department and there was no way they could get all the way out to Frank's property within ten minutes, even with lights flashing and sirens blaring.

Katie continued taking pictures. She needed to document, but she also found some semblance of comfort in looking at the scene through something, using her camera's viewfinder to put a barrier between herself and the horrors unfolding in that clearing. The fire still raged in the background, but the primary focal point had shifted to the person pulled from somewhere inside the burning barn.

Three emergency medical technicians hopped out of the ambulance, but even Katie with her limited medical training as a police officer could tell that the person was no longer alive. There was no movement, and the body had been burned beyond recognition. The skin was black and papery, like a marshmallow that had been dropped into a campfire.

"There's no hope," one of the EMTs said almost immediately. "This one is already gone." He was a man who looked to be twice Katie's age with prematurely thick grooves etched into his skin likely from years of stress.

George stood next to the EMT, shaking his head. "Can you tell who it is?"

"Nope. You can ask the medical examiner when she gets here, but I doubt we're going to be able to get an ID without running DNA. It's just too hard to tell when they are in this condition. It would probably be a fair guess to say it's the property owner, but you and I both know Frank. If anyone made it out of a fire like this alive, it would be that weasel."

Katie recognized the EMT as a townie, like George, but she didn't know him by name. And he was right about Frank. He wouldn't get caught up in a fire at his own barn. He rarely left the property. He had to know it like the back of his hand. The thought made a shiver run up Katie's spine, and she couldn't shake the feeling that she was being watched.

"If that's not Frank," George said, turning to scan the tree-tops, "I better start looking for him. This case just changed from a manufacturing charge to a murder investigation."

*Shit*, Katie thought, pushing herself back into the foliage as George's gaze swept past her.

If she'd moved a half-second later, George would have seen her. It was probably time for her to wrap up her own investigation. She needed to get out of there before he started traipsing around in the woods and ran straight into her. But she was also reluctant to do so. This would probably be her best opportunity to gather evidence. Otherwise, the defense would have to rely on whatever evidence George found, and Katie hadn't seen him take a single picture so far.

*No*, she decided. She wouldn't allow it. Her job was to even the playing field between prosecution and defense, and she couldn't do that running from George with her tail between her legs. If he found her out here, so be it. Sure, she would have some explaining to do, but it wasn't a crime to take crime-scene photographs, and there wasn't anything preventing her from being on Frank's property.

Just then, her phone buzzed in her pocket. Most phones didn't work on Frank's property, but Katie used a local carrier that was more expensive but also more reliable. She pulled it out and studied the screen. It was a text message from Ashley.

*I just finished Aubrey Miller's sentencing hearing. I haven't heard from you. Are you okay?*

Katie unlocked the phone and typed a message back. *I'm fine. How'd Aubrey's sentencing go?*

*Shitty. I'll fill you in later. What's going on out at Frank's?*

*It's a mess. A firefighter pulled a body out of the wreckage.*

*Is it Frank?*

*I can't tell. The body is too burned. George doesn't think it's him. He's treating it as a murder.*

*You be careful. I'd feel better if I knew where Frank was.*

*I'm fine*, Katie typed back, but it was a lie. The heat from the fire had leached nearly every ounce of moisture from her, and she still had that eerie sense that someone was watching her.

*Another murder. Could this day get any worse?*

Katie understood Ashley's reluctance to represent a client in a murder case. If it was like any of Ashley's past cases, the whole town would get involved. Lately things had been quiet. Ashley hadn't received a death threat for over six months, which was a record for her, and Katie wasn't eager to start receiving threats of her own.

*That's all for now*, Katie typed. *I'll let you know when I have more.*

*Great. Thanks.*

Katie pocketed her phone and turned back to the scene in front of her. The fire was still burning hot and wild. Which was bad enough on its own, but what made matters worse was that the wind was picking up and it was blowing in her direction. Long tendrils of fire pointed at her in an almost accusatory way. It was like they were telling her to *get out, get out, get out!*

She started to back away. It was probably time to leave. At least until the firefighters could get the fire under control. The drought had turned the woods into excellent kindling, and she didn't want to end up like the poor person pulled from Frank's barn.

But just as she was starting to back out, she heard one of the firefighters shout, "We've got a second one!"

Katie leaned forward, despite the harsh heat of the fire.

"There's a second body in here. It could be a child!"

*A second body*, Katie thought. *And a child.*

That made things a whole lot worse. The first body could have been Frank, even though nobody seemed to believe that it was him, but the second—that most certainly was not him. Frank was not a small man. But who was it?

There was another gust of wind, pulling Katie out of her thoughts and forcing her to jump back. She wanted to take pictures of the second body, but it was getting too dangerous to remain hidden in the woods. If the fire jumped from the buildings to the woods, there would be little chance of her getting out undetected. The entire time she'd been there had been a gamble. Katie wasn't much of a gambler—especially when it came to her life—and it was best to quit while she was ahead, or she might not be around to play the next hand.

# 7

## ASHLEY

Ashley had no doubt that Katie was a crucial asset to her team, but it was times like these—when there was a potential murder trial pending in the not-too-distant future—that Ashley truly appreciated her investigator. Before Katie came along, Ashley had to do all the legal work and investigating on her own. Back then, it hadn't mattered how many hours she worked, she was always one step behind the prosecution. Mostly because she could not be two places at once. But now, with Katie at her side, she could.

That didn't mean that Ashley had less work to do, though. It might seem that way, but she had no problem filling that extra time with the needs of other clients. And that was what happened the moment she'd finished texting with Katie. Her phone starting ringing, and a familiar number populated the screen.

"This is Ashley," Ashley said, bringing her phone up to her ear.

"Ashley, it's Morgan. Morgan Stanman..." Morgan was an on-again, off-again client of Ashley's. Her current charge was for burglary of an unattached garage. She was out on pretrial release.

"I know who it is. What's going on?"

Morgan's voice had been high pitched and squeaky, the way it always was when Morgan was panicking. It immediately put Ashley on edge.

"I need...there's a...he said...*help me!*" Morgan dissolved into a fit of tears.

"Calm down, Morgan. I can't help you if I don't understand you. Are the police interrogating you?" The number that Morgan had called from belonged to the police department.

Morgan cried for several more moments, then hiccupped and seemed to gain some semblance of control over herself. "No...I mean, maybe...I don't know. Can you come?"

"Yes. I'm on my way. Don't say anything to anyone until I get there. Got it?"

"Umm, yeah."

Ashley would have preferred a little more confidence behind Morgan's words, but she'd take what she could get. "I'll be there in five minutes."

"Okay."

Ashley was already headed for the door. She was still at the courthouse from Aubrey's sentencing. She'd intended to visit Aubrey at the jail right away to make sure she was settling in okay for her thirty-day sentence, but Morgan sounded like she was in genuine crisis, so she took precedence. The police department was next door to the courthouse and connected to the jail, so she'd go see Aubrey after she was done with Morgan.

It had been a long time since Ashley had seen Morgan in a condition that was anything above barely scraping by, but she hadn't been prepared for what she saw when she walked into the interview room. Morgan was pacing back and forth along the back wall with her hands balled into fists, muttering to herself. Her baggy T-shirt was ripped in several places, and her shorts were flecked with dirt and what appeared to be dried blood. Her legs and arms were peppered with welts, scratches, and darkened spots that would later turn into bruises.

"Morgan," Ashley said, hurrying into the interview room and closing the door behind her. "What the hell happened to you?"

Morgan stopped pacing and looked down at herself as though shocked by her appearance.

"You look like someone beat you with a switch. And is that blood on your shorts? Who did this to you?"

"The blood is mine, probably. And nothing...nobody, I mean, hurt me."

"Okay," Ashley said, disbelieving.

"I...umm...I don't know how to say this. It's nothing, though. I had a mishap with a tree, I guess."

It was a hell of a lot more complicated than a "mishap with a tree," but Ashley knew the line where questioning a client could hinder her ability to represent them, and this was it. Any story Morgan told Ashley now would have to be the one she stuck to on the stand when or if she was charged with a crime. Although, looking at Morgan now, she seemed more like the victim than the perpetrator.

"Okay," Ashley said slowly. "What's going on?"

"I can't go back to jail. I can't."

It was not an answer, but it was a start. It also wasn't truthful. Morgan had a pending burglary charge, and she was out on pretrial release. If she'd done something to violate the terms of that pretrial release, then she could and would go back to jail and wait there until her trial date.

Morgan was starting to hyperventilate again, and she was

clenching her fists so hard that her nails dug into her palms, drawing blood. *Well, that explains the blood on her pants*, Ashley thought. "Let's talk about why you are here. Who brought you in?"

"I don't know. Some deputy." Morgan motioned to what looked like a mirror that encompassed almost the entire side wall. It was long and thin and at eye level. It was supposed to be discreet, but anyone who'd ever seen a cop show would recognize it as a one-way window. If cops wanted to fool people, they needed to come up with something better—like one that looked like a picture instead of a mirror.

"Did he put you in handcuffs?"

"No."

"Then how did he get you here?"

"He said I needed to come voluntarily." She used air quotes around the word *voluntarily*. "Which isn't very voluntary, now, is it," she said, turning to the mirror and shouting that last bit straight at it.

"Screaming at them is not going to help, Morgan. Even though it might make you feel better." Ashley completely understood how Morgan was feeling. She'd once been wrongly incarcerated, and she, too, had the urge to rage at them until they set her free.

"But I can't go back. You know I can't. I can't handle it. *You hear me!*" She began shouting and banging on the one-way window, her fists leaving small circles of blood on the mirror. "*Let me out of here, you fucking assholes!*" Then she sank to the floor sobbing.

"Stay here, Morgan. I'll be right back."

Ashley empathized with Morgan's position but couldn't handle the hysterics. Not because they were unjustified, but because Ashley simply didn't have the emotional tools to properly address them. She knew Morgan had been abused as a child and she'd developed a phobia of small or confined spaces—a particularly difficult phobia to have when facing incarceration in a jail cell—but Ashley's personality wasn't one that was equipped to provide reassurances that everything would be okay. Especially since Ashley didn't know if it would.

"*Ash-ley!* Don't leave me," Morgan began to wail, high pitched and whining, drawing Ashley's name out into two distinct syllables.

"Stop it," Ashley said in the harshest tone she could muster. Sometimes her clients needed tough love, and this was one of those occasions. She wasn't Morgan's therapist, she was her attorney, and she needed Morgan to understand the difference.

Morgan didn't stop crying, but she did quiet down.

"I'm going to step out for a few minutes. I need to find out why they are holding you. Then I'll be back. Okay?"

"Okay."

Ashley stepped out into the hallway and banged on the door leading to the room on the opposite side of the one-way window. Since Morgan was in the interview room, it only seemed logical that someone would be watching through that window. A moment passed, then she heard the shuffling of feet before the door opened.

"Zachary Brinks," Ashley said. He was a sheriff's deputy. New to the department within the past year, but she and Zachary had already had a few skirmishes in the courtroom. All of which she had won, of course.

"Can you tell your client to stop banging on the window?"

"Tell me why she's here, and I'll consider it."

Zachary stared at Ashley for a long moment, eyes narrowed to slits, but he finally relented. "Violation of pretrial release is all I know."

"How did she violate it?"

Zachary shrugged. "You'll have to ask George. He's the one who requested the warrant."

"George Thomanson?"

"Yeah."

"I will do that. Is he planning on turning up anytime soon?"

Zachary shrugged again, his big shoulders bobbing up and down. It was an action that Ashley thought he really should avoid. It made him look like a big, dumb animal. Like a bear with half a brain. "He's busy at the moment."

"Yeah, I know. He's out at Frank Vinny's place."

"How do you know that?"

"I know everything, Zachary. The sooner you figure that out, the better," Ashley said before turning on her heel and marching back into the interview room.

Morgan was on the floor curled into the fetal position, which was only marginally less dramatic than she'd been when Ashley had left.

"We are waiting for Detective Thomanson to get here, whenever that will be." Ashley mumbled that second part under her breath. "But Deputy Brinks says that you are here for a violation of pretrial release. Do you know what that's all about?"

Morgan shook her head and sniffled.

"Seriously, Morgan. You have no idea? No clue as to what you could have done?"

"Nooooo..." Morgan wailed. "I didn't do anything."

*That might be the problem*, Ashley thought as she dropped into one of the two seats at the interview table. Part of pretrial release was treatment and meeting with a pretrial release officer. If Morgan truly had done *nothing*, it could be almost as bad as if she had committed a crime.

Ashley sighed and reached into her laptop bag, removing a stack of paperwork. It sounded like it would be a while before George would decide to grace them with his presence, so she might as well get some paperwork done.

In any event, she needed something to distract her from Morgan's pathetic figure balled up in the corner of the room. She was calmer now that Ashley had returned and was clearly sticking around for a while, but she hadn't made any moves to pick herself up off the floor.

Morgan had always been a bit theatrical, but this time felt different. She'd never thrown a fit quite like this one. It made Ashley wonder if Morgan had done something far worse than violating her pretrial release, something that would result in a far longer term of incarceration. She hoped not, but with the way Ashley's day was shaping up, she had to expect the worst.

# 8

## ASHLEY

The first fifteen minutes that Ashley waited with Morgan hadn't bothered Ashley, but after that, she'd grown impatient, glancing at her watch every few minutes. She hated waiting—especially when it was George Thomanson's fault—but she was willing to give him a little leeway because he was at the fire, and they were dealing with a body. Once the thirty-minute mark passed, though, she was no longer quite so generous.

Morgan was back up, pacing along the back wall. Fortunately, she wasn't sobbing or muttering to herself anymore. Ashley's constant presence had quelled the most destructive part of Morgan's panic, but she still wasn't calm by any stretch of the imagination.

Ashley picked up her phone, unlocking it to check for messages on social media. Many of her clients used Facebook Messenger to contact her. Ashley preferred phone calls or emails but would accept any form of communication when the alternative was disappearing until a warrant was issued. Before she could click the Messenger icon, her phone started buzzing in her hand.

"Katie," Ashley said, picking up the call. "How's it going?"

"Not good." Katie sounded breathless, like she was running from something.

"What's wrong?"

"Hold on."

Ashley could hear Katie's breaths and her footfalls as they crunched in what sounded like gravel. A few moments later, there was a click, followed by a dinging sound and the sharp slam of a car door.

"All right," Katie said. "I'm in the car. That was intense." Katie was holding herself together, but Ashley could hear the telltale shudder in her voice. She was scared.

"What? What was intense?"

"The fire is getting out of control. It looks like it could spread to the woods. I feel like I barely made it out of there alive."

"Are you okay?"

Ashley hadn't thought about the risk Katie was taking. Sure, she'd been worried about what Frank would do if he encountered her out there in his woods, but she hadn't even thought about the danger the fire posed. She'd known there was a chemical fire and she'd known that Brine was in a severe drought, yet she'd still sent Katie in there. It was like a death trap. What kind of boss was she?

"Yeah. I'm fine now. But we've got a problem."

"What kind of problem?"

"They found another body..." Katie paused for a long, tense moment. Ashley allowed the silence to stretch out, giving Katie time to gather herself. "They think it's a child."

"*A child?*" Ashley jumped out of her seat, shocked. She hadn't known what to expect, but this wasn't it.

"They don't know for sure, but I think the firefighter was basing it on the size of the body. I wanted to stick around to see if I could hear more or get some pictures, but that's when the wind shifted, and I had to get out of there. Sorry..."

"No, no," Ashley said, shaking her head. "Don't apologize. You've gotten far more than I expected. And it was dangerous. I should be thanking you for risking your life for a case that isn't even officially open yet."

"The medical examiner is supposed to be on her way, but I doubt she's going that direction if they don't get the fire under control. We should know more after she's examined the bodies. Hopefully, we can get an identification on one or both."

"A child..." Ashley said. "Why would Frank have a child at the barn?"

Morgan visibly flinched when Ashley mentioned the words *child* and *Frank*, and she started to grow agitated again. Her pacing picked up, and her lips moved as if she were talking, but no words followed. Ashley watched Morgan for a moment, then focused back on Katie.

"Frank doesn't have any children, and nobody would ask *him* to babysit. Unless he stole the kid, but I don't remember hearing any recent AMBER Alerts. Do you?"

"No. But I think we're getting a little ahead of ourselves. There's a possibility that the body belongs to a small woman. It doesn't make the situation a whole lot better, but child victims are the worst to deal with."

"I agree." Ashley had represented people accused of crimes against children in the past, and it had never been easy. They rarely took full responsibility for their actions, and the public always blamed Ashley if she ended up with a good outcome at trial.

"I'm headed back to the office, but I'm going to stop by my house to shower first. I smell like burned flesh, which, it turns out, is the worst smell in the world. I should be back at the office in about an hour. If you're done with Morgan, meet me there, and we can go over the pictures together."

Ashley's gaze darted to Morgan. Her fingernails were digging back into the skin of her palms. Blood dripped from both of her hands, beading up and dropping on the floor every few minutes.

"Yeah, I think it's going to be a while. We've still got to wait for Sir Georgie."

"I think George is on his way. I was on a path that ran parallel to the driveway when I left. I could hear him walking up to his car, too."

Ashley froze. "Why would he come here? He just discovered a second body. Unless..."

"Yup," Katie said. "He seems to think Morgan knows something about the fire."

"Why does he think that?"

"I don't know. I overheard him on the phone with Morgan's pretrial release officer as he walked up the driveway. He was asking her a lot of questions about Morgan's whereabouts."

"Shit," Ashley said with a hiss, her gaze shifting to Morgan. "I'll finish up here, and then I'll meet you at the office. If charges are coming soon, we better get moving on our end of the investigation."

"See you then," Katie said, and they both hung up.

Ashley turned to Morgan, studying the welts on her arms and legs in a new light. What if she hadn't been struck by a switch, but instead whipped by branches as she ran? That was what George would see when he stepped into this interview room, and Ashley was powerless to stop him from discovering that vital piece of evidence.

# 9

## KATIE

Katie drove home with all four of her windows down. The scent of smoke and burned flesh clung to her, like the stink from a skunk. She tried to keep her mind busy by turning up the radio, but her thoughts kept wandering back to the bodies found in Frank's barn. They had been so charred. Had pieces of them floated through the air along with the other ash from the fire? Did she unwittingly breathe in parts of dead people?

*Stop!* she chided herself. No good came from thoughts like these. It wouldn't get her home any faster. But, oh, how she longed to get into the shower and crank the heat up as high as she could stand and wash away the horrors of the day.

Frank's barn was out in the country—about forty miles south of town. It normally would have taken Katie a good forty-five minutes to get back to her apartment, but this was the one time in her life that she allowed herself to speed. Within thirty minutes, she was turning onto her street and parking in her usual parking spot. When she did, she hopped out of the car and jogged toward the front door. She couldn't wait to get inside. She was almost there, but she froze when she reached the steps leading to the front of the building.

A man was leaning against the railing, his arms crossed and eyes shifty. He had aged a great deal, and he was a few pounds lighter than he had been the last time she saw him, but she would recognize that profile anywhere. It was in the way he held himself—like he owned the world. Sure, his shoulders hunched forward a little more and his back curved slightly under the weight of his sins, but he still had some of that same arrogance about him even all these years later.

Katie took a few deep breaths, then forced her body to move forward, jogging up the steps two at a time until she was at the top. "Follow me," she said to the man. She had no intention of greeting him.

The man did as she asked without saying a word.

She scanned the outside of the building, looking for anyone who might have seen him standing there, but everything was still. Earlier in the day, she'd been cursing the brutal heat, but now she was thankful for it. People would stay indoors with their shades drawn at least until the sun set.

Katie entered through the main entrance and walked briskly down the shared hallway. The carpet covering the floor was stained and smelled of cigarette smoke even though "no smoking" signs lined the walls. There were three floors to her apartment building and four apartments on each floor. Hers was apartment 104. It was the second door to the left.

When they reached her apartment, she pulled her keys out of her pocket and flipped to the right one with shaking hands. It took her a moment to jam it into the lock, but when she did, she threw the door open and turned to the man. "Get inside," she said.

The man stepped past her, and she followed him, slamming the door behind her. Her breaths came quick and shallow. She was hyperventilating. She needed to get control of her emotions, but this was all too much. The events of the day had been horrific. She didn't know if she could handle this on top of it all.

"Hello, Katie," the man said.

"Don't *hello* me. What are you doing here?" Katie demanded.

"Is that any way to greet your father?"

"I have no father. He's been dead to me since I found out that everything he ever told me was a lie."

"Fine. That's fine, Katie." Michael Michello shifted his gaze to the floor. "Then call me Michael. At least until you are comfortable with me again."

"I will never be comfortable with you. Never."

Rage, fueled from years of pent-up frustration, welled within her. All at once she was that helpless sixteen-year-old girl watching her father as he was dragged away by police. Back when everything disappeared in the blink of an eye. Her mother left, the money was gone, he was locked up. She had everything one moment, then nothing the next. How could she possibly explain that to him?

"I'm glad you agreed to see me," Michael said after a long pause.

"I didn't agree to anything. You showed up outside my apartment, and I didn't want anyone to see you. That's the only reason we are speaking at all."

"So, it's true," Michael said, crossing his arms. "You are hiding from your past."

"No. I'm hiding from *your* past. I haven't done anything that would make me want to hide. You, on the other hand, you destroyed my life."

"A name change isn't going to keep this buried forever."

Katie had changed her name from Kaitlyn Michello to Katie Mickey. Deep down, she had always known that this day would come—when people opened the closet door and found the skeleton of her father's crimes. He'd been a financial planner—a successful one—right up until he was busted for embezzling money from his clients. It turned out that he'd lost all his clients' money, and the government then took everything that Michael had. The mansion with the pool was sold, the staff was dismissed, and the tuition for Katie's expensive private school went unpaid.

"The name change was working up until now. But, sure, people are going to piece it together if a notorious felon starts showing up unbidden on my doorstep saying he's my father. That doesn't leave a lot open for interpretation."

"I would say I'm sorry, but I wanted to see you."

"I wish I could say the same," Katie said with a snort.

"You do?" Michael quirked an eyebrow.

"Sure," Katie said with a sigh. "But wishing things were different is a bit like spitting in an empty pond to try and fill it. The effort is fruitless."

A small smile twitched into the corners of his mouth. "That analogy," he said, shaking his head. "You've always been my little tomboy."

"I'm not your little anything anymore. If you haven't noticed, I'm an adult, and I became a cop for six years because I hated what you did."

"Why aren't you in law enforcement anymore?"

"I don't want to talk about that," Katie said, marching into the kitchen area of the apartment and grabbing a bottle of wine and a glass. She needed alcohol if she was going to finish this conversation. She twisted the top off the bottle and poured until the dark red liquid nearly reached the lip of the glass. "I'd offer you some, but I don't like you and you are probably on parole, so you probably can't drink wine anyway."

"Yeah. I'm on parole."

"I didn't know you were out of prison. When did you get paroled?" Katie said before taking a large drink of wine.

"Last week."

*Last week?* Katie almost spit her wine out. "How did you find me so quickly?"

Michael shrugged. "I have my ways."

"That's not creepy at all," Katie muttered.

"Don't worry about *how* I found you. Let's just worry about fixing this relationship between us. Whether you like it or not, I'm your family. The only family you've got."

Katie snorted and took another drink of wine. "Mom's out there somewhere. She's probably even popped out a few more kids with that doctor from the country club that she ran off with. She'd need to do that to ensure child support if he left her."

Michael's eyes grew weary, almost sad. "Your mother always did know how to get what she wanted. I loved her, though. She apparently didn't feel quite the same way about me."

"Well," Katie said, eyeing him, "the lying and stealing certainly didn't help."

"Let's not talk about your mother," Michael said, shaking his head, like he was trying to physically knock the idea of Katie's mother out of his mind. "Let's talk about us."

A clock hung in the living room, just above the couch. Katie could easily see it from her spot in the kitchen. Everything in this tiny, shitty apartment was right there except the bathroom and bedroom, which were down a short hallway. It wasn't a bad apartment as far as apartments went, but she wanted a place of her own. Somewhere that she could hang pictures on the wall and decide the color of the living room paint. She'd been saving for years for a down payment, but she hadn't gotten very far.

"It's nearly five o'clock," Katie said. "I have to be back at the office to meet my boss and go over some things, but first, I need to shower." In all the excitement, she'd forgotten about the smell of death that she had been carrying around. All the sudden she was acutely aware of it, and she held her arms out away from her body as if that could do something to air out the stench. "The sooner, the better."

"What is that smell?" Michael said, wrinkling his nose.

"You don't want to know."

"If I leave now, will you agree to meet with me sometime soon?"

Katie knew he wasn't going to leave her alone unless she agreed to his terms. "Are you living in the halfway house in Ames?"

Ames was a college town thirty minutes northeast of Brine. It was where Iowa State University was located, but also the location of the Curt Forbes Residential Correctional Facility, or halfway house for short. The facility was the next step down from full incarceration. Inmates had to get jobs and pay rent. Once they proved they could assimilate back into society, they'd be released on full parole.

"Yeah. I'm doing some work in Brine County."

"Working?" Katie said, furrowing her brow. "Where?"

"Don't worry about that."

Oh, she was worried all right. Him working in the area presented more opportunities for Brine residents to discover her background. It was always a secret with an expiration date, but she wasn't quite ready for that day to come. But then again, she probably never would be.

"Seriously," Katie said, "I really have to get in the shower." She was past wary of him, and she just wanted him out.

"Will you call me?"

"Sure." Katie sighed heavily. "What's your number?" She grabbed her cell phone, ready to type it in.

"The same as it has always been."

She lowered her phone and met his gaze. "The same?" She narrowed her eyes. The only way that was possible was if he had been paying his phone bill all these years while incarcerated. But with what money? None of it made any sense. "I'd ask you how, but the common thread of this conversation is that you don't answer the tough questions. So, I'm not even going to bother."

"Good," Michael said with a nod. "It's better that way."

Katie doubted burying her head in the sand was better, especially considering her father's propensity to commit crimes, but she didn't have time to worry about it now. She had work to do, and she was in desperate need of a shower. So, she halfheartedly agreed with her father and all but shoved him out the door. He was a problem that she'd have to deal with, but not yet.

First, she needed to clean the ash from her skin, then she would start working on a way to figure out the identities of the two bodies pulled from Frank's fire.

# 10

## ASHLEY

Ashley eyed Morgan. Her agitation had increased notably at the mention of Frank's name. Morgan had never taken well to incarceration, but something about Frank had her well past worried.

"What is it?" Ashley asked.

"Nothing," Morgan answered far too quickly.

"Do you know something about those bodies found in Frank's barn?"

Morgan paused and looked up, but then continued pacing without saying a word.

"Did Frank kill two people and burn the barn to cover it up?"

"I don't think that's what happened," Morgan said without breaking stride.

"Then what *did* happen?"

"Nothing."

"Doesn't look like nothing to me."

Morgan didn't respond to Ashley's statement, and Ashley decided that it was probably best to leave it at that. There was no point in hounding her clients for information. She'd tell

Ashley when she was ready. Or, perhaps, she'd never tell. Which, to be honest, was the better option. Ashley preferred working at trial with a blank slate rather than being tied to whatever story her client had told her.

"We sure have been waiting here a long time," Ashley said, glancing at her watch. A full hour had passed since Ashley had arrived, and Morgan had been there even longer. "I'm going to call George and see where the hell he is." Katie had said that he was on his way, but that was forty minutes earlier. He should have been right behind Katie. He couldn't hold Morgan indefinitely. He either needed to charge her and put her in a cell or release her. The former was far more likely than the latter, which wasn't ideal, but at least they'd know what they were dealing with.

"Good idea," Morgan mumbled.

Ashley removed her cell phone and clicked on the name "Sir Georgie." George hadn't given Ashley his cell phone number, and he wasn't happy that she had it. She'd gotten it from Katie when they started working together. Since then, Ashley had badgered him enough that she assumed he would get a new number. He hadn't yet, so she was taking full advantage of the situation.

The phone began to ring, and she put it on speaker. The ringing coming from the phone filled the room, but it wasn't the only ringing sound. A phone rang out in the hallway, faint at first but growing louder.

*He must be here*, Ashley thought moments before the doorknob turned and in strutted Sir George-a-lot.

"Sorry to keep you waiting," George said, closing the door behind him.

"Are you?" Ashley said.

"Not really." George turned and came to the table, dropping into the seat across from Ashley.

"There aren't enough chairs for Morgan to sit," Ashley said, gesturing to her client.

"It seems like Morgan is fine standing. Right?" He directed the question to Morgan, but he kept his gaze trained on Ashley.

"Yeah." Morgan's voice was weaker now that George had arrived, like she had somehow shriveled and shrunken in his presence.

"Since you took your sweet time to get here, let's get straight to business. Why are you holding my client?"

"Violation of pretrial release."

"Yeah. Your deputy told me that much. But what *is* the violation? You can't just claim a violation without telling us what she's supposedly done."

George's gaze shifted to Morgan, first settling on her face, then travelling down the length of her body to rest on her ankle. "She cut off her tracker."

"She did *what*?"

Ashley whirled in her seat, staring straight at Morgan's ankles. They were both empty. There was a tan line on her left leg, the only sign of the once affixed ankle monitor. Ashley had forgotten about that added condition to Morgan's pretrial release. The judge had specifically included it in his order. This was bad. Why the hell would Morgan do something like that?

Ashley wasn't dumb enough to believe that the tracker had fallen off on its own. Those things held on with a vise grip. And even if the impossible had happened—as it sometimes did—Morgan had a duty to call her pretrial release officer and inform her of the malfunction. Then the pretrial release officer would have come straight to Morgan's residence and affixed a new one. Since there was no replacement monitor, Ashley could only assume the worst.

"Guess where I found it," George said, removing what looked like Morgan's ankle monitor from a sack. It was encased in a large plastic evidence bag, which wasn't a good sign.

Morgan's mouth opened to answer, but Ashley cut her off before she could say a word. "Morgan is exercising her right to remain silent, and I'm not interested in your silly guessing game. You're either going to tell us or you aren't, but we aren't going to make any guesses."

"Very well," George said, looking smug. "I found it in a ditch less than a quarter mile from Frank Vinny's property." He paused, letting that sink in. "You know...where that fire has been raging."

"Is that so?" Ashley said, trying to sound nonchalant even though her heart was pounding wildly in her chest.

"You wouldn't have anything to do with that fire, now would you, Morgan?"

"Do not answer that," Ashley said without turning around to look at her client.

This was bad, really bad. Ashley had already suspected her client might have been involved in the fire. It didn't bode well that law enforcement seemed to be on the same track.

Ashley had no idea what started the fire. Maybe it was arson, maybe it was a meth fire, but that wasn't the part that had Ashley worried. It was the bodies. It didn't matter if the fire was an accidental meth fire. The bodies meant that felony murder charges would follow. Either way, Morgan was looking at a hell of a lot more time than a piddly little violation of pretrial release for a burglary charge.

"I think that's enough interviewing for one day," Ashley said, placing her hands flat on the table and shoving her seat back.

"But..." Morgan started to speak, but her words were choked off by a burst of sobs.

"Be quiet," Ashley said, rising to her feet and turning to approach her client.

"I can't go to jail," Morgan wailed.

"You can and you will." Ashley grabbed both of Morgan's arms and forced her to meet her gaze. "Listen to me," she said, lowering her voice so only Morgan could hear. "This is bad. The pretrial violation is the least of your worries. You need to stay quiet and keep your head down until I can figure out what's going on and how much George has on you. Do you understand?"

Morgan nodded slowly, but she was a mess. Tears spilled down her face, mingling with the snot that poured from her nose. When Ashley released her arms, she crumpled to the floor, sobbing. Morgan was desperate to stay out of jail, but there was no way around it anymore. As Ashley headed toward the door, she could only hope that Morgan wouldn't do anything stupid, like self-harm or confess. When she reached the doorway, she stopped.

"And George," Ashley called over her shoulder.

"Yeah?"

"Don't talk to my client without me present."

"Sure thing," George said without conviction.

"I mean it," Ashley said.

Then she left the room, heading back to the office to meet with Katie. They had an investigation to conduct. She hoped that George and Morgan would honor her request and avoid speaking without her present, but deep down she knew better. Neither of them would listen to her. So long as Morgan remained in that jail, it was only a matter of time before she started talking.

# 11

## KATIE

Katie shut the door and locked it behind Michael Michello, then rushed to the window to watch him leave, all the while thinking, *Go, go, go*. She didn't know why she was doing it, because she couldn't prevent him from lingering or stop him from telling others about their connection. It was merely instinct. A way to feel like she had some control over an uncontrollable situation.

She watched him step into a black Cadillac SUV, wondering how he had scraped up the money to afford a car like that. He was freshly out of prison, and the government had drained every account the family had once owned. Shaking her head, she turned away from the window. She'd have to chalk it up to just another Michael Michello mystery. For all she knew, he could have been borrowing it, but that raised a whole separate set of questions.

Dispelling the thoughts of Michael, Katie hopped into the shower and cranked the heat up as high as it would go. The one good thing about her shitty apartment was the water pressure. Sometimes it felt like it was strong enough to strip paint, which was more than welcome to her on that day.

She'd be just fine if it stripped off the entire outer layer of her skin.

After showering, she pulled her red hair back and twisted it into a bun on the top of her head, keeping the wet hair off of her neck. Then she grabbed her keys and drove the half mile it took to get to the office. The first thing she heard when she parked and got out was music. She didn't know where it was coming from at first, but as she approached her office, it grew louder.

Katie glanced at the time displayed on her phone. It was close to 5:15 p.m., so the office was closed, all doors locked. She used her keys to open the back door and entered to the familiar chords of Nirvana's song "Come as You Are." It had to be Ashley. She had been a teenager in the late eighties and into the early nineties, and she gravitated to the harder bands like Nirvana. Katie, on the other hand, preferred modern alternative rock, like The White Stripes.

Katie headed straight for Ashley's office. The door was open like it always was—Ashley had an open-door policy—but Katie paused in the doorway before entering. It was normal for Ashley to blast music after-hours, but her posture, sitting hunched in front of her desk with her hands covering her face, was anything but normal.

"Ashley," Katie said, speaking loud enough so Ashley could hear but not so loud as to be characterized as a shout.

"What?" Ashley dropped her hands and looked up. When she saw it was Katie, she turned the music down and motioned to one of the two cracked leather chairs sitting in front of her desk. "Sorry. I was just...thinking. Have a seat."

"Did the interview with Morgan go that badly?" Katie asked as she lowered herself into the chair. Ashley looked like someone whose doctor just told them that they only had days to live.

"Worse," Ashley said, scrubbing her hands against her face, then dropping them to her sides.

Katie shifted in her seat. "How much worse?"

"I don't know," Ashley said with a sigh. "I mean, Morgan didn't say anything stupid. At least not yet, but it's only a matter of time. She's losing her mind already, and they haven't even put her in a cell yet."

"What did she do this time?" There was no point in asking *if* Morgan had done something. That woman was always in trouble.

"As far as I know, she cut off her tracker and left it in a ditch not far from Frank Vinny's property."

Katie sucked in a sharp breath. That wasn't good. Sure, someone could have found the tracker and tossed it in the ditch to frame Morgan, but that was a longshot. Mostly because the tracker should have been on Morgan's ankle, but also because Morgan was presumably the one who cut it off, and she would have chosen where to leave it.

"What else?" Katie hated to ask, but the expression on Ashley's face said that there was more.

"I don't know, exactly, but Morgan knows something about the fire at Frank's. I just know it. I started asking her about it, and she was evasive, so I quit. Now, I just," she sighed heavily, "I feel like I'm waiting for the other shoe to drop."

"Yeah. I know the feeling."

Ashley looked up, studying Katie for a long moment. "What happened to you? You look like someone kidnapped your puppy."

"I don't have a puppy. Even though it would be nice to have *something* waiting for me when I got home at night. But my apartment doesn't allow pets. So—"

"I think we're getting a little off topic here. My question

wasn't about puppies. My question was about you. What happened?"

"Aside from wearing burned flesh for the better part of an hour?"

"Yeah. Aside from that."

It was Katie's turn to sigh heavily. "When I got home, my father was standing outside my apartment waiting for me."

"Shit," Ashley said under her breath. "I was worried this would happen."

Katie furrowed her brow. "Did you know he got paroled?"

"I didn't *know*," Ashley said, "but it was inevitable. I mean, he went in on a nonviolent crime. With prison overcrowding these days, they are pushing people out quicker than ever. It just seemed like it was bound to happen sooner rather than later. Apparently, the parole board decided on sooner, huh?"

"Yeah," Katie said. They both fell quiet. The silence stretched on, punctuated every now and then by the hypnotic voice of Kurt Cobain. "But enough of that," Katie said, clapping her hands together. "We can worry about Michael Michello later. Let's focus on Morgan."

Ashley nodded. "First, we need to figure out how the fire started. I mean, was it arson, was it an accident, or was it that brief lightning storm that passed through?"

"Okay..."

That was going to be harder than it sounded. Usually, they didn't get that information until they received discovery from the prosecutor. But that wouldn't be until two or three weeks after the State had filed formal charges. Morgan was in jail, but only for violation of pretrial release. Now that she was in custody, Charles Hanson could take his sweet time deciding when and what charges to press. All the while, Morgan would be breaking down piece by piece until she was desperate to talk.

"Then we need to figure out if the two bodies had been dead before they were burned or if they had died as a result of the fire." That question would be simpler to answer. It would be part of the medical examiner's report.

"What about the identities of the bodies?" Katie asked.

Ashley waved a dismissive hand. "That'll come soon enough. Not from the prosecutor, but from the media. They'll be following every lead possible to identify the bodies. All we need to do is wait for the news to break."

"Have you heard from Frank?"

Ashley shook her head. "No. Which means he's either injured, dead, or on the run."

"I assume you want me to go back out to the scene," Katie said reluctantly. "I heard on the scanner that the fire is out, and some arson dogs from the Council Bluffs Fire Department are coming."

Ashley sat up straighter. "When is that happening?"

"Tomorrow."

"Yes. I'd like you to go see what you can find out about that. But until then, I think we should take a look at the pictures you took earlier today."

"Yes." In all the drama over the past hour, she'd completely forgotten about them. Katie had brought her camera bag inside with her and placed it on the floor when she'd sat down. She reached down and picked up her camera, removing the card from the back and handing it to Ashley.

Ashley popped it into a special drive in her computer and turned the screen toward Katie so they could both see. At first, Ashley scrolled through all the pictures to start with the ones of the actual fire. The first thing Katie noticed when Ashley stopped on the first picture was the gas can.

"Do you see that," Katie said, pointing to the half-melted plastic container.

"One point arson," Ashley said grudgingly. "Zero for accident."

Ashley flipped past a few more pictures, stopping on a photo of the front portion of the barn. Flames burst from every inch of it, reaching up toward the sky like souls locked in the underworld.

"Shit," Ashley hissed through her teeth.

"What?"

She pointed to the door of the barn. "That's a traditional barn door."

"Meaning..."

"There is a lock on the *outside*. See that bar. It's meant to keep animals inside."

"Why would Frank have a lock on the outside of the door? That makes zero sense. Didn't he want to keep people from coming in?"

Ashley shrugged. "Maybe there were locks on both sides."

"Why would he want to lock someone inside?"

Ashley's eyes shifted back to the picture. "So they'd die in a fire."

"Ugh," Katie groaned.

That was not good news overall, but maybe it was for Morgan. If Frank had barred the people inside and started the fire, that would likely get Morgan off the hook. Even if she had participated, the prosecutor would probably offer her immunity in exchange for her testimony against Frank.

"And look at this." Ashley flipped to the next few pictures, pointing at all the windows. "The windows are barred."

"It's like a makeshift jail cell."

"That front door was the only exit, and someone placed a metal bar across it," Ashley said, a note of frustration in her voice.

"Why would Frank do that?" Katie asked the question, but

she knew it would be impossible to answer. If Frank planned to get away with two murders, it made little sense. Firefighters were always going to respond to the fire no matter what, especially with the drought. So, they were always going to find the bodies. The barn belonged to Frank and Frank alone. He had to assume that law enforcement would come asking questions.

"Maybe it wasn't Frank. Maybe Frank is dead."

As a drug dealer and a criminal, Frank had all sorts of enemies. If his was one of the bodies in the barn, then there was an endless list of people who would have liked to burn him alive. If the bodies belonged to others, then the answer was still the same, but flipped. Either way, they needed to identify the bodies.

# 12

## ASHLEY

The work on Morgan's case was piling up. What exactly Morgan would be charged with was still a bit of a mystery, but Ashley felt certain that there would be charges in addition to the pretrial release violation. Because all that violation did was put her in jail pending her burglary trial. Sure, she could go to prison in the burglary case, but with prison overcrowding, she'd do eighteen months at most on a five-year sentence.

That was the nature of the Iowa criminal justice system. In truth, most of her clients would do far less time and endure less hassle if they just agreed to go to prison right away, do their time, and come back out with a clean slate. It avoided all the probation violations and halfway house situations that always led to prison anyway—unless the client was prepared to stop using drugs, which most of them weren't.

"So, I'll go back to the scene tomorrow," Katie said, pulling Ashley out of her thoughts, "and see what happens with the arson dogs. I'll need that memory card back, though, if you want me to take more pictures."

"Sure," Ashley said, exiting out of the window on her computer and ejecting the card. "But can you print them off whenever you get a chance? I want to take a closer look at them, and I get tired staring at a computer screen."

"Sure thing," Katie said, popping the card back into her camera. "We were only about a quarter of the way through them, anyway. I found this bracelet out there, too, and took some close-up images of it. The thing looked familiar to me, but I can't place why that is."

"Don't ask me." Ashley put her hands up in a gesture of surrender. "I don't know anything about jewelry. Besides, it might not mean anything. Frank is always having wild parties out there in the woods. That could have been dropped at any time."

"True," Katie said, "but I think we should still consider it."

"Sure. But not as a priority right now. Worst case scenario, we can use it as a diversion. We could claim that it belongs to some unidentified assailant if Morgan does end up getting charged. But I don't think it will lead us anywhere further than that."

Katie's phone buzzed in her pocket. She pulled it out, staring at the screen. It must have been a text message because Katie mumbled, "All right, all right. I'll be there in a second," as she typed something back.

"What's that all about?" Ashley asked.

"Tom."

The mention of his name caused a shiver to run up Ashley's spine. She'd been in love with him once, and in truth, she was probably still in love with him. But he had hurt her in a way that seemed irrevocable. Yet he still wanted to patch things up between them. That was why she made it a habit to stay away from him. Out of sight, out of mind.

"I'm meeting him down at Mikey's Tavern. I was supposed to be there ten minutes ago."

"Oh," Ashley said, shifting a few things around on her

desk. A failed attempt at creating a distraction. "Who all is going to be there?"

"Tom, Forest, me, and I think Rachel, too."

Rachel was a former client of Ashley's. She was young, beautiful, and broken. When the prosecutor dismissed all charges against her seven months earlier, Rachel had moved in with Ashley. It wasn't something Ashley typically offered her clients, but Rachel was different. She'd been eighteen years old when she was charged criminally, but only barely, and it ultimately turned out that she'd been a victim, not a criminal. The combination of events stirred a maternal instinct deep within Ashley that she'd never known existed.

"Do you want to come?" Katie asked with an expectant look on her face.

Ashley considered it, mulling the thought over in her mind. It would be nice to have a drink with friends, but she decided against it. She just didn't feel quite strong enough to spend time in Tom's presence, especially when alcohol was involved.

"I don't think so. I need to stop by the jail to speak with Aubrey. She was sentenced to thirty days, and I want to make sure she's adjusting. I don't have time to do both."

Katie gave Ashley a hard look. "Are you sure it doesn't have anything to do with Tom?"

"Am I sure?" Ashley shook her head. "No. I won't say it has nothing to do with him."

"You can't hide from him forever."

"I'm not hiding. I'm just keeping my distance. I'll tell you what," Ashley said, rising from her seat and grabbing her laptop bag. She folded her computer and placed it inside the bag along with a notepad and a few pens of varying colors. "I'm going to the jail, but I will stop by Mikey's Tavern on my way out. I need to check to see if Rachel needs a ride home, anyway."

"That'll work."

Katie and Ashley left the office at the same time, both using the front door. Ashley locked the door and waved to Katie before heading the opposite direction toward the jail. Shortly after arriving at the jail, a jailer led Ashley to the attorney-client room. Aubrey was already inside, seated in the chair designated for inmates.

"How are you doing?" Ashley said as she dropped into the only empty seat.

"I've been better," Aubrey said, picking at her nails, "but I'm fine. There are enough books in here to occupy me for thirty days."

"Good. But you'll get twenty percent good time. Remember that. So it won't be a full thirty days."

Aubrey nodded. "That's good news, because I'm already having trouble with one of my roommates."

"Who is it?" Ashley was ninety percent sure she knew the answer, but she still had to ask the question.

"Morgan Stanman."

"What did Morgan do this time?"

"Nothing to me. She's just..." Aubrey paused, chewing on her bottom lip. "She's losing her shit. She was banging her head against the cement wall when I left." She shook her head slowly. "If someone doesn't do something soon, she's going to kill herself."

Ashley straightened, her entire body growing rigid. "Listen to me, Aubrey, and this is important. Has Morgan said anything about suicide?"

"No. Not yet at least. I can just feel it coming, you know. She's got this stormy aura hanging around her. She's talking to herself and self-harming. And she hasn't been here for a full day yet. I mean, if she's already this far gone, it isn't a far leap to think she'd use a bedsheet to make a noose."

Aubrey had a point. Ashley hated suicide. It was giving up, waving the white flag. But she could also understand why someone like Morgan might make that choice. She'd been abused her entire life. Morgan never talked about the exact form of abuse, but Ashley could only assume it involved enclosed spaces, like perhaps she'd been locked in a closet for long periods of time or shut away in a shed.

"Something has to be done. I can't watch her twenty-four-seven. I've got to sleep sometimes."

"Okay. I understand," Ashley said. "And this isn't your problem or your fault. I'll talk to the jail administrator about putting Morgan on suicide watch."

Aubrey gave Ashley a hard look. One that said, *That's bullshit and you know it.*

"What do you want me to do?" Ashley said, throwing her hands up in frustration. "I'm out of ideas. She was out until she violated her pretrial release. She won't be getting out anytime soon."

"Calm down. I wasn't accusing you of anything. I'm just trying to say that where there is a will, there's a way. Morgan may not quite have the will to die just yet, but she's going to be there in a couple days. I've seen plenty of people go off the deep end, and Morgan is on the fast track to hitting rock bottom."

"Okay," Ashley said, rising to her feet. "I'll think of something."

When Ashley left the jail, she felt heavier than she had when she'd entered. She was thankful for Aubrey, happy that she was sharing a cell with Morgan. At least Aubrey would alert Ashley if the situation grew any worse. It was also nice to know that Aubrey, while unhappy about her predicament, was making the best of it.

Unfortunately, the opposite was true when it came to Morgan. It sounded like she was on a slippery slope, sliding downward. Ashley didn't have time that evening to visit her, and she wasn't sure what she'd say if she did. She couldn't tell Morgan that Aubrey had ratted her out. That would only make things worse. But she also didn't see any way to get Morgan out of jail. The only option was to speak with Kylie, the jail administrator, and hope that they had enough employees to keep Morgan safe from herself. The jail was perpetually short-staffed, so it was a longshot, but it was the only thing Ashley could think to do. She felt powerless, and she hated it.

# 13

## KATIE

Katie was thirty minutes late by the time she finally stepped through the door to Mikey's Tavern. The bar was one of several downtown, but it was Katie's favorite. The drinks were cheap, and Mikey, the owner, kept the patrons in line.

"Hey, Mikey," Katie said, waving to the man behind the bar. Mikey was a big, heavily muscled Black man with a wide nose and a generous smile. He was a family man, with a wife and several children relying on income from the bar, so he didn't allow nonsense.

"Hello there, Katie. Will it be the usual for you?"

"Yes. Thank you."

Mikey hadn't always been this friendly to Katie. They'd butted heads a time or two when Katie was a police officer. But Mikey and Ashley were friends, and Mikey fully supported the creation of the MEHR team.

"The group's waiting on you," Mikey said, popping the top off a Bud Light bottle and handing it to Katie.

Katie nodded and headed toward a high-top table near the back. Tom and Forest were seated on one side with their backs to Katie as she approached, and Rachel was across from them.

The two men were in deep conversation, but Rachel didn't appear to be paying attention.

"Hello," Katie said, stopping at the end of the table and speaking to the group.

"About time," Tom said, glancing at his watch. "What took you so long?"

The truth—that Katie's father had unexpectedly shown up and thrown a wrench in her life—was not one that she wanted to get into. All three of these people knew about Katie's past, but that didn't mean she wanted to talk about it. Her conversation with Ashley had been enough.

"I was working," Katie said, coming around and dropping into her seat. "You should try it sometime."

Tom used to be the Brine County jail administrator, but he'd left that position over two years ago when a corrupt police officer named John Jackie had assaulted Ashley inside the jail and nearly killed her. Shortly after that, he and Ashley started dating, and he resigned from his position to go back to college. He was back in Brine for the summer, but next school year would be his third year living in Des Moines.

"Very funny," Tom said, but there was a slight smile tugging at the corners of his lips. He knew Katie wasn't serious. Then Tom's smile dropped, and he turned to look behind him. "Is Ashley coming?"

Katie took a swig of her beer. She knew this would be one of his first questions because that's how every conversation with Tom had gone since his breakup with Ashley. They started with a simple hello, then proceeded to some question about Ashley.

"Later. She's at the jail right now. She's stopping by to pick Rachel up."

"Is she going to stay for a drink?"

Katie tried not to sound too irritated. "I don't know, Tom, maybe you should ask her yourself."

"I would, but she won't talk to me."

"Well, that's not my problem."

It was harsh, sure, but Katie was tired of Tom putting her in the middle. She was friends with both of them, and they wanted opposite things. There was nothing she could or would do to change Ashley's mind. If he wanted her back so badly, he needed to find a way on his own.

"All right, all right," Forest said, cutting into the conversation before it dissolved into an all-out fight. He, too, was friends with Ashley, which led to the same sort of interrogation from Tom, but on a smaller scale. But Forest still knew it was best to divert the discussion to safer ground early or else they'd spend their entire night fielding questions about Ashley. "Does everyone have a cocktail?"

Tom held up a beer glass, half full of amber liquid that was most likely the local brewer's IPA, and Forest was swirling a glass of deep red wine. Mikey's wasn't the type of place to serve nice red wines or to provide decent wine glasses, but Mikey kept those two things available specifically for Forest. Katie guessed that was the benefit of being a member on the only city council in Iowa that was seriously considering altering the local law enforcement system.

"I just got a beer, and it looks like Rachel has plenty of Sprite," Katie said.

Rachel was eighteen, almost nineteen, and she wasn't legal to drink, but even if she was of age, she wouldn't be drinking. Rachel had been through a significant amount of trauma, and she was in intensive therapy, which included antidepressant medications. She'd come a long way in the past seven months, but she still had a lot of work ahead of her. Mixing other mood-altering substances, like alcohol, would only hinder her development.

"Then let's get down to business," Forest said, knocking his knuckles against the table. "First things first, funding."

The MEHR team would need a great deal of money for startup fees. So much so that Katie felt like raising funds was all they ever talked about. They'd had plenty of heated discussions about whom they would accept money from and why. Ultimately, they decided on an all-inclusive approach, where they'd be primarily funded by donations. The council intended to provide some startup capital, but the other two members of the council refused to fund the group until they had proof that the new system would work. Until then, they were going to keep doing what they were doing now, which was siphoning whatever money they could from the police department and reallocating it to the MEHR team.

"We are on track to open our doors in two years," Forest said.

*Two years.* Katie's heart skipped a beat. The original projection had been one year from now. Katie loved working with Ashley, but the funding for her investigator position at the Public Defender's Office was precarious. Ashley had enough to pay Katie through the next year, but it was tentative at best after that. It didn't bode well for her plans to get out of that apartment and into a home of her own.

"But we have a visitor coming," Forest said, flashing Rachel his best politician smile. "Don't we, Rachel?"

"Yes." Rachel scratched at the surface of the table with her fingernail, speaking without meeting anyone's gaze. "Aunt Stephanie said she was going to stop by to make an announcement."

Katie sat back, her spine colliding with the back of the barstool painfully. Stephanie Arkman was Rachel's aunt and a member of one of the richest families in Iowa. They owned several meat-packing plants around the state, including the main facility that was about thirty minutes north of Brine, near the county border. While the meat-packing plant was likely a contributor to the family's wealth, it wasn't even close to their primary source of income. The Arkman family had their hands in every money-making enterprise in the state of Iowa, including farmland, ethanol, wind energy, and banking.

"What kind of announcement?" Katie said, her eyes narrowing.

Forest had brought Stephanie's name up during the funding conversation, and money was not in short supply for any member of the Arkman family. Stephanie could easily provide all the cash that they needed, which seemed positive on its face, but it was also a source of concern for Katie. The plan was for the *community* to fund the MEHR team, not one member of the community. The idea was that everyone would contribute so that everyone—and not only the rich members of society—would feel like they were equals in the eyes of the MEHR team.

"Why don't you ask her?" Forest said, turning and gesturing toward the door.

Katie looked up to see the door swish open and Stephanie Arkman sweep inside. She moved with the posture and grace that could only be developed through years of formal ballet training. She had long, blond hair so thick that it was unattainable without hair extensions. It cascaded over her shoulders in perfect waves, settling near the middle of her back.

*Shit*, Katie thought. She took a large pull from her beer bottle and diverted her eyes away from the new arrival.

Stephanie's family had been close with Katie's parents back before Michael Michello's very public downfall, but Stephanie was a good fifteen years older than Katie. She'd been out of the house and living in Europe by the time Katie was five years old. She'd come back stateside a few years ago to take over the business when her father's health began failing. That was the only reason that Stephanie had never recognized Katie as Michael's daughter. But still, Katie was always worried that Stephanie would look at her one day, see something of Michael in her features, and call her out for what she was—the daughter of a felon.

"Good evening," Stephanie said, coming straight to their table without acknowledging Mikey behind the bar. Her English accent grated on Katie's nerves. She wasn't English; she was only pretending to be.

"Stephanie. It's so nice of you to join us," Forest said, rising to his feet to greet her. He kissed her once on both cheeks as though they lived in Beverly Hills, then motioned at the table. "Have a seat. I'll pull up an extra chair."

"No, no, that won't be necessary," Stephanie said, waving a dismissive hand.

As Stephanie waved her arm around, a memory struck Katie like a slap to the face. It was of Stephanie's eighteenth birthday. Katie was three, almost four, and it was one of her first memories. The party had been huge, with specific items of entertainment geared toward each age group. Katie remembered the bounce houses, pony rides, and a petting zoo for the little children.

Another thing Katie remembered was the gift Stephanie had received from her parents. It was a solid gold bangle, etched with the Arkman family seal. Every Arkman woman had one, and it was rumored to have a chip buried inside it containing information on how to access that family member's trust fund.

Katie had never known if the rumor was true, but she had never seen an Arkman woman without the bangle. Even

Rachel's mother, Lyndsay, had worn hers despite being excommunicated from the family after eloping with an unsuitable man. Stephanie's had been solid gold with a light pink trim. Katie remembered it because at three years old, pink was her favorite color.

Today, as Stephanie waved her hand through the air, that bracelet was noticeably absent. And now that Katie thought of it, she wondered if Stephanie's had been the bracelet she had found and photographed while searching for evidence in Frank's forest earlier that day. It, too, had been gold with pink trim. It was possible that it was coincidence, but Katie thought not. There was only one way to find out, and that was to take a closer look at the photographs.

"I only have a few moments," Stephanie said, pulling Katie out of her thoughts. "I'm just here to tell you that I'll be providing a donation to your little team here. Five million to start, but there will be more if I like what I see."

*Five million dollars*, Katie thought. *What would it be like to just give away that much money?* And Stephanie had said it so nonchalantly, as though it were nothing more than pocket change.

Forest straightened, a smile spreading across his lips. "That should be plenty to get started. We could work on officially forming as early as tomorrow."

Part of Katie wanted to protest. This was not the original plan. If they accepted this kind of money from Stephanie, then she would effectively own them. That was what they were trying to avoid. But, at the same time, they needed that money. Without it, Katie was looking at potential joblessness in a year. That was an abyss that she had to navigate seven months earlier, and the thought of dealing with it again in a year made her feel sick.

But then again, she didn't think she could stomach

Stephanie Arkman calling all the shots. Especially if Katie could link that bangle in the forest to her. It would mean that Stephanie had a connection to Frank Vinny and possibly had her hands in another lucrative enterprise that was not quite so legal as the others.

# 14

---

## ASHLEY

After leaving the jail, Ashley went straight to Mikey's Tavern. It was down the street, so she walked. She wasn't eager to see Tom or ward off his advances after the exhausting day she'd had, but Rachel was there, and Ashley wanted to make sure she had a way home.

Rachel didn't have a driver's license, and she was not emotionally strong enough to work yet, but she also didn't like to be left home alone out in the country. So, every day, Rachel got up at the same ungodly hour as Ashley, got ready, and rode into town with her. Some days she'd spend her time at the Public Defender's Office, hanging out with Elena, learning the ropes, but other days she would go to the local library. Rachel's therapist had told Ashley that the public interaction was good for Rachel, and Ashley liked having company on the thirty-minute drive into and out of town.

It only took her five minutes to reach Mikey's Tavern, and she was starting to think she should have walked slower. Why did she come here, anyway? She could have waited for Rachel at the office. But she'd told Katie that this was what she was going to do, so that's what Katie and Rachel would be expecting. She lingered outside, taking several steadying breaths before forcing herself to push the door open and enter.

"Ashley," Mikey said, a wide grin splitting across his face. "Tom said you might be stopping by." He came around the bar, wiping his hands on a towel. "I've got a couple of things I'd like to discuss with you, if you have a minute."

The soon-to-be MEHR team was seated at a four-top table near the back of the bar. Stephanie Arkman was standing at the head of their table. She was in the middle of a monologue —probably about herself—speaking and gesturing with her hands. It looked like she was holding court.

Ashley had known of Stephanie all her life. She was older than Ashley and attended private school, but Brine was a small town. A local family with that kind of cash had often touched the lips of the Brine gossip ring. But it was only recently that Ashley had gotten to know Stephanie as a person, thanks to Stephanie's niece Rachel, and Ashley didn't like what she saw.

"Sure," Ashley said to Mikey. She had all the time in the world if it meant she could avoid Stephanie.

Whenever possible, she tried to keep her distance from Rachel's aunt. Mostly to keep the peace for Rachel's sake. Stephanie had been outright hostile toward Ashley over the past few weeks. She wanted Rachel to move in with her—to become a true Arkman—but Rachel wasn't comfortable with her aunt. Rachel's mother was Stephanie's sister, but they'd had a falling out before Rachel's birth, and Rachel hadn't met Stephanie until she was released from jail.

It felt significant to Ashley that Stephanie hadn't offered any support to Rachel when everyone thought she was a baby killer. Stephanie hadn't bothered coming around until the tides turned and it was revealed that Rachel had been the victim of sexual assault and her baby had been stillborn. At that point, Stephanie was on every news station claiming that she'd known all along that her niece would never do anything so horrible and she was happy to welcome her into the family.

"What do you want to drink?" Mikey said, pulling Ashley out of her thoughts. "I've got half a bottle of that wine that Forest Parker drinks. You want some of that?"

"Yes, please," Ashley said, pulling out a barstool and sitting down. "What did you want to talk to me about?"

"I don't mean to be nosy, but I overheard something from that group over there that I didn't like." Mikey nodded at the only other patrons in the bar, the soon-to-be MEHR team. He placed a wineglass in front of Ashley and poured a generous portion of red wine, then looked up.

Ashley took a sip, then asked, "What did you hear?"

"That Arkman lady is going to give them five million dollars."

*"Five million dollars?"*

"Shhhh," Mikey said. "Keep your voice down. I don't want them to think I was spying on them. I just know that even though you aren't on the team, it matters to you. It matters to me, too. It's the only chance that folks like me have at getting fair treatment by the cops. And I don't like that Arkman lady. She's rich and snooty. She may be nice enough, but she doesn't even notice folks like me. When she walked in, she didn't say a word. She looked in my direction, but I don't think she even *saw* me. It's always that way with people like her. They don't look at me, they look through me."

"That's not good news, Mikey," Ashley said, taking a larger gulp of wine this time. "But I don't know what I can do about it," she said after swallowing.

Mikey gave her a hard look. "There's plenty you can do about it. Every one of those people over there wants something from you, or owes you something—"

"Except Stephanie," Ashley interjected.

"Except for Stephanie," Mikey agreed. "But this is one situation where Stephanie doesn't get to make the decision."

"How so?" Ashley said, cocking her head. She was genuinely intrigued. Mikey was an intelligent man and a shrewd businessman. He saw things that Ashley didn't even consider. Sure, she was a lawyer, but a legal mind didn't automatically transfer into good business sense.

"Stephanie can try to give them all the money she wants. It's up to them if they want to accept it. If she hands them a check, they don't have to cash it. They could rip it up right then and there."

"You have a point," Ashley said, nodding. "I'll see what I can do. Thanks for letting me know."

Mikey winked. "Anytime."

She rose from her barstool and approached the group. Stephanie was just finishing with whatever speech she'd undoubtedly spent hours preparing. Ashley was thankful she didn't have to listen to her fake English accent longer than necessary.

"We'll have a meeting at my house later this week," Stephanie said, waving a hand in the air. "A small event to commemorate the creation of the Mental Health Response Team and to shore up any details before we issue a press release."

"When?" Ashley asked.

Stephanie turned, her ocean-blue eyes narrowing. They were the color of the Caribbean, an unnatural shade for eyes. She had to be wearing colored contacts. "This doesn't concern you, Ashley."

"Sure it does. I have to make sure Rachel gets there, right?"

"I'll send a car for Rachel."

"Wonderful," Ashley said, rocking on her heels and

shoving her hands in her pockets. "Money solves everything, doesn't it?" She wasn't even bothering to mask her sarcasm.

"Anyway," Stephanie said, turning away from Ashley. "My people will be in touch with your people about the details."

"I'm Rachel's people," Ashley said, using air quotes around the word *people*. "So are you saying that someone is going to contact me?"

"No. I will contact Rachel directly. Good day to all of you," Stephanie said to the table, then she turned and spoke directly to Ashley. "Except for you. I hope your day was rotten." With that, Stephanie gave a tight smile to the rest of the group, then glided out of the bar.

Ashley watched the heiress to the Arkman fortune leave with a sinking feeling in her stomach. Sure, Mikey was right when he'd said that Forest, Tom, Katie, and Rachel all needed something from her, but would that be enough to combat a force like Stephanie? Ashley hoped so, but somewhere deep in her soul, she knew better. People like Stephanie Arkman always won in the end.

# 15

ASHLEY

Forest called an end to the MEHR team meeting the moment Stephanie Arkman left. It seemed like he had accepted the funding as a done deal and there was already an informal agreement that they wouldn't proceed without their primary benefactor. Which was ridiculous, but judging by the expressions on everyone else's faces, she knew she was in the minority on that.

That didn't mean that Ashley had already forgotten her conversation with Mikey. It just meant that she was going to have to be smart about her approach. If she took that moment to make a statement, urging them to reject the money, it would come to nothing. They were too excited about the possibility of opening their doors much earlier than expected to consider the strings that Stephanie was attaching. Ashley would have to approach them individually, sowing the seeds of doubt. Only then could she reasonably make her request.

"Ashley," Tom said, catching her attention.

"Yes," Ashley said. She was careful to keep her voice even and her facial features blank, like she did in jury trials. It was the only way to hide her emotions, even though her heart felt like it was hammering loud enough for anyone to hear.

"Can I, um," Tom cleared his throat, "talk to you,"

"Another time," Ashley said, straightening her back and turning to Rachel. "Are you ready to go? The dogs are waiting on dinner."

Rachel nodded, and Ashley waved to the group before making her way toward the door. Before leaving, she turned to Mikey. "About what you said earlier..."

"Yes." He was shining a glass with a rag. He didn't look up, but Ashley knew he was listening.

"I can't make any promises, but I'm going to try."

"That's all I can hope for, Ms. Ashley."

Then Ashley turned and exited out the front door, Rachel following hot on her heels.

They walked back to the Public Defender's Office and hopped in Ashley's car. They were quiet for the first ten minutes of the drive home. Ashley's mind kept drifting back to Morgan's mental health, and Rachel was always content with silence. It was a defense mechanism she'd developed to keep the abuse from her mother's husband to a minimum. Now, after so many years, it had become a part of Rachel. So, Ashley assumed they'd ride in silence the entire way, but to her surprise she was wrong.

"You seem like you've got something on your mind," Rachel said, her head turned toward the window. She rarely looked at anyone when she spoke. Which made it difficult to tell who her words were directed at when in a group. Fortunately, Ashley didn't have that problem at the moment.

"It's nothing," Ashley said, trying to keep her tone light. "Just work stuff."

Rachel nodded, and Ashley thought it would end there, but once again, Rachel surprised her.

"I know where you work. You forget I'm with you at the office most days, and I was once a client of yours. You've always got something stressful happening, but I've never seen you like this. It's like you're carrying the weight of the world on your shoulders."

Ashley sighed heavily. The fire at Frank's, two burned bodies, Frank missing, and Morgan as a suspect were all things that Ashley could handle. She'd dealt with worse situations—namely when she'd been accused of murdering two former clients, jailed, and nearly killed by a former police officer—but the concern with Morgan's mental health was a step above all that. Aubrey had said that suicide was inevitable. Ashley had notified jail staff, but that was all she could do. If Morgan hurt herself on Ashley's watch, it would weigh on her conscience forever.

"See, there you go. You're doing it again," Rachel said, cutting through Ashley's thoughts.

"Doing what?"

"You get this faraway look like your mind isn't connected to your body."

"Okay," Ashley said. "You're right."

Then she proceeded to tell Rachel about everything, spilling all the events of the day like word vomit. She normally kept sensitive information away from Rachel, but she couldn't hold back after the day that she'd had. Rachel was in a fragile state of her own, and Ashley felt protective of her. She didn't want Rachel worrying about others when she really needed to focus on her own recovery.

After Ashley was done speaking, Rachel was silent for a long moment. An acute sense of concern lit up within Ashley's chest, squeezing at her heart. She'd said too much, and now Rachel was going to have to share the burden. Why had she done that? But, if she was honest with herself, she knew why.

The predicament with Morgan was heavy. She was having trouble shouldering it on her own, but that didn't give her an excuse to unload on Rachel. She should have talked to Katie about it instead.

"I'm glad you told me," Rachel finally said.

"You are?" Ashley asked, surprised.

"Yeah. Don't take this the wrong way, but you treat me like a child sometimes. I'm an adult. I know my head is screwed up in so many ways, but I still want you to look at me as an equal."

"I don't do that?"

Rachel shook her head. "I want a friendship like you and Katie have."

"Okay. You're right," Ashley said, nodding. As much as it pained her to agree, Rachel had a point. She wasn't the same broken child she'd been when Ashley first encountered her. The therapy was working, and she was starting to come into her own. "I'll try to be more open about things, okay?"

"Thank you," Rachel said. "Now let's figure out what we can do about Morgan."

"The problem is that no judge is going to let her out of jail. She violated her pretrial release in a big way, and she's now the suspect in a major crime."

"What crime?"

"We don't know yet. But possibly manufacturing methamphetamine, arson, murder, or even all three."

"Sounds bad."

"I filed a motion for bond review. The judge set it for nine o'clock tomorrow morning, but it's just a formality. It doesn't matter what I say, he's going to deny bond either way."

"What if I say something?" Rachel suggested.

"I don't understand..." Technically, anyone who had relevant information could testify at a bond review hearing, but

Rachel had nothing to do with Morgan or her case. Ashley had no clue what she could possibly contribute.

"Well, I know a thing or two about mental health," Rachel said, tapping the side of her head with her index finger, "with me being crazy and all. And I also know what it feels like to be in jail. Now, I didn't mind jail, but I can see why someone might be bothered by it. I'll just need to talk to Morgan and get some details on her past." Rachel paused for a long moment, then added, "It might not help, but it's better than nothing, right?"

They had just pulled into Ashley's driveway, her two dogs, Finn and Princess, chasing them up the gravel drive. Ashley put the car in park when they reached the house, then turned and looked at Rachel. "Sometimes I think you are a genius. It's crazy, but it's worth a shot."

# 16

## ASHLEY

The night crawled by, sleepless, with thoughts of Morgan plaguing Ashley's mind. Now that she was in the dark, thinking about it, she was second-guessing this plan to let Rachel speak in court. Rachel had come a long way, but she wasn't quite ready for cross examination, especially from Charles Hanson. He was not the type to hold back his punches, even knowing Rachel's background. If Ashley put Rachel on the stand, he would tear into her like he did to any other witness.

At five o'clock, her alarm finally sounded, and she rose out of bed. The lack of sleep made her limbs feel heavy and her head full of cotton. She walked into the bathroom, showered, and chose a black pantsuit to wear. It took her thirty minutes to get ready, but Rachel was seated on the couch waiting for her by the time she came downstairs.

"Coffee's ready in the kitchen," Rachel said, "and the dogs are fed."

Ashley could smell the inviting aroma of fresh-brewed coffee. She followed it into the kitchen and poured herself a cup. Then she returned to the living room.

"Are you ready to head out?" Ashley said, grabbing her keys.

Both were silent on the drive into town, content to listen to the local news over the radio. The fire out at Frank's was the only major story, so the newscasters spent most of their time harping on the same details that Ashley already knew. Fire at Frank Vinny's. Frank had a criminal history involving methamphetamine. He'd been charged with manufacturing several times. The weather conditions had not been ideal, but the "brave" firefighters were finally able to put it out. Two people perished in the fire, but they have not been identified.

"What's taking them so long?" Rachel said, motioning to the radio. "Why haven't they identified them?"

"I don't know. Maybe they have, they just haven't released that to the media yet. Law enforcement usually keeps that stuff quiet until they can notify the family."

"Oh." Rachel was silent for a long moment before asking, "Do you still want me to talk to Morgan this morning?"

"I don't think so."

"I'm not some fragile bird, you know." Rachel crossed her arms. "And if I'm going to work for the MEHR team, I'm going to have to get used to testifying."

"I know that," Ashley said, but there wasn't a lot of confidence in the words. "But you need to cut your teeth on something a little less sensational. You heard the news coverage. If Morgan's implicated in this mess with Frank, then this is going to become a real circus. It's not the time to test out your testifying skills."

"Fine," Rachel said, but she didn't sound satisfied.

*This must be how mothers feel*, Ashley thought to herself. She hated letting Rachel down, telling her that she wasn't ready yet, but she saw no other way around it.

They drove the rest of the way in silence and split ways

once they got to the Public Defender's Office. Rachel stayed out front with Elena, and Ashley holed herself up in her office. She spent the next several hours catching up on paperwork. At 8:45, Katie came into her office, dropping into the seat across from her.

"Rachel's in a mood today," Katie said.

"Well, hello to you, too."

"I mean it. What did you do?"

Ashley set her pen down and closed the file she'd been working on. "I am keeping her out of this Morgan mess. She wanted to testify about mental illness and incarceration. I agreed to it last night when I was tired and apparently delusional but changed my mind this morning. Rachel is no mental health expert, so I doubt the judge would let her testify, anyway."

Katie nodded. "I'll try to smooth things over with her, but for now, we probably better get over to court. Morgan's hearing is in fifteen minutes."

Ashley and Katie left out the back door so Rachel wouldn't see them leaving. Katie wasn't testifying, but Rachel would still see Katie's attendance as a slap in the face. She was already sensitive about the relationship between Ashley and Katie. It was best that they got to the courthouse without Rachel seeing.

When they arrived, Morgan was already there and seated at the defense table. Kylie, the jail administrator, stood next to her. Chains wound their way around Morgan's arms and legs, weighing all four of her limbs down. Morgan was so thin that the chains looked gigantic on her tiny frame. Ashley approached the table, and Katie sat in the back on the defense side of the aisle.

"Good morning, Morgan, Kylie," Ashley said in the cheeriest voice she could muster. Then, when Morgan turned,

Ashley froze, staring at her client. "What the hell happened to your face?"

Identical claw marks ran from the top of her cheek bones to the bottom of her jaw where the skin had been gouged out by fingernails.

"Morgan dabbled in some self-harm this morning," Kylie said, casting a dark look at Ashley's client.

Ashley furrowed her brow. This was precisely what Aubrey had predicted. Self-harm was sometimes the first step in suicidal ideation—or at least that's what Ashley was led to believe by mental health experts.

"I thought you put her on suicide watch."

Morgan snorted. "So, it's your fault they took my blanket."

When someone was on suicide watch, all sheets and blankets were taken from them and replaced with a papery replacement. One that would easily rip if used as a noose. Morgan must not have been sleeping well as a result, because heavy bags clung below her eyes, purple and puffy, and the whites of her eyes were shot through with red.

"No," Kylie corrected. "It's your fault." She gestured to Morgan's face.

"Someone should have been watching her," Ashley said, completely ignoring Morgan's objections.

"I know," Kylie said with a sigh. "We'll do better. We're short-staffed. Which I know isn't an excuse, but that's the situation."

Just then, the back doors to the courtroom banged open, and the prosecutor, Charles Hanson, came strutting inside. George scurried along behind him, dropping into a seat parallel to Katie but on the other side of the aisle.

"Good morning," Charles said as he approached Ashley. It was an automatic statement, something he said to everyone, because he really didn't sound like he meant it.

"Yes. You too," Ashley said, trying to keep her voice light. She hated showing him kindness, but she didn't have much of a choice. She had a favor to ask him, an appeal to make. "Listen, Charles," Ashley said, coming over to his table so that she was out of Morgan's earshot. "Can't you agree to release her?"

"Are you kidding me?" Charles said. He was actually chuckling as he said the words. "That's a joke, right?"

"No."

"She's cut off her tracker, and she's a suspect in a pending investigation. Tell me one good reason to let her out."

"Look at her," Ashley said, gesturing to Morgan. "She's a wreck. She's torn holes in her face already. I'm afraid of what comes next. She'll probably end up killing herself."

Charles moved a few papers around and opened his laptop. "Well, that's one less case I have to worry about, then, isn't it?"

Ashley's eyes widened with shock, then narrowed in fury. Charles was hoping Morgan would take her life. That was what it sounded like to Ashley. Sure, she was a criminal, and she made bad choices, but that didn't mean the best option was to give up. Morgan had been abused as a child, and that abuse led to an addiction that continued to abuse her in adulthood. Why couldn't Charles see that? She wanted to scream and rage at him, but before she could open her mouth to say a word, Judge Ahrenson and his court reporter entered the courtroom.

Ashley scurried back to her table.

"All rise," the court reporter shouted. "The Honorable Judge Ahrenson presiding."

"You may be seated," Judge Ahrenson said. "I know it's a little before nine, but it looks like all the parties are here, so we might as well get started."

Judge Ahrenson just wanted to deny Ashley's motion for

Morgan's release and get back to whatever it was he did all day in chambers. Even Charles could see that, judging by the faint smile forming at the corners of his mouth. Ashley glared at the prosecutor, but he didn't seem to notice.

"Do either of you have any witnesses to call?" Judge Ahrenson looked to Charles first.

"No witnesses, just argument."

The judge's gaze shifted to Ashley.

"Same," she said. She was feeling dejected, like the world was stacked against her.

"All right. Then I'll hear from the State first."

Charles rose to his feet. "Thank you, Your Honor. Morgan has been charged with burglary in the third degree, a felony offense. She was granted pretrial release under the supervision of the Department of Correctional Services. That was a gift." He paused to turn and look pointedly at Morgan. "One that she squandered. Within two weeks of release, she cut her tracker off and left it in a ditch near a known drug house that also burned down that very same day."

"Wait a minute," Judge Ahrenson said, interrupting Charles. "Are you saying that Ms. Stanman here is a suspect in that fire?"

"Yes. I am most certainly saying that. And look at her." He gestured to Morgan. "Not her face, those are recent, attention-seeking scratches, but the rest of her body. Her arms and legs are covered in scratches and bruises, consistent with running through a forest, like the one surrounding Frank Vinny's property. Now, we've taken swabs of her hands to see if there is any evidence of an accelerant, but we had to send those off to the DCI lab in Ankeny for testing. We don't have results back yet."

The Division of Criminal Investigations Criminalistics Laboratory (or DCI lab for short) did all the major testing in the state of Iowa. It could take a while before Charles would have results back, but it could be soon if they put a rush order on it. Yet, Morgan hadn't mentioned anything about law enforcement swabbing her hands. They must have done that before Ashley arrived yesterday. That seemed like a pretty big detail to forget, and Ashley wasn't happy to hear it for the first time from the prosecutor.

"I don't mean to get into details," Judge Ahrenson cut in, "but wasn't that fire out at Vinny's property a meth fire?"

"It's unlikely," Charles said.

Everything Charles had said up until then—aside from the hand swabs—had come of no surprise to Ashley. But that did.

"Why is it unlikely?" the judge asked.

"Because Frank was one of the two bodies found inside the barn. He died in that fire. And there is evidence to support that he and the other victim had been locked inside using a lock on the outside of the door."

*Frank is dead*, Ashley thought in complete shock. It was always a possibility, but one that she'd pushed to the back of her mind. One that wasn't realistic, at least not until now. To her, Frank was like a cockroach. The nuclear apocalypse could come, and he'd still be scurrying around committing crimes.

"Weren't there other exits?" Judge Ahrenson said.

"No. All the windows had bars on them."

"Why?"

"I'm not going to pretend to understand Frank Vinny's living situation, Your Honor. It certainly wasn't safe. But Frank knew better than to cook inside a closed structure, especially while locked inside."

"And you believe Ms. Stanman here had something to do with that door getting locked?"

"Yes. That, and possibly lighting the fire."

"Okay. I think I understand your argument, Mr. Hanson.

Ms. Montgomery," the judge said as he turned his ice-blue gaze to her. "You better have a good argument for release."

She didn't, but she still tried. She pointed out Morgan's new wounds and what Kylie had said about suicide watch and being short-staffed. She told the judge about Morgan's childhood and her addiction. It wasn't a great argument, and she hated to grovel at the judge's feet, but sometimes that was all there was left to do, so grovel she did. But in the end, the result of the hearing was exactly as she had expected.

"I understand your position," Judge Ahrenson said to Ashley, "and I sympathize with it. However, I believe that Ms. Stanman is a danger to this community. As such, her bond will remain the same."

With that, Judge Ahrenson stood and left the room, leaving Ashley to deal with the aftermath. Morgan screamed and crumpled to the floor, tears streaming down her face as she sobbed, *I can't, I can't, I can't.*

"Tell her if she cuts out the hysterics and agrees to talk," Charles said to Ashley in a low voice, "then we might be able to come to an agreement for something less than a life sentence."

Charles had been speaking softly, and Morgan was so out of control that Ashley felt certain she hadn't heard the prosecutor's statement. But she'd been wrong.

"I will," Morgan said, shooting to her feet. "I will talk. Anything, anything to get out."

"He didn't promise to let you out, Morgan," Ashley said with a sigh.

This was the problem with proffer agreements. The State rarely agreed to much, and defendants gave away lots. Charles had said *something less than life.* Which wasn't much of a concession if Morgan took the time to really think about it. A fifty-year sentence would be less than life, which sounded at least a little better, but it was still a life sentence for Morgan. She was in her thirties, and she'd lived life hard with all the drugs and alcohol. It would be a miracle if she made it past eighty years old.

"I still want to do it, Mr. Hanson. Please. Let me do it." Morgan sounded so pathetic. It was truly disgusting how she begged for scraps.

"I will come and see you later today, Morgan," Ashley said, pulling her away from the prosecutor. "We will discuss it then."

"What time? I need to do this. Soon."

"I can't give you an exact time, but as soon as possible."

Ashley then told Kylie that she could take Morgan back to the jail. She watched her client leave with a heavy heart, wondering how long she would truly make it. She was losing her mind in custody. But Ashley had done all she could to get her client out of there. Now it was up to the jail to keep her alive, and the jail was not within Ashley's control.

# 17

## KATIE

Ashley didn't stick around after the hearing. She packed up her things and left the courtroom without saying a word to anyone. The stress of Ashley's work was weighing on her. It always had, but it seemed like she was taking it extra rough over the past few days. Katie made a note to check on her, but she had more pressing things to deal with, like grilling George for more details on Frank Vinny's death.

"Some hearing, huh?" George said.

Katie looked up, startled. She was still seated in the bench-style seat in the courtroom, and he was standing at the end, shifting his weight from his heels to the balls of his feet.

"Sure," she said dryly. "Another win for the State."

"You've been working with Ashley for too long. She's rubbing off on you."

"I'll consider that a compliment," Katie said, rising to her feet.

Two years ago, Katie would have deemed that the worst insult—even more serious than calling her a *see you next Tuesday*—which would without a doubt set Katie's blood boiling. But that was before she got to know Ashley.

"Consider it how you like." George paused for a long moment. "How are you these days?"

"I'm fine." Katie kept her response short, not out of rudeness, but because she didn't want to discuss her circumstances.

Technically, she was *fine*, but her life seemed unstable these days. She didn't like the direction they were going with the MEHR team—not that she would discuss that with George, anyway—and her father had made a sudden, unexpected reappearance, threatening to pull her hard-kept secret straight out of the bag.

"But I don't want to talk about me," Katie said.

"You want to discuss Frank, don't you?" George was smiling now, apparently pleased that he could still predict her thoughts.

She would have liked to say no, just to screw with him, but she was in the middle of an investigation. Her work came before petty social squabbles. "Yeah. Are you sure that Frank is dead?"

"Unless he found a way to give another corpse his DNA, then yeah, he's dead."

"So, DNA, then. That's how you identified him?"

"With that forty-eight-hour cold-case rule, we put a rush order and got the positive identification early this morning. It matched with his DNA sample in the national criminal database. He's in it, of course."

"Naturally. He's got, like, a zillion felonies to his name."

George eyed Katie. "You still aren't sure he's dead, are you?"

"Honestly," Katie said with a sigh, "yes and no. It seems fitting for Frank to die in a fire. He's been playing with it nearly all his life. But I also don't see him going down that easily. Especially locked inside a building like a rat in a cage.

Frank was, I don't know..." She paused, chewing on her lip. "He was notorious. And not in a good way. It seems like he should have a death that better fit his personality."

"You watch too much TV."

Katie snorted, and she was about ready to respond by saying she doesn't have cable, so nice try, but she held her tongue. When she was young, her mother used to tell her that *you catch more bees with honey than vinegar*. She'd been a bit of a hot head even when she was small. It was a rare occasion when she thought of her mother as right, but that saying was accurate when it came to dealing with George.

"What about the other victim? Do you have an ID on them yet?"

George shook his head. "There's no record that matches her in CODIS, so she doesn't have a criminal history like Frank."

"Her?" Katie said, latching on to the only word that told her anything.

"Don't tell anyone I said that," George said, looking to his left and then to his right. It wasn't necessary because they were the only ones left in the courtroom, but George seemed extra jumpy about this case. "But yeah, the medical examiner has confirmed that the second body is female. We don't have a name yet, though."

"What about age?"

"Young. Not a child, but maybe a teen or a young adult."

Katie's heart seized. Young deaths were always the most tragic. "Is Morgan your only suspect?"

"What makes you say that Morgan *is* a suspect?"

"Umm, the prosecutor. I think he actually said those exact words. 'Morgan is a suspect.'"

"Okay. You've got a point. Yeah. Right now, Morgan is our target."

"Why?"

"You did listen to Charles Hanson a few minutes ago, didn't you?"

"Yeah. I did. But Morgan's presence doesn't mean she lit the fire or locked Frank inside the barn."

"Let's wait to see what the DCI lab has to say about her hand swabs before we start doubting my theories, huh?"

He was speaking down to her again. It felt just like old times. "And if there's no trace of accelerant on Morgan's hands, what then?"

"Then she washed her hands."

Katie rolled her eyes. "Why are you zeroing in on Morgan alone?"

George quirked an eyebrow. "Do you have information that would tell me to do otherwise?"

"No," Katie said, a heated flush creeping into her cheeks. "I'm just saying it could be any number of people. Frank had lots of enemies. There were rival drug dealers from other counties. People who wanted to take over his territory. And then there are the families of users whose lives were destroyed by him. All kinds of options."

"Like the users themselves, right?"

Katie huffed in exasperation. "Why would Morgan want to kill Frank? He was her dealer. She *needed* him. His death causes a whole lot more problems for her than it solves."

"I don't have to prove motive."

Katie hated that line. She heard it far too often. No, motive was not an element of any crime, but it was helpful to the prosecution. She wanted to shout that straight in his face, but she restrained herself.

"I can see what you're thinking," George said, his smile widening. "But consider this. Maybe Morgan owed Frank money. A lot of money. And he was refusing to give her any more dope until she paid up. That sounds an awful lot like motive, now, doesn't it?"

"You have no evidence to support that."

"I don't? Morgan hasn't worked a single day in as long as I can remember. Yet she's been downing dope like she was getting it for free. And you and I both know that Frank isn't a generous person. What does that add up to? Debt."

Katie opened her mouth to respond but then closed it again. George had a point. Usage at Morgan's addiction level would cost hundreds of dollars a week. Morgan wasn't from money, and she wasn't working. So how was she paying for all those drugs?

# 18

### ASHLEY

Ashley kept her phone on silent during hearings, and she'd missed a call from the jail during Morgan's bond review hearing. It couldn't have been Morgan because she was with Ashley, so it had to be one of her other incarcerated clients. Once Morgan was taken back to the jail, Ashley clicked on the message and listened. What she heard had her tearing out of the courtroom and headed straight for the jail.

Ashley ran down the steps of the courthouse and across the street. She called the jail, letting them know that she would be there in a few minutes. When she arrived, a young jailer took her straight to an attorney-client room where Aubrey was already waiting. Ashley thanked the jailer, and he left. When the heavy iron door slammed closed behind him, Ashley turned to her former client.

"What the hell is going on?"

"I don't know. Like I said in my voicemail. Morgan won't stop talking about Frank. She was up all night chattering about him and the fire. Is someone giving that girl drugs in jail? She acts like she's high or something. I mean, she's freaking out one moment, and then she's somewhat normal the next. Then I wake up this morning to her clawing her eyes out. Blood was everywhere, by the way. It was disgusting."

It was a mistake to assume that Morgan wasn't high just because she was in jail. The jail staff did everything they could to keep illegal substances out, but as Aubrey pointed out yesterday when discussing Morgan's suicidal ideations, *where there's a will, there's a way.*

"She wasn't clawing her eyes out," Ashley said, responding to the only thing she knew for sure. She didn't lie to her clients, and she wouldn't claim Morgan was sober if she didn't know.

"It sure looked that way to me."

"She just scratched her face a little, is all."

Aubrey grunted. "If that's a scratch, then a stab wound is a bruise."

They were getting off topic here. Morgan's self-harm wasn't the issue right now. It was her inability to keep quiet. It could destroy any chance they had at trial. "You said that Morgan was talking about the fire. Who was she talking to?"

"Erica."

"Elsberry?"

"Yup."

"Ugh," Ashley groaned. "Why? Why would she do that?"

Erica was one of her clients as well, but she was a back-stabber. Even before she got into drugs. Ashley had known her in high school, and she'd been one of those truly horrible mean girls that never seemed to grow out of the nastiness. The fact that she was hooked on drugs and in jail did not lessen that element of her personality. In fact, it had done the exact opposite.

"If you want my opinion, I think Erica baited her into it."

Ashley knew the implications and the reasoning as to why Erica might do that. It was the same reason Morgan wanted to talk to Charles. They thought their personal situation would get much better if they snitched on someone else. Sometimes that was true, but they never took a moment to look at the larger picture. If none of them ever rolled over and turned State's evidence, then they all would be in a better situation. Not just one of the few. But Ashley had been unsuccessful at explaining that to any of her clients.

"Is there anyone else sharing a cell with you?"

"Nope. Not at the moment, but you know how quickly things can change."

"Yeah. I know." They were one drug bust away from filling the female side of the jail to full capacity. "What is Morgan saying about Frank? She hasn't confessed, has she?" That would be bad, really bad. There weren't even official charges filed against Morgan yet. That meant they had a chance of avoiding formal charges altogether if they played it smart. A confession to another inmate would surely change that fact.

"Not exactly."

"What does that mean?" Ashley said, rubbing a hand over her face. "Either she is confessing, or she isn't. There is no middle ground on something like that."

"Well, she said that she's happy that Frank is dead. Actually, Erica agreed with her on that one. I think Morgan said something to the effect of, 'Devils deserve to die in hellfire.'"

"She said that?"

"I can't be exactly sure, because it wasn't like I could record it or write it down. But it definitely was something like that."

"Fuck," Ashley said, groaning. It wasn't a confession, but it could be presented to the jury as one. And the timing mattered. This conversation would have taken place before anyone outside of law enforcement knew that Frank had died in the fire. Sure, Ashley could argue that it was Frank's barn, so it was logical to believe that Frank was one of the bodies, but it sounded like the conversation was a lot more definite than a conjecture. "Are you sure that Morgan didn't say that Frank was *probably* dead?"

"Like I said, I don't remember her exact words, but I don't think so."

Ashley groaned. "And Erica agreed with Morgan?"

"Yeah. She wasn't as vocal about it, but she definitely agreed. I don't know if that was to keep her talking or because she felt the same way, but she definitely acted as though they were on the same page on that."

Ashley felt Aubrey was right on this one. Erica had no reason—at least that Ashley was aware of—to want Frank dead. Then again, neither did Morgan, but her words clearly indicated the opposite. Ashley had to assume that Erica planned to turn State's evidence, but maybe there was a way to talk her out of it.

"What are you going to do about it?" Aubrey sounded almost bored, but it was an act. Jail inmates lived for gossip like this. Aubrey would be incarcerated for nearly a month; she needed something to occupy her time.

"I'm going to have a little chat with Erica."

"Is Morgan getting out of jail today?"

"Nope. Her bond remains the same. No bond. So, she'll be here for the foreseeable future."

"Great," Aubrey said sarcastically. "Twenty-nine more days with that psycho. Seriously, Ashley, she's nuts. Certifiably insane."

"I wish," Ashley said with a sigh. "Because if that were true, I'd have a nice insanity defense. And also, you'll get twenty percent good time. It's not twenty-nine days, it's twenty-three."

"It still feels like an eternity. At least with that loose

cannon bouncing around the cell, peeling her skin off with her fingernails. That girl's not right in the head."

"Are any of us?" Ashley asked.

"You got me there."

Ashley glanced at her watch and realized with a start that her meeting with Aubrey had taken a full hour. It was already 10:30, and she had piles of work to do. Yet she still needed to carve out time to talk Erica out of screwing herself and Morgan. Ashley groaned inwardly. It was shaping up to be a rough day, indeed, and it was still morning. There was plenty of time in the day for shit to go horribly wrong.

# 19

KATIE

When she'd extracted all the information that she could about the police investigation into Morgan, Katie ended her conversation with George. She could tell that he would have liked to linger, but she had nothing to say to him anymore.

Even though he was sorry for the way he had treated her —he'd apologized more times than Katie could count—she still couldn't bring herself to completely forgive him for causing her to lose her job at the police department. Sure, she was happy working with Ashley, but it had stung to be rejected by the agency that she'd devoted her life to for more than six years.

"Where are you going?" George said, following her out of the courtroom. "We can walk together."

Katie pulled out her phone and held it up. "Sorry, I've got to call Ashley."

"Sure, sure," George said, shoving his hands in his pockets. "We'll catch up another time, then."

"Yeah," Katie said with absolutely no conviction. Then she pressed Ashley's name and the phone began to ring.

She had more than one reason for calling her boss in that

moment. True, it got rid of George, but she also wanted to know what had caused Ashley to go tearing out of the courtroom like a bat out of hell after Morgan's hearing. When Ashley ran off like that, it usually meant there was an emergency, and she would need Katie's help.

"How fast can you get over here?" Ashley said. Her voice was heavy with exhaustion.

"Well, hello to you, too," Katie said.

"Ha. Ha. No, seriously. You should get here. I'm at the jail."

"Sure," Katie said. "I'll be there in a few minutes."

She hung up the phone without saying goodbye. They'd see each other soon enough.

Ashley was waiting for Katie in the jail common area, arms crossed, toe tapping. "Took you long enough."

"I didn't run, if that's what you mean. What's going on?"

"Well, I've got one hell of a story to tell you," Ashley said. Then she launched into the details about her meeting with Aubrey Miller.

Apparently, Erica Elsberry was trying to cause trouble, and she was succeeding. That came as no surprise to Katie. Erica had become addicted to methamphetamine somewhat recently. Before that, she was the town's self-proclaimed queen bee. People didn't challenge it mainly because they were scared of her. She was the prototypical mean girl. She lapped praise on anyone who took her side and gossiped mercilessly about anyone who didn't.

"So," Katie said after Ashley was done filling her in, "what do you want to do about it?"

"I'm going to meet with Erica now, try to talk her out of using the information she got from Morgan to turn State's evidence."

"And if she doesn't listen..."

Ashley shrugged. "I'll have to withdraw from her case. I

can't have two clients testifying against one another. Then we'll have to find a way to blame Erica for the fire."

"She was arrested in the farm field behind Frank's place for trespassing and possession."

"Yeah," Ashley said, chewing her lip. "It's the fact that she had drugs on her that worries me. It makes it seem like she bought drugs and left. Frank would have been alive at that point."

"True," Katie said. "But she could have also stolen the drugs, then burned the barn, or burned the barn after buying meth. I mean, just because she made a purchase doesn't mean she didn't kill Frank, right?"

"To me, it makes it less likely, but I still want you to start looking for a way around that. I mean, Erica wasn't exactly denying she was involved either during her conversation with Morgan. From what I understand, Erica was saying the same things Morgan was. Or at least agreeing with her. Sure, she can say she was saying all that stuff to get Morgan to confess, but she still said it."

"Are you two ready?" Kylie said. The jail administrator was behind the glass partition, watching Ashley and Katie as they talked. She would have had to allow Ashley to come out to meet Katie, and Ashley must have told her that they'd be going back in. "I don't want to rush you, but I can't wait around all morning."

"Right, sorry," Ashley said. "We're ready now."

Kylie pressed a button, and the lock on the heavy door leading back to the jail clicked. Ashley pulled it open, and Katie followed her into the jail.

"Erica's already in the interview room waiting for you, and she's not happy about it," Kylie said, leading them down the long, depressing hallway. The walls were unadorned cinder block, and the floor was painted cement. "She's scheduled to have a visit with her son, but that's been postponed until tomorrow since Ashley said this meeting was urgent."

"Yeah, well, Erica only has herself to blame," Ashley said.

Which was true. Erica's son had been removed from her care because of her methamphetamine use. If she would stop using, she would get her son back and she would stop getting arrested. It seemed like a win-win scenario to Katie. But then again, she never did understand addiction.

"Good luck telling *her* that," Kylie said. Then she unlocked the door to the interview room and motioned for Ashley and Katie to enter.

Erica was not sitting in either of the two chairs; she was instead standing near the back door, looking impatient. She waited until Kylie was gone before she said, "You better be coming with news of my release, because I'm—"

"You're missing a visit with James," Ashley cut her off.

James Elsberry was well known to both Ashley and Katie. He was Erica's son, now eight years old. He'd been sexually assaulted by one of Ashley's clients a few years earlier. From what Katie had heard, the kid was starting to show signs of sexual deviance himself now. Which wasn't shocking. Most sex offenders were victims when they were children. While that would have been enough of a reason for social services to be involved, Erica's newfound drug habit was also an issue.

"Don't *you* use my son's name. Not ever. Either of you." Erica looked furiously from Ashley to Katie, her eyes flashing and her nostrils flaring.

Erica needed their help, and she knew it, but there were times that she didn't want it. This seemed to be one of those times. Katie had been the lead investigator when James was assaulted, and it might seem like that would have made Erica like Katie, but she despised Katie more than she did Ashley. Katie had screwed up the search warrant that led to the suppression of much of the incriminating evidence against James's abuser. That was a mistake that Erica would never forgive. Not that Katie ever expected her to.

"Sit down and shut up, Erica," Ashley said.

Katie startled at the sudden sharpness in Ashley's tone. The way she spoke to clients in private was something Katie was still getting used to. When she was a police officer, she'd thought Ashley excused her clients' choices and babied them. Now that she'd spent some time working with Ashley, Katie knew it was the exact opposite. Yes, Ashley wanted people to think she liked all her clients, but that was just an act. In private, she could be harsh on them, especially when they needed tough love.

"I'm here to talk to you about your conversation with Morgan last night."

Erica snorted and dropped into the seat across from Ashley. "So, you've been spying on me lately, huh? You're tired of your boring life, so you have to go somewhere else for entertainment."

"Don't flatter yourself, Erica. I don't care about you enough to spy on you. What I do care about is your attempts to torpedo Morgan's future case while potentially incriminating yourself."

"I don't know what you mean."

"Then let me spell it out for you." Ashley leaned forward, tapping her index finger against the desktop. "If you plan on running to the prosecutor and turning State's evidence against Morgan, you might as well tell me now. I, of course, never encourage snitching, but I definitely can't represent you if you are going to testify against another one of my clients."

Erica leaned back and crossed her arms. She'd grown frail over the past few years as the drugs melted the weight off of her formerly voluptuous figure. "What are you talking about?

I seriously don't know." The hard edge had disappeared from her eyes, a note of fear replacing it.

"Your conversation last night. The one where you goaded Morgan into saying that she was happy that Frank was dead."

"I didn't goad Morgan into anything. I don't know where you are getting your information from, but I said the same things as Morgan. We're both happy he's dead. That doesn't mean that we killed him."

"Why would you be happy that he's dead?" Ashley said, shaking her head. "It doesn't make any sense. Frank was your dealer."

"It makes perfect sense if you knew Frank in the way that me and Morgan did."

"And how do you know Frank?" Katie asked.

At first, she'd been content to sit back and listen, but there was something about what Erica had said that had her investigative mind tingling. Frank was their dealer, everyone knew that, but the implication here was that there was something more going on behind the scenes that was still a secret.

Erica shook her head. "You wouldn't believe me."

"Try me," Katie said, even though deep down she knew Erica was probably right.

"Who even told you about my conversation with Morgan? Was it a jailer? They hang around, lurking in the shadows like a bunch of filthy cockroaches, watching us. It's creepy. This isn't the first time I've been in jail, but it is the first time I feel like I'm being watched even when I'm peeing."

"This may be hard for you to stomach, Erica, seeing that you think everything is about you," Ashley said, "but they are trying to keep Morgan safe."

"Why? She's in jail. Do they think I'm going to hurt her? Because I wouldn't. Morgan's my friend. And the other girl that shares our cell—Aubrey—she's not a friend, but she's not an enemy either."

"Suicide watch," Ashley said.

Erica scrunched her nose. "Who said Morgan was suicidal? That's bullshit. Morgan wouldn't hurt herself."

"Have you seen the scratches on her face?" Ashley asked.

"Well, there's that, but she did that more for show. A manipulation so the judge would let her out. It didn't work, obviously, because Kylie brought her back to the cell this morning, but it was worth a try. Seriously?" Erica looked hard at Ashley and then shifted her gaze to Katie. "Who is telling you this stuff?" When they were both silent, Erica gasped. "It's Aubrey, isn't it? That little snake."

"I'm not saying it is or it isn't Aubrey," Ashley said. They were losing control of the interview, and they needed to get it back on track. "But what if it was, what would you say to that?"

"I'd say Aubrey has as much motive to kill Frank as either of us do. She's a user too, right? That's why she's in jail. A thirty-day sentence for possession. Or, at least, that's what she told us. Apparently, she's a liar, so that could be made up, too."

"She's in for possession," Ashley said, "but what do you mean that Aubrey had as much reason to kill Frank as you and Morgan?"

Erica shook her head. "I don't want to talk about it."

"Come on, Erica," Ashley said, her tone soothing. "It sounds like something bad was happening down at that property, and if I'm going to properly defend Morgan, I need to know everything. Does this have something to do with those parties that Frank used to throw?"

The location of Frank's property was no accident. It was in the country and heavily forested for good reason. Privacy. Frank would have big parties on his property at least once a month. It was invitation only, and he hired a security firm to work the perimeter of the property to keep prying eyes out. Nobody knew where he got the money for all that—not even law enforcement—but it likely wasn't the drugs. Meth-amphetamine was lucrative, but not that lucrative. But whatever went down at that property was kept a close secret. Not even the junkies would speak of it.

"Yes, and no," Erica said.

"I don't follow..." Ashley said.

"Frank had these girls. He calls them '*his* girls.' I wasn't one of them, mind you, because I'm too old for all that. So is Morgan, and Aubrey for that matter. He likes them young, thank God."

Katie pulled out a notebook and a pen and began rapidly scribbling notes. This was a bit of information she'd never heard before. A glimpse behind the shade that shrouded Frank's activities back there in the forest.

"What does he do with these 'girls,' and what does it have to do with his parties?" Ashley asked.

"I've never been invited to Frank's parties. Neither has Morgan, and I suspect Aubrey is the same. That used to bother me, because I knew there were girls there because Frank would casually mention that his girls made sure everyone had a good time.'"

"What does that mean?"

"I didn't know for sure, at least not until recently. He kept his girls away from us older ones. The only way I knew they existed was because of the things Frank said."

"Okay. If they were such a secret, how did you find out about them?" Katie asked.

"I don't like being kept out of the loop, and that's what Frank was doing. After a while, I got tired of not knowing. So, I convinced Morgan to go with me and check it out. Frank doesn't have security when there isn't a party, so I figured we could walk right up if we came in any other way than the driveway."

"Okay..." Katie was writing so furiously that her wrist was starting to cramp.

"So, we did. This was before Morgan was arrested for burglary. She didn't have that ankle monitor on."

"How long ago?"

"Three weeks, maybe?"

"That would have been around the time Mr. Winters's barn was burglarized."

"Yeah," Erica said.

"His place is down the street from Frank's."

When Ashley said, "down the street," it really wasn't all that close. The properties outside of town were acreages, so Mr. Winters's farm was a good five miles away from Frank's property, but it was on the way if Morgan and Erica had been coming from town, which was likely.

"I didn't have anything to do with that," Erica said. "Morgan needed cash, so she popped in and took a few tools to pawn later."

Ashley shook her head, and Katie knew what she was thinking—that Morgan was desperate and dumb. Selling the tools to the pawn shop had led to her criminal charges, but now there was an eyewitness. That wasn't great for Morgan's defense, at least in that case.

"Okay, so you snuck onto Frank's property without him knowing," Ashley said, steering Erica back to her original story. "Then what?"

"Well, we saw him with this girl. She was young, and she was high as fuck."

"How do you know that?"

"She couldn't walk on her own. She was stumbling all over the place. Frank was holding her by the arm, and that was the only way she was standing at all. He led her to the shed out back of the barn, put her in, and shut the door. Then he locked it from the outside."

"He locked a girl in the shed?" Katie repeated, shocked. "How old was she?"

Erica shrugged. "I don't know. Pretty young. She looked to me like a teenager. Her hips were still narrow, and she had that gangly, awkward look that girls sometimes have when they are in middle school. But I have no idea. It's not like Frank was telling me any of this."

"Okay. Then what happened next?" Katie asked.

"Then Frank left to go back inside the barn, and that was it."

"That was it?" Katie said, her tone incredulous. "You didn't do anything to help the girl?"

"What kind of psycho do you think I am? Of course I did something. I ran over there when the coast was clear and knocked on the door. There weren't any windows, but the girl responded. Like I said, she was fucked up. On what, I'm not exactly sure, but she sounded very groggy when she responded."

"What did she say?"

"I don't know. She wasn't speaking English. I couldn't find the key, so I left."

"You left her there?" Katie and Ashley both said in unison.

Erica crossed her arms. "So did Morgan. It's not like we knew what to do. I couldn't exactly call the cops. What would I say? 'Morgan and I were trespassing on Frank's property after we committed a burglary, and we saw him lock a girl in a shed.' That's worse for us than it is for Frank. We would have been arrested, and nothing would have happened to Frank."

"Still..." Katie started, but Ashley cut her off.

"No, Katie, she has a point." Ashley was speaking to Katie

but kept her gaze locked on Erica. "Do you have any idea what Frank was doing with the girl?"

"I don't *know*, but I can make an educated guess."

"And that is..."

"That he was using her for sex. Exchanging drugs for sex. That's why I said I thought it had something to do with Frank's parties. Based on what he's said in the past, I assume that's what he meant when he'd said that he had a good time with his girls."

"So, you believe he's giving these girls drugs at no cost. Yet, he's charging you," Katie said, narrowing her eyes and setting her pen down.

As a rule, Katie rarely believed anyone, at least not without corroborating evidence. And here was a fantastical story, told by a criminal. It seemed a bit more trustworthy since Erica admitted to her presence while Morgan committed a burglary, but then again, she hadn't really admitted to anything either. She'd said Morgan burglarized Mr. Winters's place, not her.

"This isn't a jealousy thing, if that's what you're getting at. Like I said, Frank isn't giving drugs out for charity; he's offering them to get the girls nice and addicted. Once they are on the hook, he starts charging them. And it isn't cheap, if you ask me."

"Where are this girl's parents? And you implied that there are other girls. It sounds like you only saw one."

Erica narrowed her eyes. "I don't know about parents. Like I said, I'm making a guess at her age. She could be twenty-five for all I know. And I did only see one girl. But, like I said, Frank mentioned more."

"But you haven't seen any others?"

"Did I say I saw others? No. I said I saw one. That's all."

"And then you left without saying anything to anyone?" Katie knew she was pushing Erica too hard, but she needed to know. Maybe that same girl that they'd seen in the shed was the body found in the barn with Frank.

Erica sighed heavily and crossed her arms. "I only just found out a few days before the fire. And the girl didn't speak English. I had no way of talking to her. I couldn't go to the cops for obvious reasons. What did you expect me to do?"

"Did Morgan do anything with the information?"

"I'm not Morgan's sitter. Maybe, maybe not."

"Okay," Katie said, chewing on her lip. "You mentioned Aubrey earlier in the conversation. Did she know about these girls?"

"Yes. At least that's what she told me."

"How did she find out?"

"I don't know. You'll have to ask her."

"Do you have any idea where the girl came from?" Ashley asked.

"Mexico, maybe. I don't know. Like I said, I couldn't talk to her. And that's all I know. Maybe Morgan knows more, but I wouldn't talk to her today. She's pretty upset that she isn't getting out."

Katie was silent, thinking. Maybe these "girls" were the key to Morgan's defense. Morgan might know more, but Katie at least had something to start working on. She would have to track these girls down, but presumably they didn't live all that far away. They must have families or some ties to Iowa. Otherwise, why would they be here? For all Katie knew, a family member of one of these girls burned the barn in a desperate attempt to break the girl's addiction by cutting out the manufacturer and destroying the factory. It wasn't a great place to start, but at least Katie had something to do.

## 20

### ASHLEY

If what Erica was telling them was true—and that was a big *if* —Frank was disgusting, but it didn't quite rise to the level that would prove helpful in Morgan's defense. Two people died, presumably in the fire, although cause of death was still up in the air. Ashley would need something more than *Frank was trading drugs for sex* as a defense.

The fact that the girl was locked in the shed suggested a lack of consent, but that was only if that bit of information could be believed. Ashley's assumption was that the second body belonged to one of these girls, but the body was in the barn, not the shed. That contradicted Erica's story. Ashley groaned and rubbed her hands over her face.

"What is it?" Katie asked.

They were still in the attorney-client room. Kylie was taking Erica back to her cell, and Ashley hadn't decided whether she wanted to meet with Morgan or Aubrey next. Kylie was letting her think about it while she was getting Erica situated. Then she'd be back.

"Nothing fits," Ashley said. "All their stories are different. I mean, it's good that Erica isn't snitching on Morgan. And I think we got at least some relevant information from her, but I still don't have a clear picture as to what was going on down there at Frank's barn. I feel like we've gotten half-truths from everyone so far."

"And that's different than other cases because..."

Katie had a point. Nobody ever told Ashley the truth. Honestly, it didn't matter all that much in most criminal defense cases. All that mattered was what the State could prove. But Ashley was trying to end an investigation before formal charges were ever filed, so it wasn't exactly the same.

"I don't know, it just is."

"Well," Katie said, rising to her feet. "I think I'll let you handle the next few meetings with Morgan and Aubrey. I'm going to follow up on some of the leads from Erica, and I probably better get back out to the scene. The arson dogs are supposed to arrive today."

"Good plan," Ashley said, but there was little excitement in her voice. She was running herself ragged, but there wasn't much she could do about it. She'd catch up on sleep when things settled down.

"I want to track down some of these girls, but I'm not sure where to start. Do you think I should check the missing persons lists?" Katie asked.

"Maybe, but I'd talk to Elena first."

"Elena?" Katie seemed shocked. Ashley supposed it was because she had never suggested that Katie check with their office manager when it came to any part of an investigation.

"Yeah. Her parents work at the meat-packing plant, and they are undocumented. They probably know something about girls that go missing from their community. Wouldn't you think?"

"Yeah," Katie said. "Good plan."

They waited in silence until Kylie returned. By then,

Ashley had decided that she would meet with Morgan despite Erica's suggestion otherwise. Kylie let Katie out and was back with Morgan within ten minutes. Ashley gasped when she saw her client. She looked horrible, shrunken in a way that she hadn't been earlier that morning.

"I want to proffer," Morgan said.

Proffering was when a criminal defendant met with the prosecutors and gave them information in exchange for leniency. Ashley didn't like it because it was just a formal arrangement for snitching, but she had to allow it when her clients really wanted to do it.

"I'm sorry, Morgan, but I don't think you have any information that the State is going to want or need."

"I do," Morgan insisted.

"Okay," Ashley said, crossing her arms, "then tell me first. What is it that you think you know that is important enough to encourage the prosecutors to not charge you with double homicide and arson?"

"Frank has these girls."

"I know," Ashley said. "Erica told us all about them."

Morgan shook her head. "She doesn't know what I know."

"Well, she told me an awful lot."

"Did she tell you about the card game?"

"The what?" Ashley said, genuinely confused. Erica hadn't said anything about gambling.

"That's what I thought. She probably told you about the girl that we saw him put in the shed, but she didn't tell you about any of the others."

"Do *you* know about the others? It sounds like the girls might be immigrants that he is trafficking from the border."

"Some are. Or, at least, a few have been. But the others, they're just girls from broken families. Runaways that ran into the wrong man's arms."

"How do you know this?"

"I was invited to one of Frank's parties. The one that happened a few months ago." Morgan used air quotes around the word *invited*, and she said it with such total disdain that it surprised even Ashley, who was rarely shocked by her clients anymore.

"What do you mean by 'invited'?"

"I bought some drugs, and I made the mistake of using while there. I got too fucked up to leave. What happened next was..." A tear trickled down her cheek, and she brushed it away. "It was horrible."

"What did Frank do to you?" Ashley lowered her tone so it was softer, less harsh. She'd represented Morgan on multiple occasions. She'd seen her scream and rage about incarceration, but she'd never seen her cry like this. It was the silence in this suffering that had Ashley immediately on edge.

"It wasn't Frank. Well, it was, but it wasn't."

"I'm not sure that I follow."

"Well, you probably don't know this, but he only invites men to his parties, and he's extremely selective about who is allowed in. They have to be discreet, and they've got to have a lot of cash. They pay big bucks just to get onto Frank's property, and then they pay more to play the game."

"What is this game?"

"Frank gets out a stack of cards. Everyone who wants to participate pays him a fee, then they draw a card. Those with the highest cards go first, the ones with the lowest go last."

"Go? What do you mean by 'go'?" Ashley thought she knew what Morgan meant, but she needed to hear it from her lips.

"Sex. They'd have sex with the girls. And that night, since I was too fucked up to leave, Frank went ahead and used me in the same way. Luckily, I'm older, and most of these men really like them young, so I only had the overflow."

"The overflow." Ashley didn't want to ask, but she knew she had to. "What does that mean?"

"A deck has fifty-two cards, right?"

Ashley nodded.

"Well, the overflow is when there were so many people paying that Frank had to go to a second deck."

"What about cards that were the same number?"

"Frank had a way to handle that. It always went in this order—diamonds, spades, clubs, hearts. He said he had to keep it fair. As if any of it was fair to us."

"Us," Ashley said, leaning forward. "Who do you mean by *us*?"

"Me and the girl. I never caught her name, but she wasn't the same girl I saw him lock in the shed when I was with Erica. That girl was Mexican or something, but this girl, she spoke English, and she was blond. I don't know much about her other than that."

"What happened to her?"

"I don't know. I never saw her again. I hope that she went back to her family."

"And if she didn't?"

Morgan shook her head. "I don't want to know."

It was yet another angle for Ashley and Katie's investigation to follow. Frank's parties had been going on for as long as Ashley could remember. If this was the true nature of *all* his parties, she shuddered to think just how many women had been gang-raped over the years. It did solve one question that had been lingering in Ashley's mind. She now knew where Frank came up with so much money. He was charging each one of the men to have their way with his girls. Depending on how much he charged, it probably brought in a large chunk of change.

She hoped Katie was making some leeway in discovering the identities of some of these girls. They would all have motive to murder Frank and burn his property to the ground. If Morgan's story turned out to be true, Ashley completely understood the person's reasoning. Frank did deserve to die.

# 21

## KATIE

Elena was alone at her desk when Katie entered through the front door of the Public Defender's Office.

"Hey, Elena," Katie said as she came around the unoccupied reception desk that separated the waiting room from the employee area of the office. "Where's Rachel?"

Rachel had been coming to work with Ashley every day. Sometimes she stayed at the office, and sometimes she didn't. It just depended on the day. When she did stay, she usually remained out front with Elena. Rachel was only a year younger than Elena, so it made sense that the two girls were drawn to one another.

"She went to the library. Why? What's up?"

Katie was lingering beside Elena's desk. It wasn't something she ordinarily did unless she needed something.

"Listen, Elena," Katie said, pulling up a chair. "I need to ask you some rather sensitive questions."

"Okay," Elena said, removing her long, thin fingers from the keyboard of her computer and placing her hands in her lap. Katie had her full attention now. "What kind of questions?"

"Questions about your family. Well, actually, not *your* family specifically. They are more about the community as a whole."

Elena cocked her head to the side, confused.

"I can tell that I'm not making a lot of sense. So, I'm going to just come out and say it. We have some witnesses that are claiming that some girls from the immigrant community have gone missing. Do you know anything about that?"

Elena shrugged. "I don't know, but I can find out. Do you have ages for these girls?"

"No." Katie shook her head. "Not for sure, but probably teenagers."

"I'll ask around. I overheard my mom one time talking about children getting snatched while immigrating, but she didn't say where they'd disappeared. I was pretty little at the time, so I never asked my mom about it. She wouldn't have told me. But she probably would now. She has another doctor's appointment this afternoon. I can ask her about it if you'd like."

"Yes, thanks," Katie said, rising to her feet. "That'll be a huge help."

Elena nodded, turning back to her computer, and Katie headed down the hall to her office. She wished she could do something more to follow up on the lead, but she didn't know anyone else that had ties to the meat-packing plant other than Stephanie Arkman, and she doubted Stephanie would even acknowledge that she employed undocumented workers. She suspected that Stephanie knew plenty about the disappearances, but that was only a guess. Besides, she was trying to keep her distance from Stephanie, not seek her out. The last thing she needed was for an Arkman to realize she was Michael Michello's daughter.

When Katie reached her office, her body's autopilot

snapped on, following the same steps she had for the past seven months. She flipped on the light, pulled out her chair, shook her computer mouse, turned on the scanner, and then typed in her computer's passcode. She was just about to open her email when the scanner crackled to life with George Thomanson's familiar voice.

"You could at least send *one* deputy out to Frank's," George said.

"You know why I can't do that. Conflict of interest." Katie instantly recognized the gravelly tone of Sheriff St. James.

"Oh, don't pull that same bullshit excuse. Frank's dead. I don't care that you are second cousins twice removed or whatever familial connection you have always claimed. You should get your ass out here and do your job. This is *your* jurisdiction, not mine. I'm running on fumes here."

"Don't take that tone with me. Your boss agreed to this. Chief Carmichael decided a long time ago that he would take all calls to that residence."

"That was then, this is now."

"Nothing has changed," Sheriff St. James growled.

"Everything has changed, and you know it."

Katie leaned so close to the scanner that her nose was almost touching it. Sheriff St. James and George were in a pissing match over the fire at Frank's. She wasn't sure how she and Ashley could use that to their advantage, but it was possible. Then George said something that had her even more intrigued.

"Listen," George said with a heavy sigh. He sounded far more defeated than Katie had ever heard him. "I'm on my way back out to the scene. I'd appreciate it if you would send someone to assist me. The arson dogs should be here in the next hour. They are coming from Council Bluffs, and I'd like to have some support from you. If for no other reason than to show solidarity. If you can't provide that, then I guess I'm on my own. But I'm telling you that you want to be involved in this. If those arson dogs identify an accelerant and Morgan's hand swabs come back with the same, then we are going to move in for the arrest. It's an election year for you next year. You can either be a part of this huge story or not. Either way, that's your problem."

Sheriff St. James was silent for a long moment, then he said, "Fine. I'll send Deputy Brinks. But that's all. I can't spare any others."

Katie seriously doubted that. The sheriff's department was fully staffed, and they had more than twice the positions as the police department. She almost felt sorry for George, but then she reminded herself of what he'd done to her. If he hadn't thrown her to the wolves, their roles might be reversed. So, really, this was just a version of karma playing out.

She rose from her seat and grabbed her camera bag. The sheriff might not be all that eager to find out what those arson dogs were going to do, but Katie was. She typed a quick text message to Ashley as she made her way down the hallway to the back parking lot.

*Going back to Frank's. Arson dogs here within the hour.*

A bubble immediately popped up. Katie watched it for a few moments, then Ashley's message came through.

*Sounds good. I'm just finishing up with Morgan. I'll call you after that to fill you in. She gave me some interesting details.*

*Is her story different from Erica's?*

*Not really.*

*Okay. I'm leaving now. If you can't call in the next thirty minutes, then text. I won't be able to answer my phone once I make it to Frank's.*

Katie didn't want to tip off any of the officers, especially George. He wouldn't be happy to hear that Ashley and Katie had already started an investigation of their own. Then she tucked her phone in her pocket and hopped into the car. The drive out to Frank's land took about forty minutes if you were driving the speed limit, but Katie intended to move a little faster than that, banking on the fact that all officers would be tied up with the investigation or elsewhere.

It turned out that speeding was a gamble worth taking, and Katie made it in record time. She parked in a gravel area a quarter mile down from Frank's property, then jogged the rest of the way. As she approached, she noticed George's cruiser at the top of the driveway, but his was the only vehicle.

*No Deputy Brinks yet*, Katie thought. She wondered if the sheriff would actually send the deputy for backup or if he was only saying that to get George off his back.

She continued jogging, staying close to the tree line for some camouflage. When she got closer, she realized with a start that George was sitting inside his vehicle. Luckily, he was looking down, focused on his phone screen. Katie picked up her pace, then ducked onto the trail she had used the last time she'd snuck onto the property.

When she reached the bottom of the trail, near the clearing, she heard the familiar sound of tires crunching on gravel and the opening and closing of car doors. Moments later, she heard a dog bark. The arson dogs had arrived, and she'd gotten into position just in time. She pulled out her camera and crouched down behind a patch of thick underbrush, ready to start clicking photos as soon as the dogs came down the driveway.

It didn't take long before George and a tall, burly man made their way toward the clearing. They had two Labrador retrievers with them, one black and one yellow. The black dog looked older based on his size. He was barrel chested, whereas the yellow dog was thin and gangly—like she wasn't quite a puppy, but she wasn't full grown either.

The black dog trotted alongside his handler while the yellow lab bounded around, sniffing everything with curiosity.

"Don't mind Missy," the man said to George. "She's not the real arson dog. Rex, here, is." He patted the black dog on the head. "Missy is only here to try to learn a thing or two from her elder."

"She doesn't seem to care what her elder is doing right now," George said, his tone incredulous.

Katie hated to agree with George on anything, but here, she had no choice. Missy was now leaping around in the underbrush dangerously near Katie, paying no attention to her handler or the other dog. It was an unfortunate turn of events. Katie would have a lot of explaining to do if the dog caught her out there.

Luckily, Missy froze a couple of yards away from Katie and started digging furiously at the ground. The dog dug for a few minutes, then she raised her head. She had something in her mouth. It was a long bone—Katie could see it as clear as day —and it didn't look like one that would come from an animal. It was too long, too familiar. It brought Katie back to her school days, to the science classroom that had a life-sized skeleton hanging in the corner. She hated science, so she used to study that skeleton, thinking of her own set of bones below her skin and muscles.

*Holy shit*, Katie thought. This bone, the bone Missy had clutched in her jaws, looked just like one of the long bones of that human skeleton. A human femur. And she doubted this bone was plastic like those in her science classroom. This was human, and it didn't belong to either of the bodies in the barn. As convoluted as this investigation had been so far, it had just gotten a whole lot more complicated.

## 22

### ASHLEY

Morgan seemed more broken than ever by the time she was through telling Ashley her story. At first, Ashley had wondered about Morgan's honesty, but those doubts had dissolved by the end. There was too much detail. Too much emotion in her eyes. Nobody spoke that convincingly without theater training, and Morgan was no actress.

It was the kind of story that she couldn't stop thinking about. Visions of sexual assaults at Frank's direction played through her mind. They were vivid in a way that Ashley couldn't unsee. And one thought kept her wondering. *How?* How could these unforgivable acts have happened in her town right under her nose? And how had it remained hidden for so long? The only viable solution was that Frank had a strangle hold on his "girls" and the men who attended those parties. Otherwise, there would have been rumors.

But there was nothing, which increased Ashley's concern for the poor girls that Frank forced to participate in his disgusting card game. Where were they? She didn't think Frank would allow them to return home to their families. That would be relinquishing control and could lead to reports to law enforcement. That was a risk Ashley knew Frank would be unwilling to take.

It was possible that Frank was holding the girls somewhere. She'd have to look into rental storage spaces, but that was probably a longshot. If Frank still kept these girls, he'd been smart about it, and Ashley probably wouldn't track them down until it was too late to save them from starvation or dehydration. The other option was that Frank had trafficked them elsewhere. It was the more likely option because it would lead to a payout to Frank and ensure that the girls remained silent. While the thought was repulsive, it was preferable to being locked in a storage locker without food or water.

"So, now you know everything," Morgan said. "The whole disgusting truth." She kept her head down, glancing up at Ashley through strands of her straggly hair. "Do you think less of me?"

"Do I?" Ashley said, placing a hand on her chest. "You're asking me that question?"

"Yeah."

"No, Morgan. Absolutely not. You were the victim of a crime. I wish that I could have helped you."

"Will you talk to Detective Thomanson?" Her green eyes grew wide and hopeful. In that moment, she looked like a broken flower that was trying to bloom despite a damaged stem.

"I don't know," Ashley said with a sigh.

"I can't stay in here," Morgan said, throwing her arms up in the air and shooting to her feet. She began pacing again, desperation radiating from her in waves.

Despite the detail in Morgan's account, part of Ashley still wondered if this whole story had been concocted by Erica and Morgan to manipulate the justice process. Which wasn't something Ashley was above doing. She was a defense attorney, after all, and she was willing to win at all costs, but she also needed to know what she was getting herself into. It wouldn't be the first time she relied on a defendant's version of events just to show up at trial to have the prosecutor completely destroy it with a single rebuttal witness.

"You are going to need to calm down, Morgan."

"I can't, I can't, I can't." She began pulling at the ends of her hair, twisting it like she intended to rip a chunk straight out of her head.

"Listen to me," Ashley said, gritting her teeth and lowering her voice to a growl.

Morgan stopped pacing for a moment. Her gaze met Ashley's, then flickered away.

"Thank you," Ashley said. "What you have told me is helpful to your defense. It's one of the two classic trial defenses."

"Which are..."

Morgan should've known the answer to this question considering her criminal history, but she'd never taken a case all the way to trial. She'd always wanted to cop to a plea right away so that she could get out of jail with probation and a suspended sentence. Ashley had been powerless to stop her. Defendants got to choose two things when it came to their cases, whether they wanted to testify, and if they wanted to plead. That was how conviction after conviction had stacked up against Morgan, making her criminal history far worse than some of Ashley's other clients who had the stomach to sit in jail and wait for the trial process to run its course.

"The two primary trial defenses are, one," Ashley held up her index finger, "I didn't do it. And two," Ashley held up a second finger, "he deserved to die. Considering the evidence that we have gathered so far, 'he deserved it' seems like a pretty viable option, don't you think?"

"Umm, yeah."

"But if we tell the prosecutor your story now in an attempt to secure your release, we are going to lose the element of surprise. I know Charles Hanson, and he'll find a witness that will refute your version of events."

"But I'm telling the truth."

Ashley gave Morgan a hard look. "Trials aren't about truth. They are about proof. And for once, we have the element of surprise here. We can't give that up."

In the trial world, there were few advantages for defendants. Surprise happened to be one of them. Prosecutors had to list every witness and provide a brief outline of their testimony. So long as the defense didn't take depositions of the State's witnesses, Ashley would never have to provide a witness list to the prosecutor, and that could be a real advantage. Especially when dealing with a shocking defense like this one.

"I want you to use it to get me out of here."

"It's not going to get you out of here," Ashley said, groaning. "Can't you see? They are going to keep you in here at all costs. You can tell them any sympathetic story you like, and it wouldn't make a difference. Your mother, sister, grandmother, dog, and child could all die in the next week, and they wouldn't agree to let you out to attend their funerals. Do you understand me?"

"I thought I was innocent until proven guilty."

"Not to the prosecutor you're not," Ashley said. She almost added, *And to nobody else either*, but she kept that particular criticism of the criminal justice system to herself.

"I still want you to try."

"What makes you think it will make any difference to George or Charles Hanson?"

"Because it is horrible, and young girls were hurt."

"You said yourself that you don't know their ages. That the girls could have been twenty-five but looked much younger. And you don't know where the girls are now. Don't get me wrong, it's a sad story," Ashley said, putting up her hands, "but it does nothing to help the State. They can't use the information to track down other victims because you don't know where any of them are. They can't even use it to punish Frank. He's dead already. So, what do you think they will do with it?"

"I don't know…"

"Exactly." Ashley slapped an open palm down on the table, and Morgan flinched. It hadn't been her intention to scare her client, but she didn't regret it either.

"I can't stay in here." Morgan gestured around her. "The walls are getting smaller and smaller, closing in on me. I can't stand it." She gripped her hair again at the base, tugging. "I'm losing my mind."

"I just need some time," Ashley said, rubbing her temples. "A little bit of time is all I'm asking."

"Time, unfortunately, is not on our side."

Ashley looked up, her brow furrowing. "What does that mean?"

Morgan crossed her arms and stuck her nose in the air, refusing to answer.

"Is that a suicide threat?"

"I'll give you two days," Morgan said, holding up the same two fingers Ashley had used when she was discussing defenses. "If I'm not out of here or likely to get out of here, I'm taking matters into my own hands."

"What matters will you be taking into your hands?" Ashley said, shooting to her feet.

As a defense attorney, she carried a weighty burden. She was her clients' only possibility at freedom. It was a lot of responsibility, but she managed it because at the end of the day, her clients still had other options. A guilty verdict was not the end. There was a whole appeals process followed by a post-conviction relief process. Years of potential litigation. But suicide, that was final. There was no second set of judges that could overturn that decision.

"It doesn't matter."

There was a wild glint in Morgan's eyes that hadn't been there earlier. It reminded Ashley of something Aubrey had said. *That girl is on something.* For the first time, Ashley wondered if it was true. It wasn't easy to smuggle drugs into the jail, but it was possible.

"It sounds like a threat to me."

"It's not a threat. It's an ultimatum."

"Okay, so what will you do if you aren't out in two days?"

"I'll go to the prosecutor myself. I'll write a letter and file it with the court."

Ashley sighed heavily. Her job was hard enough, why did her clients insist upon making it harder? "I can't stop you from doing that, but you shouldn't. It will completely blow your defense."

"Maybe it will help," Morgan said with a shrug.

"Probably it won't."

"Oh, well. There are always other options. More final options."

"What does that mean?" Ashley asked, but she knew Morgan wouldn't answer.

It was a suicide threat, but Morgan was careful to keep it implicit. If she stated it any more plainly, Ashley would have something tangible to report to Kylie. Morgan would find herself not only on suicide watch but also alone in solitary confinement, all utensils that she could possibly use to harm herself taken.

*All right*, Ashley thought. *Two days. I have two days to develop this defense before Morgan either torpedoes it or hangs herself.* It wasn't nearly enough time, but she had to try. Morgan was her responsibility, and she would do everything she could to get her to trial alive, and to convince that jury to say *not guilty*.

## 23

___

KATIE

The dog handler whistled. The yellow lab puppy—or at least Katie thought of the dog as a puppy since she clearly wasn't well trained—popped her head up. She still had that femur bone in her mouth as she rooted around, possibly looking for more bones.

"Missy!" the dog handler shouted, whistling through his teeth. A high-pitched sound that hurt even Katie's ears. "Get over here *now*."

The dog bounded through the underbrush, headed back toward George and her handler. Katie released a heavy breath that she hadn't even realized she'd been holding. *That was a close one*, she thought. Missy had been right by her. If those bones hadn't been there to distract her, she would have discovered Katie's position and revealed it.

There was no telling what George would have done if Katie had been caught. She wasn't supposed to be out there, and they both knew it. Sure, there was no explicit sign saying "police line," but Katie had been an officer in the past and she knew better. Lately, George had been trying to patch up their friendship, and maybe that would tip the scales in her favor, but then again, maybe not. She didn't want to find out.

"That doesn't look like an animal bone," George said when Missy reached them.

The dog carried her finding like an Olympian displaying their gold medal. She trotted straight up to her handler and dropped the bone at his feet, wagging her tail furiously.

"No, no, it doesn't," the handler agreed as he leaned over to peer more closely at the bone.

Katie carefully removed her camera's lens cap. The dog wasn't near her anymore, but that didn't mean there was no risk of discovery. Katie had no doubt that if either of those dogs saw her—especially the trained one that the handler called Rex—they would sound an alert. Whether it was barking or pointing, it really didn't make a difference to Katie. She'd be screwed either way.

"Are you going to call DCI?" the dog handler asked.

Katie zoomed in on the bone at their feet, rapidly pressing the shutter button. Nobody had made a move to pick it up. The two men seemed stunned.

"No," George finally said. "Not yet. I don't want to bring them in until I know more. This could end up being a sick joke. A prop from a play or part of a Halloween costume."

The handler straightened and looked George in the eye. "That's a pretty realistic Halloween costume. It looks like there are still bits of skin attached."

"I will call the medical examiner and get a feel of what exactly we're dealing with here," George said irritably. "It's possible that these bones are so old that they won't make a difference to our investigation one way or another."

"Sure," the dog handler said, but his voice held little conviction.

Katie agreed with the dog handler. George was delusional

if he actually thought these bones were so old as to not matter. They'd have to be at least a hundred years old for that to be the case. And even then, there were family members to notify. Distant relatives or grandchildren. Most likely someone was related to the owner of these bones, and they had to be informed of the discovery. Then there was the cause of death issue, which could blow this whole thing wide open.

"I'll go make the call," George said. He was already headed up the driveway toward his police cruiser. "You wait here."

Katie had hoped that the dog handler would take his dogs and go with George. If for no other reason than to give her a few moments to breathe easy, but that wasn't going to happen.

While George was gone, Katie whipped out her phone and started typing a message to Ashley.

*I think the arson dog just found a human bone in the woods.*

Three bubbles appeared, and Ashley's response came through a couple of seconds later. *I'm not following you. Whose bone?*

*Dunno*, Katie typed back. *George is calling the medical examiner. It was buried in the forest. The dog dug it up.*

*You're sure it is human?*

*Not 100%, but yeah, it sure looks like it. Maybe a femur.*

*Another fire victim?*

*No.*

*You sound sure.*

*I am. This one was out in the forest. It looks to me like an unrelated death.*

*And it's older, right?*

*It would have to be. It's completely decomposed. I'm not an expert, but I'd think it had to be out here for at least a couple months.*

*This could be good for us.*

*I know.*

Katie glanced up to see George making his way back down the driveway, his boots crunching against the gravel.

*I've got to go,* Katie typed. *I'll fill you in as things unfold.*

*10-4.*

Katie rolled her eyes. Ashley sometimes used officer codes. She thought it was ironic since Katie used to actually use those codes, but it felt more like a bad mom joke to Katie. She pocketed her phone and focused back on the two men and the dogs.

"I just got off the phone with Chief Carmichael," George said to the other man. "Since these dogs are already here, he wants us to complete our arson investigation. He's going to call the medical examiner and try to get some cadaver dogs out here, but he said the medical examiner has been busy and she probably won't want to come out here unless we have more proof that the bone is human."

"Oh, it's human," the dog handler said. "I've spent my whole life hunting, and I've never seen an animal that had a bone like that."

"I know, but you know these professionals," George said, clapping the dog handler on the shoulder. "They don't trust us grunts out in the field."

"They should, but they don't."

"Either way, the chief doesn't want the dogs anywhere other than the clearing where the fire was. There's no reason for them to be out in the underbrush, anyway."

"Agreed." The dog handler pulled a leash out of his pocket and clipped it onto Missy's collar. "This one here is a bit of a loose cannon. She's supposed to be learning from Rex, but I don't want to chance her running off again. Next time she might come back with a skull. And it could be gooey."

"That would be gross," George said. "And the opposite of what we want."

They made their way to the clearing, and Katie watched them through the viewfinder of her camera. The dog handler handed Missy's leash to George. George wouldn't go any further, and neither of them seemed to want Missy to either. The handler stepped forward and motioned with his hand, and Rex, the big black Labrador, stilled. The handler whistled two times in quick succession, and Rex sprang to action.

Katie did as well. Her Nikon was not capable of recording footage, so she pulled her phone back out and started recording. The camera lens couldn't zoom like her Nikon, and the dogs were far away, but there were ways to enhance videos later. At this point, all she was worried about was getting the footage. It didn't look like either George or the handler had bothered to record the interaction. George would have had to reach up to his chest area to turn on his camera, and Katie hadn't seen him do that, and she doubted the dog handler would have that kind of equipment.

At the handler's signal, the dog's nose dropped to the ground, but he waited for his handler to move first. When the Council Bluffs firefighter began walking forward, the dog moved alongside him. Katie marveled at the kind of training Rex must have received. She'd seen arson dogs at work before, but they almost always had to be kept on leashes and guided by their handlers.

When Rex and his handler reached what had once been the front door to the barn, the dog sat down.

"See that," the handler called to George. "Rex is signaling already. Some form of accelerant was used on the door here."

"And the door had been barred from the outside," George said. "That sounds like murder to me, how about you?"

The dog handler nodded, then continued deeper into the barn. Rex signaled seven more times in various locations around the outside of the barn. He didn't signal anywhere inside the barn.

All the while, Katie continued taking pictures, growing less at ease each time that the dog sat back on his haunches. Maybe the femur bone would turn out to be something Ashley could use in Morgan's defense. But this accelerant all around the outside of the barn—it was bad. Very bad. Especially if Morgan's hand swabs came back positive.

## 24

### ASHLEY

Ashley was on her way out of the jail when her phone started buzzing. It was a text message from Katie saying, *The arson dog found a human bone in the woods*, and her jaw dropped.

Initially, the information had worried Ashley. They were already dealing with Frank's body and the body of an unidentified young female. Two bodies were bad enough for Morgan, but a third would have made things far worse. Three added up to serial killer, and that was always a major news story. And publicity was a problem for the defense side.

Ashley practically did a jig when Katie clarified that the femur bone found by the accelerant dog couldn't have had anything to do with the bodies in Frank's barn. That was information she could use, assuming she could prove that Frank had something to do with the end of that person's life and the placement on his property. Juries had little sympathy for the death of a killer. But she was getting ahead of herself. She first needed to find out more about that bone and its owner.

*I wonder if Morgan, Aubrey, or Erica know anything about it?* Ashley thought. All three of them had been invited to Frank's property on multiple occasions. Aubrey wasn't as hard into meth as the other two, but she still would have had to be around the same people. Maybe there were rumors about the bones. Ashley doubted it since today was the first day she'd heard anything about Frank's disgusting card game and the unforgivable acts that came with it. But maybe Ashley hadn't been asking the right questions.

Ashley turned on her heel and marched right back into the jail.

"I know I'm lovable, but back so soon?" Kylie said, a smile tugging at the corner of her lips.

"Yes, you are pretty awesome, Kylie, but something has come up, and I need to see Aubrey again."

"This feels a bit like the jail version of musical chairs. One comes in, another comes out, then the other goes back in. It's a circle of client meetings," Kylie said as she typed the request into her computer. The jail kept records of every person that came in and out of the jail, even attorneys.

"Yeah, sorry. It's just..." She trailed off, biting her lip.

Ashley considered Kylie a friend, but the jail was part of the sheriff's department. That meant that Kylie was technically law enforcement. She didn't act like it. She treated Ashley's clients very well, and she never tried to get information from them or intervene in any way with their cases, but Ashley still had to be cautious.

Kylie gave Ashley a curious look, but she didn't ask any questions. Instead, she slid an electronic signature pad through a small hole in the partition and said, "Sign here."

Ashley used the stylus to scrawl her signature, then waited for Kylie to unlock the jail door. Within minutes, both Ashley and Aubrey were back in the interview room.

"Are they moving Morgan?" Aubrey asked by way of greeting.

"No. At least not yet."

"Then what's this all about?" Aubrey said, her brow furrowing.

"Have a seat." Ashley gestured to the open chair across from hers. "I want to talk to you about something sensitive."

The room was small, so it only took Aubrey a few steps before she was beside the chair. "Sensitive?" she asked, dropping into the chair with a heavy *thump*.

"Private. Sensitive. Secret. Call it what you want to call it, but I'm going to ask you about something, and I want you to promise me that you will keep quiet about it."

"For how long?" Aubrey leaned forward, her interest piqued.

She was hungry for the information, and Ashley didn't blame her. Gossip was an important part of an inmate's life. News was power. It was something that could be controlled— to tell or not to tell—which had a form of freedom to it.

"Until I tell you otherwise."

"And that will be..."

"I don't know, Aubrey. Can you make me that promise or not? Otherwise, I'm going to ask Morgan or Erica instead." Ashley placed her hands on the table in front of her and started to push herself up from her chair.

"No, no. Don't do that." Aubrey put up a hand. "I'll give you my word. I won't say anything."

"Okay," Ashley said, sitting back down. She wasn't sure how much she could rely on Aubrey's *word*, but at least that was better than nothing. "The cops found a bone out on Frank's property."

"A bone?"

"Nothing is certain yet, but there is reason to believe it belonged to a human."

"A human bone?" Aubrey repeated.

Her demeanor had completely changed. She was always

somewhat serious, but she had grown gravely so in the last few moments. And the intensity with which she looked at Ashley was almost unnerving. It was like Aubrey was trying to see into Ashley's soul.

"Yes."

"In a grave?"

Ashley shrugged. "That, I don't know yet. Maybe never buried, but it couldn't have been a deep hole if the dog dug it up."

"A dog," Aubrey repeated. "A dog dug up my sister's body?"

"Whoa," Ashley said, leaning back in her chair. "What the hell are you talking about?"

Ashley didn't know anything about Aubrey's family. She'd only moved to town a year ago, and she never spoke about family. Ashley had assumed that, like most drug addicts, Aubrey was the black sheep and her family had disowned her.

"My little sister," Aubrey said. Her eyes grew glassy and got this faraway look to them. "I've always been a fuck-up. I've always gotten bad grades. The teachers never thought I had a chance to make much of myself. Obviously," she gestured around her, "they were right. I got involved with the drug crowd when I was thirteen and never got out of it. But everyone thought Maxine would be different. She's twenty years younger than me."

"Twenty years?"

"We share a dad. Her mom is my age. I never grew up enough to move out of the house, so you can imagine how tense it was."

"I bet so."

"Anyway, Maxine always got good grades. Her mom was always drunk or high, and a year and a half ago I wasn't so hard into drugs that I couldn't pay attention to Maxine's schooling. The teachers heaped praise on her. When she turned thirteen, I started to worry that she'd end up like me and start running with the wrong people, but that didn't happen, and I was relieved. Then, a year later, when she was fourteen, it did. She met some dude named Frank."

"Wait a second," Ashley said, putting up a hand. "Frank Vinny?"

"Yeah. It was my fault, really. By then I was getting harder into the drugs. I met Frank at a party. A mutual friend introduced us. Actually, it was a guy I dated for a while."

"Who was this mutual friend?" Ashley asked. She had her pen poised and ready to write the name down. This man could be one of the men that attended Frank's parties in the woods. He might have either participated or witnessed Frank's card game of rape.

"I don't know."

Ashley narrowed her eyes. It was a lie, of course. Because who didn't know the name of the person they had dated? Yeah, dating in the drug scene was different than traditional relationships, but Aubrey would have known a first name or a nickname. The fact that she was keeping the information back meant that she was protecting this man.

"Okay," Ashley said slowly, in a way that indicated that she did not at all believe Aubrey. "How did that bring Maxine and Frank together?"

"I started hanging out with Frank on and off. Mostly to buy dope. A couple times, I was really in a bind, and I ended up meeting him while Maxine was in the car. After that, I guess he found her on Instagram and started messaging her."

"How do you know he was sending her messages?"

"I hacked into her account after she ran away."

"She ran away?"

"Yup. The day after her fourteenth birthday. That's why I came to Brine. I knew Frank was here, so I followed."

"Why didn't you go to the cops?"

Aubrey scoffed. "You know how they view runaways. Especially druggie runaways. They'll open a file, ask a few questions, then close it without giving it more than a cursory investigation. They don't care what happens to us."

It was sad but true. "I can't believe I've never asked you this before, but where did you move from?"

"Fort Dodge."

Fort Dodge was a medium-sized city—at least by Iowa standards—in the northern part of the state. Most Iowans referred to it as "Dirty Dodge," and that was for a reason. The town was an industrial town in its heyday, but most of those jobs had left for one reason or another, and that led an already blue-collar city to further deterioration.

"Okay, but why do you think that those bones might be your sister's?"

"Because within two weeks of running away, Maxine's social media went silent. She just stopped posting. And you know girls at that age. They're practically glued to their phones. And sure, she could have lost internet connection, but there's been nothing since. Radio silence. She's dead. I know it."

Ashley nodded, careful to keep her expression somber. The information that Aubrey was giving Ashley was invaluable. It was horrible for Aubrey, and Ashley's heart went out to the girl, but it was great news in Morgan's defense. This story that Aubrey had just told Ashley created a perfect motive for murder. And Aubrey hadn't been in jail at the time of the fire, and she didn't have a pretrial release officer supervising her or an ankle monitor. She'd been free to come and go as she pleased.

What was even better was that Aubrey had been sentenced. That made her a former client, not a current client.

This conversation was not covered by attorney-client privilege. Meaning that Ashley could use it in Morgan's trial to point the finger at Aubrey. It wasn't a rock-solid defense, but it would help when added to her currently forming "he had it coming to him" defense. And for once, things were starting to look up for Morgan.

# 25

## KATIE

Crouching, Katie quickly discovered, was not an activity easily maintained for long periods of time. Her thighs and calves were on fire, screaming at her to stand and shake them out, and she felt certain her back would have a permanent bend to it. But she maintained the position, at least until the Council Bluffs firefighter, George, and the two dogs were well past her and almost to the top of Frank's driveway.

Katie breathed a heavy sigh of relief once she was finally alone. Rising to her feet, she stretched her arms high in the air and bent over from one side to the next. There would be a lot of waiting involved in the remainder of Katie's workday. George had said that a cadaver dog was on its way, but he didn't say where the dog and handler were coming from. It could be anywhere within the state for all Katie knew.

She dropped to the ground into a cross-legged position. A tickling sensation drew her attention to her right leg, and she looked at her knee in time to see a small spider scurrying along. She flicked it away, and suddenly her whole body felt itchy, like spiders were crawling all over her. Her instinct was to jump up and brush off every part of her body, but she forced herself to remain calm, reminding herself that it was a trick of her mind. Like how her head would instantly feel itchy when anyone mentioned head lice.

*I'm going to have to check for ticks after this*, Katie thought to herself. She should have brought bug spray, but she hadn't thought that far ahead.

A buzzing passed over her shoulder, and she flinched, thinking it was a bee, but it was only a fly. God, she was jumpy. But she wasn't cut out for this kind of thing. She had grown up in a pampered environment. Her mother thought staying anywhere other than a resort with a spa was roughing it. Her father had been the same way. Some people loved it, camping and nature, but spending time in the wilderness was not part of Katie's DNA.

After swatting four mosquitoes, she was about to call it quits. But then she heard the bark of a dog and stilled. At the same time, her phone buzzed. She pulled it out, unlocked it, and read the message.

*What's happening now?* It was Ashley.

*The cadaver dog is here*, she typed back.

*Which one?*

*I don't know. I haven't seen it yet. Is there more than one?*

*In this area, no. It should be a mostly black border collie. If it is, that's Bartholomew Jackson and his dog, Phantom.*

Katie studied the screen. *How do you know all this?*

*I know everything.*

*Ha. Ha. No, really, how do you know?*

*Barty used to be the medical examiner. He retired ten years ago and started training his dog as a cadaver dog for fun.*

*Not my idea of fun.*

The slamming of car doors told Katie it was time to bring the text conversation to a close. She tapped out a quick message—*Leave me alone now, I'm busy*—then sent it to Ashley before pocketing her phone and turning back toward the gravel drive. She needed to be more vigilant now. There was no expectation that this dog would remain in the clearing like the arson dog had. But presumably, this dog would be trained well enough to ignore her presence. The dog was not looking for her; she was still alive, after all. It was still a bit of a gamble, but one she was willing to take.

Moments later, an elderly Black man came walking down the gravel drive. His frame was wiry, but his back was straight, and he moved easily. A border collie trotted along beside him. It looked a little different from traditional black-and-white border collies, because this one was almost entirely black. He had a small white spot on one ear and on all four paws, but all were freckled, so even the white looked like it was speckled with black paint.

*Bartholomew Jackson*, Katie thought to herself. It had to be the former medical examiner that Ashley had mentioned in her text message. He was the right age for retirement, and his dog was a border collie. George followed a couple of steps behind Bartholomew. He was uncharacteristically silent.

"Now, son," Bartholomew said, coming to a stop at the clearing, "where did you say it was that the other dog found the bone?"

George motioned in Katie's direction. Katie fought the urge to duck. She was tucked deep in the foliage. It was an excellent hiding spot unless she moved and caused the bushes to shake. It was a difficult instinct to fight, but she managed it.

"It was somewhere over there. Is that where you want to start?"

*Don't start here. Don't start here*, Katie silently pleaded. If they were going to discover her, she hoped that it wouldn't be until later in the search. That way, she would have learned some helpful information before she was kicked out.

"I don't think so," Bartholomew said. He placed his hands in the pockets of his khaki shorts and turned away from Katie, strolling in the opposite direction. He stopped when he reached the edge of the clearing, scanning the trees. "We know there's something over there. Phantom, here, will alert to it right away." He patted the border collie on the head. The dog had matched Bartholomew stride for stride and remained at his side. "What we don't know is if there's anything anywhere else."

"That seems like the reverse of what you should do," George said.

"I'm sorry," Bartholomew said, turning to meet George's gaze. "I didn't realize you were so well versed in searching for cadavers. How many times have you done this before?"

George grumbled something that Katie couldn't decipher.

"What was that?" Bartholomew placed a hand behind his ear. "I'm old, and I'm hard of hearing. You'll have to say it louder."

"I said *none*."

"Very good," Bartholomew said, chuckling and patting the dog on the head. "Then it's my advice we'll be following today, huh?"

Katie instantly liked Mr. Jackson. In five minutes, he'd done what so many others could not do: put George in his place.

"Phantom," Bartholomew said.

The dog looked up at him, and Katie snapped a picture. Not because it had any evidentiary value, but because she couldn't resist. It was a beautifully intimate moment between dog and handler. There was trust and affection radiating between the two of them, a natural love that came from working side by side day in and day out.

"Search," Bartholomew said, gesturing in front of himself with his hand.

Phantom stood and lowered his nose to the ground. He moved straight forward, crawling under trees and pushing through underbrush with ease. After several minutes, the dog dropped into a lying position and turned his gaze back toward his handler. This was the first time Katie had caught sight of the dog's eyes, and she realized with a start that he only had one. His right eye was dark brown, but his left eye socket was empty.

"Looks like Phantom already has a hit," Bartholomew said. He removed a packet of bright orange markers from a bag and joined Phantom in the brush, placing a marker labeled as number one near the dog's front paws.

George followed. "I don't see anything."

"Naturally. Because it's buried. See that?" He motioned toward the ground near Phantom's feet. Katie snapped a picture. "The ground is disturbed. The foliage isn't as developed as it is over here," he motioned to his left, "or over here." He motioned to his right.

"I still don't see it."

"Well, then, you need to have your eyes checked," Bartholomew said. He gave Phantom a treat, then whistled once, and the dog returned to attention. "Search."

Phantom continued forward. After another twenty yards, the dog dropped to the ground once more. Katie continued taking pictures, shot after shot, watching in complete awe. Both dog and handler moved fluidly, predicting the other's movements before they occurred.

"Are you sure the dog isn't confusing human and animal remains?" George asked after Phantom lay down for the third time and Bartholomew placed a marker with the number three next to his dog's feet.

"Yes. I'm sure."

Bartholomew had used ten markers before making it anywhere near where Katie was crouched. When they came to Katie's area, Phantom sniffed all around her, but as she had hoped, he completely ignored her. It was a testament to the dog's training. By the time the search ended, Bartholomew had used fourteen different markers.

"Are you telling me that there are fourteen bodies out here?" George said with exasperation.

"No," Bartholomew said, returning to George's side. "I'm telling you that Phantom here," he patted the dog on the head, "signaled fourteen times. That doesn't necessarily mean fourteen separate bodies, just fourteen pieces of bodies."

"One dismembered body, then?"

"To say that would be purely conjecture. Maybe, maybe not. But you'll need to get a forensics team out here to start searching, now, won't you?"

"We don't have a forensics team."

"Then call DCI."

"But..."

Bartholomew was already headed back up the driveway. He turned and gave George a hard look. "This is serious, George. I know you think you can do anything, but there's a lot of evidence out here. If you move in yourself, you're going to screw it up. Call in the experts. Me, I'm going to make a call to Wendy."

"Wendy Thomas? The medical examiner? I already had Chief Carmichael call her. She's busy."

"She's never too busy for me," Bartholomew said, shoving his hands in his pockets. "That's the benefit of mentoring someone. When they take the reins, they are skilled and they will come when you call. I heard you were once mentoring a young female officer. What happened to her?"

A small smile formed at the corners of Katie's lips.

"Budget cuts," George said, somewhat awkwardly.

"Yes, but you maintained your position, didn't you?"

George didn't answer.

Katie was smiling now. She'd never met this man before, but he was taking her side. It made her think that others in Brine felt the same way. She watched George and Bartholomew until they disappeared up the long, winding drive. She waited to move until she heard the slamming of car doors. Bartholomew would be leaving, and George was likely putting a call into DCI to request that they send agents and a forensics team.

It was time for Katie to leave. Those DCI guys would find her if she tried to spy on them during their investigation. They were specially trained investigators, and they weren't overworked and underfunded like the Brine Police Department.

She had just risen to her feet when her phone buzzed. She pulled it out, assuming it was another text from Ashley, but it wasn't. It was from Forest Parker, about the MEHR team. It was a group text to Katie, Tom, and Rachel.

*Stephanie wants to meet this evening. We all need to be there at six o'clock sharp.*

*There?* Katie texted back. *Where is "there"?*

*Stephanie's house.*

*Doesn't she live way out at the northern border of the county?*

*Yes. I don't want any excuses. Everyone needs to be there. Stephanie is donating a lot of money. We have to keep her happy.*

*Fine*, Katie typed back, then pocketed her phone. It continued buzzing with responses she assumed were complaints coming from Tom and Rachel, so she didn't bother looking.

This was precisely what had bothered Katie about Stephanie's donation. Five million dollars dwarfed the amounts that others gave, and it was making Stephanie feel like she was the owner of the team, rather than a donor. Someone was going to have to put Stephanie in her place. Katie hoped it wouldn't have to be her—especially considering that Stephanie could recognize her as her father's daughter and oust her at any moment—but she'd do it if she had to.

After meeting with Aubrey, Ashley finally returned to her office. She'd been gone all day, which only meant that the work was piling up. All this Morgan stuff was taking too much of her time. She usually carried a caseload of around seventy cases, but lately it had been higher than that. Which meant she really needed to turn away from Morgan, Aubrey, and Erica and focus on some of the others for a while.

"Hey, Ashley," Elena said when Ashley came through the front door.

"Hey." Ashley came around the desk and into the employee area of the office. "What's been going on around here?"

"The usual. You've missed a couple calls today. Nothing urgent, but you may want to call Mick Froyman back. He sounded drunk."

Ashley grabbed a stack of mail and started flipping through it. Bill, bill, bill, letter without a return address. She tossed the last one in the trash without reading it, something she had taken to lately, since those letters were usually hate mail. As a defense attorney, she wasn't a beloved member of the Brine community, and some people thought it was important that she knew it. Of course, they weren't brave enough to do so *and* sign their signature, which was why she never read them.

"Why do you think Mick was drunk?"

"He was slurring his words so badly that I could barely understand him. Then, when I told him that you weren't in, he called me a 'fucking spic' and hung up."

Ashley slammed the letters she was holding down on the table. "He called you *what*? No, no," Ashley said, putting up her hands, "don't repeat it. That motherfucker. I'm going to give him a piece of my mind. Who the hell does he think he is?"

"A drunk white man who wishes he could go back to the good ol' days when people like me were shining shoes while people like him spit on the backs of our heads."

"Yeah, well, those days are gone. I've got half a mind to withdraw from his case. You know what, I'm going to. He can have one of those shitty contract attorneys who do half-assed work. He'll probably like them better, anyway. Most of them are old, fat, White men, too."

Elena chuckled, but then she grew serious. "Thank you," she said, her voice soft. "For supporting me, I mean."

"There's no need to thank me," Ashley said, patting Elena on the shoulder. "It's just common decency."

"Unfortunately, it isn't all that common."

"Well, it should be. And one day it *will* be."

Elena nodded, then turned back to her own work. Ashley made her way down the hallway and into her office. She grabbed Mick's file and scanned it for his number, then picked up the receiver to her office phone and dialed.

"Ashley," Mick said by way of greeting. "Took you long enough. I had an emergen—"

"I'm going to stop you right there," Ashley said. "I don't really give a damn about your emergency. Using racial slurs with anyone, but especially my staff, is wrong."

"But I—"

"No buts. It's wrong. Period. Exclamation point. Now, the question is, what am I going to do with you? You're obviously drunk. I can practically smell the booze from here, and you have a pending charge for your third OWI." OWI meant operating while intoxicated. It was Iowa's drunk driving law. "I've told you countless times to get a substance abuse evaluation and get into treatment, but you won't.'"

"I don't have a problem."

"Oh, bullshit, Mick. You've got legal problems, drinking problems, and judging by the way you spoke to my office manager, you've got social problems. The day you don't have a problem is the day the Catholic Church starts ordaining women as priests. Which, by the way, is likely never."

"Well, I wanted to talk to you. Okay? Is that so bad?"

"What did you want to talk to me about?"

"I want to know when I will get my driver's license back."

"Umm, let me think about it." Ashley tapped her chin with her index finger. "The answer to that question is also never at the rate you're going. The DL suspension on OWI third offense is six years. So, at best, six years, but probably far more than that considering you can't stop *driving drunk*. Now, I've said my piece, and I'm done."

"But I have more to say—"

"I don't care. Tell your new attorney. I'm withdrawing."

"No. You can't."

"Watch me," Ashley said, cradling the receiver. *Ugh*, she thought, dropping into her worn yet comfortable office chair.

She could hardly believe the nerve of some people these days. Everyone was so demanding, so entitled. They thought they could say whatever they wanted to whomever they wanted and there would be no repercussions. Well, her clients weren't going to treat Elena poorly. Ashley could understand anger directed toward her, because she at least had control over their cases. But her staff, they didn't have control over anything.

*I better get to this Motion to Withdraw*, she thought.

Otherwise, something would come up and she'd get sidetracked. And she wanted Mick Froyman off her case list ASAP. It only took a few minutes to draft the motion. She used a simple form, alleging "a breakdown in attorney-client communication," and added her electronic signature. Then she logged in to the court's electronic filing system and e-filed the document. Usually, Elena did all the filing, but Ashley was not going to ask her to do this one. Mick was Ashley's problem.

When she was done filing the document, she checked for new notifications. All new events in case filings involving Ashley's clients came through on the electronic filing system's notification page. She started at the bottom—the older filings—and scrolled through, glancing at each one. They were run-of-the-mill discovery responses, orders setting pretrial conferences and trial dates. But she froze once she got to the top. There was a new appointment order. One for State v. Morgan Stanman, FECR019376. It was a new case number, which could only mean one thing.

"They charged her," Ashley said aloud, rubbing her hands over her face.

After all the work she and Katie had done to avoid it, Charles Hanson had still filed the indictment, charging Morgan with arson and two counts of murder. *Damn it*, Ashley thought, slamming a hand down on her desk. She allowed herself a moment of fury, then tamped it down. She hadn't met her original goal, so she'd adjust it. They could still use the information they were gathering in Morgan's defense at trial.

Ashley clicked on the Trial Information, the formal charging document, and read through each of the charges. Count one alleged the willful, intentional murder of Frank Vinny. Count two claimed the same for Jane Doe, an unidentified female. The final count was the arson charge.

*The girl still hasn't been identified*, Ashley thought.

That might have been common in larger cities, but the Midwest was rural. It was a rare occurrence when nobody came forward to claim an unidentified body as their missing teenager. In fact, that had never happened in Ashley's twelve-year career as a defense attorney. Every indictment named the victim, like it had on count one with Frank. To her, the fact seemed significant. It made her think that the key to Morgan's defense could lie with the identity of that one girl.

Ashley made a note of her thoughts on a legal pad, then moved on. There was no point in dwelling on problems that were not yet solvable. She then clicked on the Minutes of Testimony, which was a fancy way to say a list of witnesses and what the prosecutor expects them to say. The name of a criminalist at the DCI laboratory in Ankeny caught her eye. She quickly scanned the testimony.

*This witness will testify that he is a criminalist employed by the Iowa DCI Criminalistics Laboratory in Ankeny, Iowa. He will testify as to his background, training, and experience. This witness will testify that he tested a hand swab submitted by Detective George Thomanson. He will testify that the hand swab came from the Defendant, Morgan Stanman. This witness will testify as to methods used in the testing process. He will testify that the swab tested positive for trace amounts of accelerant, specifically gasoline...*

"Fuck," Ashley said out loud. "Shit, shit, shit."

This was bad. Why hadn't Morgan washed her hands? On

its face, it looked like the State had a pretty strong case. They had Morgan cutting off her ankle monitor, then throwing it in a ditch near Frank's property. They picked Morgan up outside of town, walking from the direction of Frank's property. And now they had accelerant on her hands.

It all added up to a big problem for Morgan, and Ashley by extension. Ashley couldn't bring this information to Morgan just yet. She was already in a delicate state. Telling her, "Oh, by the way, the State filed charges, and it looks like you're going to be in there for the rest of your life," would put her over the edge. She needed to come with *some* positive information to mix in with all the depressing news. She needed to identify Jane Doe.

## 27

### KATIE

During the drive back to the office, Katie grew more and more irritated with Forest's text about a meeting later that evening. It was only the night before that Stephanie had even made the announcement, but she was already making demands of them. What if Katie already had plans? She didn't, but Stephanie hadn't known that. Yet she still felt entitled to insist that four people—Katie, Forest, Tom, and Rachel—clear their calendars and rush out to her home, all during the dinner hour. It was bullshit, and Katie intended to make that fact known. Stephanie may be rich, but that didn't mean she could push Katie around.

By the time she was parking in her spot near the Public Defender's Office, she had made up her mind. She was not going. If Forest passed over her for the position, so be it. She didn't want to work *for* Stephanie Arkman, anyway. She'd had a job where she took orders and followed them blindly, but she'd been out of that kind of work for nearly a year. Now that she had a taste of freedom, she wasn't about to return to a more restrictive work environment. And the MEHR team was supposed to be a different kind of law enforcement. This all was starting to feel like the same thing with a different name.

She hopped out of the car, feeling lighter now after making a decision, and walked down the street, heading for the back door of the office. She could tell that Ashley was in her office the moment she opened the door. Music wafted down the hallway. Another 90s tune, Alanis Morissette's "Ironic." Katie went straight to Ashley's office, pausing just outside the doorway to listen to Ashley sing along. Ashley sounded angry when she said the words. She wasn't really singing; she was more talking at the same time as Morissette.

*Ashley's day must have taken a turn for the worse*, Katie thought. She stood there another few seconds, gathering energy for whatever bad news Ashley would likely share, then knocked on her doorframe and stepped into her office. "All right," Katie said, dropping into a chair. "What happened?"

"What do you mean?" Ashley said, looking up. Her features were twisted with a mixture of fury and devastation. "Everything's fantastic. Good. Great. Grand. Wonderful. Other than the fact that Morgan was just charged with double homicide and one count of arson. And, yeah, she had accelerant on her hands. So, yay for that news. All that work for, psshhh." She made a blowing-up motion with her hands.

"Now you're just being dramatic."

"You're not being dramatic enough."

"Okay," Katie said, leaning forward, "what if I told you that I have news that might help with that whole double homicide thing."

"Then I'd stop this song, and depending on the news, I might start playing something a little more upbeat. Perhaps some Backstreet Boys."

"God, no. I change my mind." She pretended like she was

going to stand. "Keep wallowing. I will do anything to avoid hearing *Larger Than Life*." Katie was too young to partake in the Backstreet Boys days, but her hatred of boy bands ran deep.

"Fine. Fine. I promise not to torment you with bad nineties music."

"Okay. You are never going to guess how many times the cadaver dog signaled."

"I don't want to guess. I want you to tell me."

"Fourteen."

Ashley sucked in a deep breath. "That's good. Oh, my God, that's good. I mean, not for whoever is buried down there, but for Morgan, definitely. When are they going to start digging?"

Katie shrugged. "I don't know for sure. They were calling DCI. I won't be able to get away with creeping around in the forest anymore. They'd catch me. Which means I'm going to be useless for a while. Unless you have something else for me to do."

"As a matter of fact, I do."

"What's that?"

"I need you to find out the identity of Jane Doe. The girl who died with Frank. We are gathering a lot of ammunition to prove that Frank was a real shit that deserved to die, but what about the girl? A 'not guilty' verdict on one murder but 'guilty' on the other still earns Morgan a life sentence."

"Okay," Katie said. "I'm still waiting on information from Elena. She's supposed to talk to her parents about the girls missing from the immigrant community, but I could take a second look at the pictures I took at the scene that day. I don't remember seeing anything that would give any hints, but then again, I could have missed something in all the excitement."

Ashley nodded toward the end of her desk. "The pictures

are right there." Katie had printed them off the day before and given them to Ashley, as requested. "I still haven't had time to go through them. The last couple of days have been busy."

Katie grabbed the photos and started flicking through, this time from the beginning. The first four were photos of the path that Katie had used to access Frank's property. It was overgrown and barely visible, but there were broken twigs and crushed leaves that made it clear that it had been used before Katie had ever entered.

The next couple were foliage as she'd made her way along the path, but she froze when she reached photos ten through sixteen. They were the close-up pictures of the bracelet that she'd found on the forest floor. It had felt familiar to her when she originally saw it, but she hadn't taken the time to study it in detail. All she'd done was pick it up and take pictures of it from all angles.

"What is it?" Ashley said, setting her pen down.

Ashley had been looking from Morgan's indictment and copying important details onto a legal pad. Katie couldn't see it from where she sat, but she'd worked with Ashley long enough to know the pad likely contained questions about the indictment with initial follow-up ideas and possible defenses.

"Remember how I found a bracelet out in Frank's forest?"

"I completely forgot about it until now, but yeah, I think I remember you mentioning something about that."

"And that I thought it looked familiar."

"Yeah, but I also recall you saying that you were no jewelry expert."

"I did say that, and I stand by that statement, except when it comes to *this* bracelet."

"Okay," Ashley said, leaning back in her chair. "What do you know about this one?"

"It belongs to Stephanie Arkman."

"You're sure about that?"

"Positive. She's worn it since she was eighteen. All the Arkman women have one. See that?" She pointed to a design carved into the gold. "That's the Arkman family crest."

"Okay, but how are you so sure it's Stephanie's?"

"Because hers was missing. I noticed when she came into Mikey's Tavern and announced her donation."

"Maybe she took it off?"

"No," Katie said with absolute certainty. "I grew up around them, remember? My dad and Stephanie's dad were buddies. It has something to do with their inheritance. I don't remember exact details off the top of my head, but I know that all the Arkman women kept theirs on. Even Rachel's mom, who had been estranged from the family. I bet if you look at pictures taken of her by media outlets, she's always got hers on."

"Well, now, that is something. Why would Stephanie Arkman's bangle be out there in the forest? She wouldn't have any reason to be there, would she?"

"No. She's so prissy. I can't imagine her walking along that path. But then how did the bangle get out there?"

"That's something you'll have to find out," Ashley said, a smile tugging at the corners of her lips.

"Well, Stephanie called for an emergency MEHR team meeting. She's demanding everyone come to her house tonight. I was going to blow it off. Because who is she to tell me what to do, right?"

"That's the Katie I know and love."

"But now, I guess I should go. I can excuse myself to the bathroom at some point and start looking around. Maybe I'll find something that links her to Frank."

"Sounds like a needle-in-a-haystack search, but if anyone can uncover the truth, it's you."

Katie didn't feel quite as confident, but she wanted to do this for Ashley. She had been so dejected when Katie had first arrived back at the office. But now there was hope.

# 28

## ASHLEY

Ashley and Katie were still in Ashley's office when Elena poked her head in. She looked nervous, which wasn't uncommon for her, but it was when she was around Ashley. They'd grown close over the past year they'd been working together.

"What's wrong?" Ashley said.

Ashley was trying to keep the concern out of her voice. Elena had enough to worry about. Her mother was sick, and even though there was no diagnosis, the symptoms sounded serious. Ashley's mother had died of cancer four years earlier, and the situation with Elena's mother didn't sound all that different.

"Umm, nothing," Elena said, shifting her weight. "It's just that Tom is here. And, well, I didn't know if you would want to see him."

"Oh, he's here for me," Katie said with an irritated sigh. "He's picking me up so we can drive out to Stephanie Arkman's house together. We're carpooling since it's a forever long drive, and I doubt Stephanie will be reimbursing us for gas." She pushed herself up out of her seat and stretched, turning to Ashley. "Do you want to say hello? I mean, you don't have to if you don't want to, but with the funding for the MEHR team coming through, he's going to move back to town and finish his degree through online courses."

"Are you sure the funding will be coming through?" Ashley asked. "Considering our discovery about the bracelet, you might not want to accept that money."

"Oh, I think the opposite is the case," Katie said.

"How so?"

"If Stephanie was involved in that fire, she's going to find her way to a jail cell, which is perfect for the MEHR team."

Ashley still wasn't quite following.

"We get the money, and we don't have to deal with her. It's a win-win for everyone."

For the good of the town, Ashley hoped Katie was right. Unfortunately, she'd had a lot of experience dealing with the Arkman family, and as was common with the extremely wealthy, they were slippery. Even if that bracelet belonged to Stephanie, she'd find a way to wiggle out of charges. She'd claim someone stole it from her and must have pawned it for drugs, or something like that. A story that was plausible enough to pull Stephanie out of hot water, but not firm enough to result in charges against someone else.

"I'm not sure what you two are on about," Elena said, "but Tom is waiting. Do you want me to tell him you'll be out in a little while?"

"No. I'm coming," Katie said, then she turned to Ashley. "If you're going to be running into him more regularly"—she shrugged—"you might as well try to be friendly."

"It's not that I don't want to be his friend," Ashley said, her heart pounding wildly. The mere thought of patching things up with Tom caused a physical reaction within her body. "It's that I'm not sure if I *can*."

"I totally get it. But avoiding him isn't going to make things any easier."

"You have a point, Katie," Ashley said, rising to her feet. As painful as the breakup with Tom had been, this separation had been even harder. She needed it. It was the only way for her to heal. But she had missed his companionship. They'd been friends for years before they ever became romantic, and it would be nice to be able to go back to that. "I'll come with you."

Elena led the way down the hallway, back toward the front area of the office, and Katie followed next. Ashley brought up the rear, her mind racing. It had been a long day full of frustration. She'd likely rubbed all the makeup off her face, and her hair was back in a limp ponytail. She probably looked like hell, but she reminded herself she shouldn't even care. It didn't matter to her what Katie thought of her appearance, so why should Tom's opinion matter? They were to be friends and nothing more. Yet, she couldn't help wishing she had five minutes to freshen up a little.

When they came out into the reception area, Tom was leaning against the front desk, his head down, studying something on his phone. He was lean with just the right amount of muscle, strong but not bulky. He was in a T-shirt and light-colored shorts, with sunglasses sitting on top of his head. He must have heard them, because he looked up, and Ashley's heart stopped. Tom had always had the bluest eyes she'd ever seen. They darted from Elena to Katie.

"You ready for this..." Tom was talking to Katie, but his voice trailed off when his gaze settled on Ashley. "Oh, hey," he said after a long beat of silence.

"Hey," Ashley said, giving him an awkward wave.

"How are you?"

"Ummm, fine."

It was such an uncomfortable conversation. A far stretch from the way things used to be between them, even before they had started dating. They'd known each other since they were children. They both attended the same elementary, junior high, and high school. He'd been part of the popular crowd, and Ashley was a bit of a loner, but they'd always been friendly. Then he took a job at the jail, and she became a public defender, and their jobs overlapped often. Never in their lives had they been this awkward.

Part of it was his fault for lying to her and causing their romance to implode, but she couldn't assign all the blame to him. She had been dodging him, refusing to take his phone calls, and altogether avoiding him for seven whole months. She'd be a fool to think that the separation hadn't been at least a piece of the problem now. If she'd nipped it in the bud a long time ago, been cordial at least, then some of this weirdness wouldn't exist.

"Well, are you ready?" Tom said to Katie, pulling Ashley out of her thoughts.

Katie's eyes darted from Tom to Ashley. "Do you want to come with us?" She said the words slowly, cautiously, like Ashley was an angry cat that might swipe at her.

"Would you?"

There was so much hope in Tom's voice, and it would probably be a good opportunity to start working toward that elusive *friend* category, since Katie would be in the car the whole time and able to steer the conversation in the right direction. But then again, this was a meeting for the MEHR team, and Ashley had no part in that.

"I don't think Stephanie would like it."

"Rachel would," Tom said. "She might already be there. You know she'd invite you anywhere."

Ashley smiled at the thought of her young houseguest. It

was nice to feel needed sometimes. "But it's Stephanie's house, her space."

"If for no other reason, Ashley," Katie said, "come along to help me do some snooping."

Ashley paused. She hadn't thought about that. If she came along, there would be two sets of eyes searching, rather than Katie doing it on her own. "Maybe..."

"Snooping?" Tom's gaze darted from Ashley to Katie. "What's that all about?"

"Umm." Katie looked to Ashley for guidance.

Ashley shrugged. "It's not a secret. At least not one we plan to keep for long. I'll be waving those pictures in front of the prosecutor's face as soon as I can establish some connection between Stephanie and Frank."

"Stephanie and Frank," Tom repeated. "Frank Vinny? You think Stephanie was involved with *him*?"

As the former jail administrator, Tom had plenty of experience dealing with Frank Vinny, and none were likely positive. Frank had always been a bit of an ass, but he was a nightmare once he was behind lock and key.

"Maybe," Ashley said, "but we aren't sure. We can fill you in during the drive."

It was nice having something to discuss that didn't have anything to do with their failure to maintain a romantic relationship. The words had come easier, and they weren't heavy or sharp. The conversation had been flowing well enough that Ashley decided, against her better judgment, to join them on their trip to Stephanie's home.

"So, you're coming?" Tom's face broke into a wide grin. He had a mouth full of perfectly straight teeth, and his grin stretched all the way across his face.

Ashley's heart skipped a beat. Oh, how she had missed that smile. "Yes."

Just then, her cell phone started buzzing in her pocket. She grabbed it, partially as an excuse to break free of the emotionally charged moment. It was the jail. She looked up and said, "Sorry, I've got to take this."

She stepped away to create some privacy, then picked up. "This is Ashley."

"Ashley, it's Kylie." She sounded breathless, panicked, and Ashley was immediately on edge. The jail administrator was usually so even keeled. Nothing got under her skin.

"What's wrong?"

"The ambulance is here. You need to come now."

"Ambulance? What happened?"

"Actually, don't come here. You should head straight to the Brine County Medical Center. They're taking her to the hospital."

"Who?"

"It's bad. Real bad."

"Kylie!" Ashley shouted. "Get a hold of yourself. I don't understand a word you are saying. Who is hurt?"

"Morgan. Morgan Stanman."

"Okay. How did she get hurt?"

"You were right. She hurt herself. We had her on suicide watch, but we don't have enough employees. It's all my fault, Ashley. She can't die. I'd never forgive myself."

"How did she do it?" Ashley said.

She was already heading back to her office to grab her keys and her laptop. Depending on how bad things were, she might be spending a good deal of time at the hospital, and she would need to do some work while she was there.

"A shank made out of a toothbrush. She slit both her wrists. I still don't understand how she did it without her cell mates noticing."

"We'll figure it out. Okay? I'll meet you at the hospital in ten minutes."

"Thank you, Ashley."

Ashley hung up and headed back out front. "Change of plans," she told Tom and Katie. "I can't go with you anymore."

"What happened?" Katie asked, her brow furrowed with concern.

"Morgan just slit her wrists. I need to go to the hospital."

"Oh, no," Tom said. His smile had already disappeared with the change in Ashley's demeanor. "Go. We completely understand."

"Do you want me to come?" Katie asked.

"No. You've got to go to Stephanie's. It'll probably be the only opportunity for you to look around her house. She doesn't know we know she has some involvement in this mess, so it's our only chance to catch her off guard. I'll deal with Morgan."

"Okay," Katie said uncertainly, "but keep me posted."

"Ditto."

Then they split up and went separate directions, Tom and Katie to Stephanie Arkman's house, and Ashley to the hospital.

## 29

### KATIE

Tom's truck was idling out front of the Public Defender's Office when they got outside. Katie looked at him and raised an eyebrow. "You're trusting. This isn't exactly a crime-free zone."

A smile spread across Tom's lips, and he hopped into the driver's seat. "I'm not worried about someone stealing this old girl." He patted the dashboard. "She's got one foot in the grave. If someone takes her, she'll break down before they get far."

"Maybe we should take my car, then," Katie said, getting in and buckling her seat belt. "This is going to be a forty-minute drive. I don't want to be stranded in the middle of nowhere."

"It'll be fine," Tom said, putting the truck in gear. It sputtered for a moment, then lurched forward. "Probably."

"Fine, but I'm never going to let you live it down if this thing falls apart halfway there."

"Deal. But if that happens, we'll just ask Stephanie to send a limo to retrieve us."

"Maybe for you," Katie said.

Tom looked at her, a confused expression on his face. "You don't think she'd do the same for you?"

"Do you know Stephanie Arkman?"

"Umm, no. Not well, at least. But I know that she is donating a lot of money to a good cause. And that money is going to make it possible for me to move back to Brine and fix things with Ashley. By the way, that went well at the office, don't you think?"

"Yeah. It went surprisingly well. I guess Ashley is turning a corner. And if I were you, I'd put the brakes on that 'Stephanie Arkman is a saint' train that you are riding."

"You don't like her?"

"I never said I didn't *like* her."

Tom gave her a hard look. Katie never had much of a poker face, not that she'd been really trying to hide her feelings.

"I don't know her, okay," Katie said. It was only a partial lie. She had known Stephanie when she was a child, but that was a long time ago and during a whole different life. "I'm just saying that you should be cautious. She may not have completely altruistic reasons for her support of our team."

"I don't follow. Does this have something to do with whatever it was you and Ashley were talking about at the office?"

"Yes and no."

"That's ambiguous."

Katie sighed heavily and then told him about the bangle she'd found out in the woods. She didn't explain how she knew it belonged to Stephanie, and he didn't ask. It was one of the things Katie liked so much about Tom. He somehow knew when to take Katie's word as truth and when he should challenge it.

"Then there's all the money she's donating. That, coupled with the bangle, makes me suspicious," Katie said.

"Why?"

"Because, think about it, she could be involved in a crime."

"That seems like a stretch."

"Just hear me out, and then you can comment," Katie said.

"Okay. Sorry."

"Her bangle is found at a crime scene. A place she would never go. So, let's assume she was somehow involved in that fire. She wouldn't want the police department to have the funds to investigate it. So, she provides money to our team. She's the sole reason we are able to exist, so naturally, we owe her something. Or at least she thinks that we do. Judging by how easily she could schedule this meeting, making us all drop our evening plans with little notice, I'd say that we feel at least somewhat indebted to her."

"You have a point."

"I know. And the police department is a mess right now. Her donation is going to encourage city council to siphon more money from them. She's distracting them and buying us at the same time. It's the ideal way to get away with a crime."

Tom was silent for a long moment. "So, you think Stephanie is an evil genius? This isn't a comic book, Katie."

"I know that," Katie said, crossing her arms. The softness in his tone irritated her. It felt like he was trying to placate her, and she found it demoralizing. "I'm just saying it is something we should all be considering. And Stephanie is smart. If you believe a well-planned devious plot is above her, you're wrong."

"Okay," Tom said without confidence, "I'll consider it."

Stephanie's home was straight north of Brine, off of Highway 169, and they reached the turnoff onto her side street in thirty-five minutes. They were making good time. The road leading to Stephanie's home might have been the only side street out in the country that had been paved. Katie wondered who footed the bill for that, the county or Stephanie. She doubted it was the latter.

"Stephanie said we drive several miles down this road and it'll be on our left..." Tom's voice trailed off as a heavy iron gate came into view. It was at least nine feet tall and ran parallel to the road.

"This must be it," Katie said, watching the fence as they drove by.

It was wrought iron and looked as though it surrounded the entire property—somewhere in the ballpark of twenty acres—at a cost that Katie couldn't even imagine. It was ornate fencing, but Katie doubted its primary purpose was decorative. It was too high for that. A simple four- or six-foot fence could have done a nice decorative job, but nine feet was overkill.

"I don't know," Tom said uncertainly. "I can't see the house."

Trees lined the inside of the fence, making it impossible to see into the property. It was the Arkmans' family compound, Katie felt certain. The entire family lived in separate houses on the same property—almost like the royal family in England. That was the way it had been when she was young, and she assumed it was the same way now.

"This is it," Katie said as they pulled up to a large double gate.

It, too, was iron, but it had a familiar design cut into it. The Arkman family crest. Katie had brought a copy of one of the bangle photos with her, and she pulled it out of her pocket. She'd been right. The symbol carved into the bracelet was exactly the same as the symbol on the gate. She grabbed her cell phone and took a quick photo of the gate.

"How do we get in?" Tom asked.

"Beats me. This place is locked up tighter than a prison."

Katie didn't say so, but she couldn't help wondering, *Why?* What did the Arkman family have to hide? Sure, it was common for rich people to have fences for security reasons, but that was when the homes were in the city. This house—or set of houses—was way out in the country. There was nobody but cows to bother them. So, why so much security? It didn't make sense unless the family had something to hide. But the question was, were they trying to keep people out, or were they preventing someone's escape?

"I think there's an intercom over there," Katie said, pointing to a lion-shaped statue on one side of the gate. "Pull up there and see if there's a button to press."

Tom did as Katie instructed, and as she suspected, there was a punch pad inside the lion's open mouth and spots on its nose for an intercom.

"How'd you know that?" Tom said with surprise. "Do you have to use lions to get into friends' houses often, or was it just a guess?"

Katie shrugged. "I wouldn't call Stephanie a *friend*."

In truth, it had come to her in a flash. A wave of memory in the form of déjà vu. Her, as a child, watching her father drive up to that gate and up to the lion-shaped intercom. He'd named the lion Fred. He would lean out the window of his black Jaguar, punch in a code, and pat the lion on the head as the double gate rumbled open. *Attaboy, Fred*, he'd say. *You're a good friend.*

"What do I do now?" Tom said, pulling Katie out of her thoughts. He was hanging out his window, studying the buttons. "Is there a specific code?"

"I'm sure there is a code, but I don't know it. There should be a button somewhere on there that calls for assistance or something."

"There's one that says 'call.' Is that the one?"

"Probably. Try it."

Tom pressed the button, and a ringing sound came from the lion's mouth. It sounded like he'd swallowed a phone.

"Arkman residence," came a brisk-sounding voice from somewhere deep in the lion's stomach. It was so clear that it was almost disconcerting hearing it come from inside the belly of a beast.

"Umm, yes," Tom said, clearing his throat. "This is Tom Archie, and I'm with Katie Mickey. We have an appointment with Stephanie Arkman today."

"Yes, yes. You're a little early, but I'll open the gate. The other members of your party are already here. You can wait with them in the formal sitting room. When the driveway forks, go straight."

"Thank you," Tom said.

Within seconds, the huge iron gate began to rumble open, retracting at both ends to allow them entry into the Arkman family compound. Tom put the truck in gear, and they drove inside. Again, Katie was struck with a strong sense of déjà vu. The driveway was wide and whitewashed so clean that it nearly sparkled. Large shade trees towered over them, casting most of the property in shadow. Large hydrangea plants with perfect symmetrical balls of pink and blue flowers lined both sides of the driveway.

"This place is...peaceful," Tom said almost breathlessly.

Katie would not have described it in the same way. Beautiful, yes. Quiet, yes. Imposing, yes. But definitely not peaceful. There was a stillness on the property that made Katie's skin crawl. A density in the air, a sense of controlled perfection that was not natural. With trees this size, Katie expected birds to be chirping and squirrels to be scampering around, but there was no wildlife that she could see. Not even bugs.

After driving a quarter mile into the property, the driveway came to a fork. At the end of each of the prongs, there was a large house. Mansions, really. Katie could see them all from where she was, but only barely, because they were set so far apart from one another.

"It's like a gated community in here," Tom said in awe.

"Yeah. I guess it is."

Tom stopped the vehicle when they reached the fork in the road, looking left and then right.

"Go straight, like the lion said."

"Okay," Tom said, easing his foot off the brake.

The truck lurched forward, and they drove another half mile until they were right in front of the middle mansion. It was three stories high with large pillars. The Arkman homes were all built in that same plantation style, like they belonged in the Deep South rather than Iowa.

"Look, there's Forest," Tom said, pointing to the front steps. Forest was coming toward them, motioning for them to park next to his Mercedes.

Tom parked, and they both got out.

"Thanks for coming, both of you," Forest said, smiling broadly. "This donation is important to our cause, and I'm happy to see that both of you are taking Stephanie's request seriously."

"Sure," Tom said.

Katie merely nodded. She was not there at Stephanie's request. In fact, she'd been refusing to come until she realized that the bracelet found on Frank's property was most likely Stephanie's.

"Follow me," Forest said, turning around and heading back up the steps to the front door of the mansion. "Rachel is already here. Stephanie should be ready for us in a few minutes," he called over his shoulder.

Katie motioned for Tom to go first, and she reluctantly brought up the rear. But once she was halfway up the stairs, something to the side of the house caught her attention. It was a black four-door sedan. A Jaguar similar to the one her father used to drive. She stared at it for a beat, and then a man came out of a side entrance of Stephanie's house. He was tall and of moderate build with a full head of thick gray hair. The man trotted down a side path and hopped into the Jaguar, driving off without looking at his surroundings.

"Hey, are you coming?" Tom said.

Katie looked up. Forest had already gone through the front door, and Tom was hanging halfway out.

"Yeah," Katie said, casting one more sidelong glance at the Jaguar as it made its way toward the gate.

There was no mistaking that man, not for Katie. It was her father, and apparently, he'd been spending some time with his old family friends. The question was, why? What would the Arkman family, especially Stephanie, want with a convicted felon?

# 30

## ASHLEY

Kylie was in the hospital waiting room when Ashley arrived, sitting in a chair with her head in her hands. She was the only person there, and the room was silent. Ashley headed straight for her.

"Hey there," Ashley said, placing a soft hand on Kylie's back.

Kylie looked up. "Hey." Her voice was strained, and her face was puffy, as though she'd been crying. Kylie was a sensitive person. Ashley had learned in the last year that Kylie's rough exterior was just for show. The person beneath all that brawn was softer than most.

Ashley sat down beside her. "How are you doing?"

"I've had better days."

"Me too," Ashley said. "But that's the thing with down days. Eventually, things usually go back up."

If circumstances had been different, Ashley would not have been comforting Kylie. After all, she'd warned the jail that Morgan might do something like this, and it had been their responsibility to ensure her safety. They were housing her; the least they could do was keep her alive. Liability was going to be clear on this one, but that wasn't something Ashley would worry about. Morgan—or some random family member smelling money—would likely hire a personal injury attorney and file suit against the jail.

But Ashley also understood what it felt like to be short-staffed and drowning in work. It had been that way for her before she could scrape together the funds to hire Elena and Katie. And she understood how Kylie felt. She didn't have enough jailers to handle the number of inmates, especially those who needed special attention, like Morgan. It created an environment where it always seemed as though the bottom was just about to fall out. The level of stress that came with it was unmanageable.

"Do you think she's going to die?" Kylie said. Her head was back in her hands, and she was hunched over. "I'm not sure if I'll ever forgive myself if she does."

"I hope not," Ashley said, rising to her feet, "but I suppose I better try and find out. You hang in there." She patted Kylie on the back for a second time. It was the only thing she felt like she could honestly say considering the circumstances. She couldn't tell Kylie that everything would be all right, because she didn't know if that was true.

A nurse was seated at a nearby nursing station, and Ashley made her way toward the woman. She had long, brown hair drawn back into a bun so tight that it pulled at the corners of her eyes.

"Hello…" Ashley said, studying the woman's name tag, "Jamie. I'm an attorney, and I'm here to see a client."

Jamie stiffened and slowly looked up at Ashley. Her eyes held clear contempt.

"I'm a criminal defense attorney," Ashley added. "Not medical malpractice or anything like that."

The severe expression lifted from Jamie's features, smoothing out her brow. "Who is it that you need to see?"

"Morgan Stanman."

Jamie pressed a few buttons on a desktop computer, then met Ashley's gaze. "She's in room 142. The doctor has not cleared Ms. Stanman for visitors yet, but she's making rounds now, so I'll check with her and let you know."

That was a good sign. If the doctor was considering visitors, then Morgan's circumstances weren't quite as dire as Kylie had feared. "What's the doctor's name?"

"Doctor Malloy," Jamie said. She was distracted by her computer screen and spoke absent-mindedly.

"Doctor Ruby Malloy?" Ashley said, trying to contain her excitement.

Jamie looked up, her full attention returning to Ashley. "Yes," she said cautiously. "Do you know her?"

Ashley could feel the smile spreading across her lips. She did know the good doctor. She'd treated Ashley when Rachel Smithson's stepfather had poisoned her in a failed murder attempt. "She treated me almost a year ago. But that was in Des Moines. What is she doing here?"

Jamie shrugged. "You'll have to ask her, but I believe she moved out here for family reasons."

"Family reasons?"

"I'm not going to tell you more than that," Jamie said, shaking her head. "I've probably told you too much already. Dr. Malloy is a very private woman and extremely professional. We are lucky to have her, and I don't want to do anything to jeopardize that."

"Agreed," Ashley said. "Will you let her know that I'm here? I need to speak to her about my client's condition, and I'd like to give her a personal hello."

"Sure," Jamie said. "Name?"

"Ashley Montgomery."

"I'll let her know."

Ashley returned to her seat next to Kylie and filled her in on the information. Kylie's body language and expression started relaxing the more Ashley told her. But she returned to the same taut position when Ashley reminded her that she was just making educated guesses and she didn't know anything concrete about Morgan's condition.

"There was just so much blood," Kylie said, shaking her head. "It was like a murder scene in there."

Ashley and Kylie were sitting side by side looking straight ahead, but Ashley turned her knees toward Kylie so she could look at her straight on. "Tell me how it happened," she said softly.

Kylie shook her head. "I don't know for sure. She wasn't supposed to have a toothbrush. She must have gotten it from one of the other women. They were all questioned, but both Erica and Aubrey denied giving it to her. Neither were willing to produce their toothbrush either. It's like they had planned it. We're going to search their cell later, but even if we do find a toothbrush, there's no way to determine whose it is so long as both Aubrey and Erica continue to keep their stories the same."

"Huh."

Ashley's mind started spinning with thoughts going in all different directions. All three women had been friendly. There weren't strong reasons to believe that Erica or Aubrey would want Morgan dead. The only change had been the fact that Morgan was begging to proffer with law enforcement. Ashley had warned Morgan to keep that information to herself, but she'd been losing control. She easily could have slipped up.

Maybe one of them wanted to prevent her from talking. But which one? Erica had been with Morgan when they witnessed Frank locking the girl in his shed, but it was Aubrey who was fed up with Morgan's antics. Aubrey was the one that kept running to Ashley, trying to get her to shut Morgan up.

Unfortunately for everyone in this situation, Ashley did not have that level of client control. Not over Morgan or any other client. If she did, none of this would be happening. And she didn't mean Morgan's suicide attempt. She meant everything surrounding this garbled mess of a job. If her clients actually listened to her, Frank would probably be alive because he would have stopped manufacturing drugs long ago. Without the drugs, Frank would not have been able to control and victimize his girls. But nobody cared about her opinion until after it was too late. Hopefully, it wouldn't be too late for Morgan.

# 31

## KATIE

They had been seated in Stephanie Arkman's formal living room—Katie, Tom, Forest, and Rachel—for a good fifteen minutes, twiddling their thumbs, before anyone else entered the room. That was when a woman with long dark hair and thickly accented English brought in a tea tray along with four teacups, all sitting atop matching saucers.

The woman poured Katie a glass and handed it to her. "Ms. Stephanie will be right in."

Katie nodded and studied the teacup. It was made of fine bone china, delicate with one pink peony stretching across it. "Thank you," she said, setting the cup on the saucer without taking a sip. She didn't like tea, and the expensive chinaware made her nervous.

When the woman left, the room fell back into an intense silence. Nobody looked comfortable, not even Rachel, who'd been to Stephanie's home on many occasions. The room was intimidating, and Katie assumed that was intentional. It was the high ceilings and museum-quality decorations that bothered Katie the most. The way everything was spotless and white, including the couches, tables, and square-patterned carpet. A whitewashed fireplace sat in the corner of the room with a large mirror directly above it, reflecting the crystal chandelier that hung from the ceiling.

As the silence stretched on, Katie's mind wandered back to her father. She wanted him to disappear from her life, but she also wanted answers from him. Why had he been at Stephanie's home? What game was he playing? She didn't know what he was up to, but Brine was her town, her home, and he was weaseling his way back into her life. Which was something she did not want to happen.

"Thank you for waiting." Stephanie's voice came from behind Katie. It was strong and echoing in the cavernous room.

Katie startled at the sudden sound, and she was thankful she'd set down her cup of tea. Otherwise, the pristine couch that probably cost more than her yearly salary would have been ruined. She turned to look at Stephanie as she breezed into the room, holding her head high and her shoulders back.

"I was held up with an emergency."

A large white grandfather clock sat nearby, its golden guts swinging hypnotically. Katie studied its hands, then turned back to Stephanie. "Must have been some emergency, since we've been waiting here for more than thirty minutes."

"Yes, well, it was," Stephanie said with a tight smile.

Forest shot Katie a warning look, but Katie was already far too annoyed to rein in her temper. Yes, Stephanie was offering to donate enough money to start the Mental Health Response Team, but money didn't take the place of common decency. She'd demanded their presence and kept them waiting, yet she offered no apology for her behavior.

That was the problem Katie had with people like Stephanie. She was fake. She pretended to be kind on the outside, and everyone believed it, because she did all the right things publicly. She attended church and donated generous amounts of money, but deep down, she lacked respect. Others were beneath her. Simple as that. And Katie, Forest, Tom, and even her niece, Rachel, were among those that Stephanie believed were below her level.

"So, what's this all about?" Katie asked. "I assume it's important as well, since you didn't give us hardly any notice and this meeting was mandatory."

Again, Stephanie issued a tight smile. One that said, *I'm annoyed with you, but I'm classy enough to keep those thoughts to myself.*

"Should we get started?" Tom's tone was much kinder than Katie's had been, but he was an overall nicer person than Katie. Even though it didn't sound like it on the surface, Katie could tell that Tom was running low on patience as well. After all, he'd had the opportunity to go with Ashley to the hospital to see Morgan. It would have been an excellent chance to further mend their friendship and move one step closer to romance.

Stephanie either didn't notice Tom's growing irritation or she didn't care. It was probably the latter. "I wanted to discuss the donation announcement and the unveiling ceremony," Stephanie said, looking around the room.

A flash of anger ran up Katie's spine. This was about a party. Stephanie had demanded their instantaneous appearance to a party plan. *What a fucking joke*, Katie thought, but she certainly wasn't laughing.

"Forest would like the money as soon as possible, and I quite agree," Stephanie continued. "There will be a sensitive news story that will soon break about my family, and I'd like this announcement to be simultaneous."

Katie gritted her teeth. "So, I'm here at, what time is it now," she paused and looked pointedly at the grandfather clock, "six forty-five at night to discuss a PR plan with you? Like I've got nothing better to do than to worry about your 'sensitive news.' Which, by the way, what the hell is that sensitive?"

A flash of rage passed behind Stephanie's eyes, but she maintained her composure. "My divorce. My husband will be filing sometime next week, and I expect it will be big news."

*Big news, my ass*, Katie thought. Nobody cared about Stephanie Arkman's marriage. Then a sudden, frightening thought crossed Katie's mind. Were Stephanie and Katie's father dating? Oh, God, that would be horrific. Michael Michello was a good fifteen years older than Stephanie, but that wasn't an impossible age gap.

It could be true, and Katie's father was a convicted felon. Maybe that news was the "sensitive" part of the divorce. If that was the case, the jig was up for Katie. Everyone would know by sunrise tomorrow that Katie's real last name was Michello. The thought sickened her but also brought a small semblance of relief. She wouldn't have to hide anymore or wonder who knew what about her past. Everything would be out in the open, and that had its benefits.

"Anyway," Stephanie said, clapping her hands together, "it's important that we get this news out immediately. I'll have my team prepared to send out an announcement to all the major media outlets in Iowa. We just need to select a date and a location."

The movement in Stephanie's arm as she clasped her hands together caught Katie's attention. The bareness of her left wrist was obvious to Katie now, especially since there was a light tan line where Stephanie's bangle had once rested. It was still missing, and Katie had found it. The question was, how did that bracelet get onto Frank Vinny's property? It reminded her of her primary purpose for responding to

Stephanie's demand for her presence. To search for a connection.

While Katie was lost in thought, Forest and Stephanie had fallen into an intense conversation, discussing the most politically advantageous details to the announcement. Tom looked bored, and Rachel's head was leaned back on the couch, her gaze staring up at the ceiling.

"Where is your restroom?" Katie interrupted.

Stephanie shot her a *you can't be serious* look, but Katie was more than serious, so she didn't back down.

"It was a long drive, and you gave us tea while we waited for your *emergency* to pass. It should come as no surprise—"

"I don't need to know details about your need to relieve yourself," Stephanie said, cutting her off. "There is a powder room right there," she gestured to a door nearby, "but Bermuda is cleaning it right now, so you'll have to go elsewhere."

*Powder room*, Katie thought. *It's a fucking bathroom. Only the truly vain would need a specific room to reapply makeup.*

"Okay," Katie said. "Then where can I go? There must be other bathrooms in this giant house of yours." Her tone was tense, but only because of Stephanie's dismissive attitude. She was actually getting exactly what she wanted—an opportunity to snoop around.

"Rachel will show you," Stephanie said, gesturing to her niece before returning to her conversation with Forest.

"Wonderful," Katie said, rising to her feet.

Rachel did the same, and she, too, looked thankful for the excuse to leave the monotony of the party-planning conversation. Tom shot Katie a pleading expression, but there was no logical reason for him to accompany them, so they left him behind. *Sorry for your luck*, Katie thought, *but I've got work to do.*

# 32

## ASHLEY

It was another thirty minutes before Ashley saw Dr. Malloy's familiar face emerge from the hallway, stepping through two double doors into the waiting area. She held herself with the poise of an empress, her head held high, her gaze scanning the nearly empty room. When her light blue eyes settled upon Ashley, she nodded and headed straight for her.

"Stalking me, I see," Ashley said by way of greeting.

Seven months earlier, Ashley had been poisoned by Rachel's stepfather, Isaac Smithson, and hospitalized. It was a failed murder attempt, but the act hadn't been about Ashley. It was about control over Rachel. She had just turned eighteen, and she had made the choice to stick with representation by the public defender over a private attorney funded by Isaac. The poisoning was Isaac's way to have Ashley removed as Rachel's attorney.

Luckily, Ashley had been in the right place at the right time, and Katie discovered her shortly after she'd ingested a high dosage of the poison. She'd been unconscious when the ambulance carried her to a hospital in Des Moines. When she woke up, she was in Dr. Malloy's care and recovered quickly.

"Stalking is a strong word," Dr. Malloy said, placing her hands behind her back.

"That's why I used it. Did you miss me?"

The doctor gave Ashley a sidelong look. Her expression was stern, but her eyes sparkled. "How are you feeling these days?"

"Just fine. What are you doing in Brine? I can't imagine you'd choose working in this dump over Des Moines," Ashley said, gesturing around her at the barren walls. The Brine hospital had to be struggling. The population was small, and most people opted to drive the hour and a half to Des Moines or the hour to West Des Moines to receive treatment. It was only the old and the dying that chose Brine for their emergency care. Dr. Malloy had to be bored in this tiny hospital.

"No. I didn't choose to leave Des Moines, but my mother lives in Carroll, and she's getting older. She needed someone close by to help take care of her. My brother lives in Montana, and my sister is in Florida." She shrugged. "I live the closest, so I drew the short straw."

"Why didn't you move your mother to Des Moines?"

Dr. Malloy's face split into a sardonic smile. "You don't know my mother. This was the far simpler option, trust me."

"Fair enough. I hear you are treating my client, Morgan Stanman."

The doctor's eyes darted toward Kylie, who was still seated but looking up at them, listening intently. No doubt trying to learn of Morgan's status. "Let's walk and talk, shall we?"

Ashley cast Kylie an apologetic look and mouthed, *I'll tell you what I can later*, then turned to catch up with Dr. Malloy.

"Self-harm," Dr. Malloy said.

"Not a suicide attempt?"

"I'm not a psychiatrist, so I don't know for sure. We don't have any on staff, so it'll take a couple days to get a full evaluation completed. But if the question is whether Morgan's a danger to herself or others, then the answer is most definitely yes."

Ashley understood where Dr. Malloy was headed with this conversation. If medical professionals determined that Morgan was a danger to herself or others, it qualified her for a court order for a mental health evaluation and continued hospitalization. Undoubtedly, that was precisely what Morgan wanted—since her only other option was jail—but Ashley still felt like she should at least give some pushback. If for no other reason than to mess with the good doctor.

"How did you come to that conclusion? That she's a danger to herself."

Dr. Malloy stopped walking and gave Ashley a hard look. "She sliced up both of her wrists. I'd say that's pretty tangible evidence that there is a significant risk she would harm herself if left to her own devices."

"Maybe she *was* a danger before, but that danger has passed."

"Past behavior is the best indicator of future actions. She is hospitalized now, but I'm primarily treating her wounds. Yes, I can prescribe a mood stabilizer, but she really needs to see a psychologist and a psychiatrist."

"Okay," Ashley said.

"In other words, there's been no serious intervention to prevent this from happening again. Until that can be arranged, I am going to stick to my current position. She is a danger to herself and potentially others."

"Why others? She didn't cut anyone else, did she?"

Dr. Malloy started walking again, her short legs moving quickly along the white tiled flooring. Ashley had to jog to catch up.

"I can't rule out her dangerousness to others, so I'm not

going to say that *isn't* the case. I won't say it *is* the case either, but I won't rule it out just because you're trying to lawyer me."

"Fair enough."

"Morgan is also suffering from methamphetamine withdrawals," Dr. Malloy said. "We're trying to keep her as comfortable as possible, but she needs substance abuse treatment. I can arrange to have a Hairstat test done, but the numbers would probably be way off the charts. I'm assuming you don't want me to do that." She paused, allowing time for Ashley to answer.

"Please don't. I think Morgan will admit she has a problem without all that extra stuff."

In truth, Ashley didn't want one more example of Morgan's blatant violation of pretrial release. Right now, the State had her cutting off her monitor near the scene of a crime, which also happened to be a known drug dealer's home. Even though pretrial release violations were the least of Morgan's worries these days, that didn't mean that Ashley didn't concern herself with it. Every case had many balls to juggle, and this was one of them. Ashley had to make decisions that would ensure Morgan the best possible outcome on all fronts, including her original burglary charge.

"Fine by me," Dr. Malloy said, coming to a stop outside room 142.

The door was closed, but Ashley could hear a TV on inside blaring the familiar sounds of *Wheel of Fortune*.

"This is Morgan's room." Dr. Malloy gestured to the door. Deputy Zachary Brinks stood a few feet away, leaning against the wall.

"I never would have guessed," Ashley said sarcastically, "what with the deputy and all." She turned to address Zachary. "It's pretty obvious who they're giving all the unimportant jobs to."

All Ashley had seen Deputy Brinks do over the past few days was stand around, guarding Morgan. He'd brought her in for her initial questioning—holding her there until George could arrive—and now he was posted outside her door.

"Ashley," Dr. Malloy said, shaking her head. Her tone was stern, but her eyes were smiling. "Go inside before you offend everyone on my floor."

"Sure thing, Doc," Ashley said, saluting. Then she twisted the doorknob and entered.

"Doesn't anyone knock around here?" Morgan shouted as the door creaked open. "What if I was naked?"

Ashley strode in, and Morgan fell silent.

"Well, hello to you, too," Ashley said, shoving her hands in her pockets and making her way toward the hospital bed. "I take it your little plan here didn't work out as swimmingly as you had hoped." She nodded to Morgan's bandaged wrists.

Ashley had been worried about Morgan since Kylie had called her with the news, but now that she was face-to-face with her client, it was pretty clear that Morgan had no intention of dying. Yes, her injuries were serious enough to require hospitalization, but Ashley doubted that she had an actual desire to end her own life. Sure, she could have accidentally caused irreversible damage, but Morgan was an impulsive person. She didn't think about all the possibilities before she acted.

"I don't know what you're talking about." Morgan crossed her arms, and she looked very much like a petulant child.

"You found a way to get yourself out of jail, I'll give you that." Ashley grabbed a chair and pulled it up to her bedside. "But it's only temporary. You're on a forty-eight-hour hold. Unless you can convince a psychiatrist that you are seriously mentally ill and in need of inpatient treatment—which is doubtful, by the way—then you are headed straight back to jail."

"I'm not going back to that jail. I will keep doing this."

"That's one way to convince the psychiatrist you're a danger to yourself. It may or may not work. But that's not a decision that I get to make. My question is, who gave you the shank, and why?"

Morgan stuck her nose in the air. "I promised not to tell."

"Do you think that person had the same thought process as you, or were they hoping you'd slice through an artery and bleed out right there?"

"I..." Morgan's voice trailed off, and her expression grew thoughtful. "I don't know," she said after a couple of moments passed.

"Who was it, Morgan? Who made the shank? Was it Erica or Aubrey?"

Morgan shook her head. "I'm not a rat."

"Oh, come on," Ashley said, sitting back in her seat, completely exasperated. "Yesterday, you wanted to talk to the prosecutor in a proffer. Today, you're saying you don't rat others out. What's the difference, honestly?"

"The difference is that Charles can help me. Ratting out my cell mates won't."

"I'm your attorney. You're supposed to tell me things. The prosecutor is the enemy. Talking to him is far worse for everyone."

"Not me."

Ashley glared at her client. This was the part of her job that she hated. So many of her clients were more than willing to throw one another under the bus in the attempt to get some scrap of a deal from the prosecutor.

"You don't know that yet. The prosecutor hasn't heard anything you've had to say. Until he does, he likely won't commit to any sort of deal. It's extremely risky, and I don't recommend it. We have better chances at trial."

"But I'll sit in jail all the way up to trial. I told you, I'm not going back. I want to proffer."

"Fine," Ashley said with a sigh. "But you're going to start by telling me whatever it is you think you know that will earn you such a fantastic deal from the prosecutor."

"There are a lot of players in this thing," Morgan said, her voice barely above a whisper. "I know them all, and I can provide information about them."

"What 'thing' are you referring to?" Ashley asked. "And who are these 'players'?"

Ashley had expected Morgan to start providing names of the men who had partaken in Frank's card game, but she didn't. That might have been information the prosecution could have used, and something that felt, at least to Ashley, more like helping than snitching. But Morgan insisted that she didn't recognize any of them—that they were from out of town, and she never caught a first name for any of them.

Instead, Morgan delved into a story that implicated more than one person that Ashley knew, including Morgan herself. Ashley listened intently, her mind whirring at the possibilities. If she were to contact George Thomanson and the prosecutor and relay this information, it could completely backfire. It could also do precisely what Morgan was hoping. But the outcome was a flip of the coin, and Ashley told Morgan as much, but her client still wanted to move forward with the proffer.

"Fine," Ashley said, rising to her feet. "I'll call Detective Thomanson and set it up. I'm going to try to nail down as many promises from them as I can, but they know you are desperate. Everyone does. That's not helpful when it comes to negotiations."

"They'll give me what I want, I know it."

Ashley shook her head and went to leave the room. She wished she could be as confident as Morgan was in the potential outcome, but she didn't have that luxury. If things went south, Morgan would blame Ashley, and then she'd be defending herself. Her advice had to be spot on, or she could end up getting sued by her client. As she stepped out of Morgan's room and into the corridor, she got out her cell phone and dialed George's number.

"Detective Thomanson here." George's familiar voice came through the line. It was loud, strong, and more than slightly irritated.

"Yes, this is Ashley Montgomery."

"Yeah, I know. I saved your number. I wanted a warning so I could steel myself for whatever harassment you intend during your not-so-welcome phone calls."

"Thanks," Ashley said flatly. Although, she supposed she deserved it. "Can you come to the Brine County Medical Center?"

"I'm kinda busy right now."

"I know," Ashley said. "You're digging up that makeshift graveyard outside Frank's barn. But I also know that you've called DCI, and they should be there by now. So, you have backup, and you can step away for a moment."

George was silent for several long seconds. Ashley was used to his maneuvers, so she didn't say anything to fill the silence. She merely waited for whatever question or accusation that would come next.

"How do you know about the bodies?"

*There it is*, she thought. His tone was so accusatory. It sounded like he was thinking that she was the one who had dug those graves and buried all those people. "Police scanner. And I have a stellar investigator. Remember? You made sure she lost her job at the police department. Which I don't think I've ever thanked you for. So, thank you for being an idiot and giving me a fantastic new employee."

"This is no time for sarcasm."

Ashley disagreed. When dealing with cops, she felt like every time was good for a little sarcasm.

"Why do you want me to come to the hospital?"

"Morgan is here, and she wants to proffer."

"I've got Morgan's arson and murder cases all sealed up. She killed two people."

"Allegedly," Ashley added.

George sighed heavily. "She killed two people," he repeated. "One may still be unidentified, and the other wasn't a stellar member of the community, but they were still human beings, and they didn't deserve to die."

"Now you're starting to sound an awful lot like Katie did back in her cop days."

George ignored Ashley's last comment. "I don't see what information Morgan would offer that would convince anyone not to put her away for life."

"What about codefendants?"

"I would be interested, but it still isn't enough."

"Okay." Ashley knew he wouldn't bite on that. They had no need to charge anyone other than Morgan. They had enough evidence to convince a jury that she lit the fire. They didn't need a whole lot more. "What if I could lead you to the identity of the girl in the barn?"

"Still not enough."

"Fine. Then what if Morgan can lead you to the identities of the women buried out in Frank's woods?"

"Who said they were all women?"

"But they are, aren't they?"

George fell silent again, and Ashley waited him out. He'd come around; she just needed to be patient.

"I'll be there in thirty minutes, but I'm not promising anything until *after* I've heard what Morgan has to say. And I'm going to have to bring the prosecutor in on this one. I can't make this decision alone."

"That's all I expected. See you soon, Georgie, and we'll hash out details."

Ashley hung up before George had a chance to respond. He wanted the information, as she knew he would, but it was what he would do with it that concerned her. Morgan was really rolling the dice here, but Ashley couldn't stop her. If Morgan wanted to proffer, she could. That was her right. It was against Ashley's advice, but this wouldn't be the first or the last time that a client refused to listen to her.

# 33

## KATIE

Rachel led Katie out of Stephanie Arkman's pretentious formal living room and down an even more ostentatious hallway where the flooring was white marble and the ceiling was lined in crown molding. Chandeliers hung every ten feet, each small copies of the crystal monster clinging to the ceilings in the formal living room and the grand entryway.

They walked side by side in a companionable silence, their tennis shoes squeaking against the brightly polished floors. Both Katie and Rachel were dressed down for the occasion, but likely for different reasons. Rachel was Stephanie's niece. She'd undoubtedly been inside the white mansion on many occasions and felt comfortable. Or at least comfortable enough to be herself. Katie was making a statement—*I don't dress up for you*—although she doubted Stephanie had noticed.

They passed one bathroom, then several other rooms, followed by a second hallway bathroom, but Rachel didn't stop. She continued walking until they reached a staircase at the end of the hallway. It was no grand staircase, not at all like the winding set near the entrance of the home.

"Where are we going?" Katie whispered. The ceilings were high and would likely produce an echo, so she kept her voice low.

"Upstairs."

"I guessed that. But why?"

"You'll see," Rachel said as she started her way up the long staircase.

Katie hesitated, but only for a moment. While it was an invasion of privacy, it was also an opportunity she knew she wouldn't get twice. Stephanie had been pressuring Rachel to move in with her, and Rachel ultimately would relent so long as Stephanie kept up the current level of coercion, so arguably this was practically Rachel's home too. They walked up the stairs and into a far darker and less elegant hallway.

"This is what Aunt Stephanie calls the servants' quarters," Rachel said. Katie must have made a face in response to the word *servant* because Rachel elaborated. "It's not as bad as it sounds. It's where the staff that works inside the home all live with their families. It's mainly the cook and the house cleaner that live up here. I think that was just the traditional name for it, so it stuck."

"I can think of other names. Stephanie could try calling it *employee* quarters, or *staff* home, or *team* private space. Any of those would do, and that's just me spit-balling. If I had time, I could come up with at least twenty other less offensive words than *servant*."

"I know," Rachel said quietly. "I agree with you, but I'm not in any position to change anything about Aunt Stephanie."

That was a fair enough statement. Rachel was barely an adult, and a damaged one at that. She was still struggling with the psychological effects of years of mental and sexual abuse. She was in no condition to argue with someone like Stephanie, not now, and maybe never. That was probably why

Stephanie wanted Rachel to move in with her. She knew she would have complete control over her niece.

"Anyway," Rachel said, stopping outside a closed door. The first in a long line of others. "This is what I wanted to show you."

Rachel twisted the doorknob and slowly opened the door. It creaked along its hinges. Katie's breath caught when she saw inside the room. It was not at all what she had expected. Not that she knew what to expect in an area of a mansion referred to as "servants' quarters." But whatever she'd thought or imagined, this was not it.

"It's a hospital room," Katie said, her voice barely above a whisper.

Rachel nodded.

The room was large with an adjustable hospital-style bed at its center. Large pieces of equipment lined the walls, most of which Katie didn't recognize, but some looked like the devices used to monitor vital signs, one of which was hooked up to whoever was lying in the bed. After a few moments, the person in the bed began stirring. Katie started backing toward the door, but Rachel grabbed her arm.

"Maria," Rachel said, her tone soft, "are you awake?"

There was more stirring on the bed, and a girl propped herself up on her elbows. Her face had several round welts that looked as though they were in the middle of the healing process, but even with the disgusting blemishes, Katie could see that Maria was little more than a girl and that she was quite a beauty.

"Frank?" Maria groaned. "More..."

Rachel walked swiftly toward the bed and sat on the end, taking Maria's hand into hers. "No, Maria. Frank is gone. It's me, Rachel."

"Need water..." The girl's English was thickly accented.

"I'll go see if I can find the doctor or a nurse. Sit tight." Rachel spoke slowly and loudly in that way that people did when they were trying to converse with someone who spoke a different language. She rose and motioned for Katie to follow her out of the room.

"What the hell?" Katie said, the moment the door closed behind Rachel. "I don't even know where to start."

"I know how you feel."

"What's happening here?"

Rachel took a deep breath but then motioned for Katie to follow her. "I've got to find a nurse first."

They walked down the hallway to the very last room, and Rachel knocked on the door. A middle-aged woman wearing scrubs and a pleasant smile opened the door.

"Rachel, my dear," the woman said. "What can I do for you?"

"Maria is awake. She's asking for water. I think she's a little uncomfortable."

The woman nodded. "Yes. It should be time for her medicine. The poor dear is struggling with withdrawals."

"What are you giving her?" Katie asked. She'd meant to sound less demanding, but she was still shocked with the presence of the girl and having a hard time piecing everything together.

"The doctor has prescribed a mild sedative to help with the anxiety and depression."

"For how long?" Katie was feeling defensive of the girl, although she wasn't entirely sure why. Maybe it was her small figure in that giant bed. Or the pick marks on her face, which Katie now recognized as a sign of methamphetamine use. Some heavy users suffered signs of psychosis, picking at their faces because they believed bugs or something equally disgusting was on or under their skin.

"She's only been here a short time. I should expect the doctor will reevaluate her medication schedule in a couple days. She may not look it, but she is starting to perk up a little."

"Thank you," Rachel said, pulling Katie out of the room before she could press the nurse for answers.

Once they were out in the hallway, Katie began firing questions at Rachel. "Who is that? The girl, I mean. I gathered the other woman is the nurse."

"She's the daughter of one of Stephanie's employees. She disappeared a month ago. I remember when it happened. Her parents kept coming to Stephanie's house for meetings. They were always upset. She's only twelve."

"Where was she found?"

Rachel shrugged. "Aunt Stephanie wouldn't say. All I know is that she turned back up here, and she was in this condition." She gestured toward Maria's closed door.

"Which day?"

"I don't know for sure. I'm not here *that* often. I just know that she wasn't here last week and now she is. I wandered up here and found her yesterday, but based on what the nurse just said, I doubt she's been here much longer than a day or two."

"Could it have been the day of Frank's fire?" Katie was thinking of Stephanie's bangle out there in the woods. Maybe Stephanie had been there to rescue her employee's daughter. Stephanie had never been one to get her hands dirty, and she was no hero, so it seemed unlikely, but it would explain the presence of her bangle in the woods. It could also create a defense for Morgan.

"Possibly," Rachel said with a shrug. She didn't know about the discovery of the bangle, but Katie also doubted that she would defend Stephanie if she had known.

"How did she get addicted to meth? I mean, I assume she wasn't that way when she disappeared."

"She wasn't," Rachel agreed. "I tried to ask what happened, but Maria doesn't speak much English. Aunt Stephanie would know more. I assume she's been using one of her other employees to interpret, but I haven't been here for that. Not that Aunt Stephanie would allow me to hear it. Whatever happened to her was bad. Possibly worse than what happened to me."

"You think she was sexually assaulted?"

Rachel nodded. "I overheard the doctor say that she was when he was here yesterday. He examined her and said there is some fairly severe vaginal tearing. He said he had to stitch her up in a couple places and that it is a clear sign of sexual assault."

"Oh, my God." Katie couldn't catch her breath. "Has Stephanie called law enforcement?"

"I don't know for sure, but I don't think so."

"Why not?"

"She's undocumented. Nobody wants cops sniffing around, asking questions. Besides, you heard what Maria said. She was asking for Frank. I think everyone assumes the person who deserved punishment has already received it. I'm sure Maria's parents want to shower Morgan with gifts."

"Morgan? Morgan Stanman?"

"Yeah," Rachel said with a nod. "She's the one charged with Frank's murder."

"But what about the girl who died in the barn with Frank?"

"Everyone around here assumes that the girl was already dead or half dead thanks to Frank."

"Why?"

"You didn't see Maria yesterday. She looks bad now, but

she's light-years better. It's amazing what a little hydration and some clean clothes can do."

"Wow," was all Katie could manage to say. "Does Ashley know about all this?"

Rachel shook her head. "I didn't know how to tell her. You know how she doesn't like Aunt Stephanie. I didn't want her to freak out and confront Aunt Stephanie before she knew all the facts. I thought that maybe you could find a way to tell Ashley that wouldn't make her so upset."

Katie doubted that was possible, but she was going to have to give it a try. First, she would need to get more information about Maria, her family, and the circumstances surrounding her disappearance. Due to her age, it was still rape whether she chose to leave on her own or not. The more important question that needed to be determined was if she was kidnapped. If Katie could prove that Frank had kidnapped and sexually assaulted a child, then Morgan's case would get a whole lot less complicated. To answer those questions, she would need to talk to a different coworker. Elena. Her parents worked in the same factory and were part of the same immigrant community as Maria's. Katie had asked Elena to speak with her parents. Hopefully, she'd have some helpful information now.

## 34

### ASHLEY

Ashley found Morgan fast asleep when she stepped back into her room after ending her call with George Thomanson. Which, she supposed, was for the best, because Ashley was going to have to do some haggling with him once he arrived.

Morgan was desperate for any deal from the State, and that was primarily because they had her by the balls. They knew it, and so did she. It didn't put Ashley on high ground when it came to the negotiations. Ashley did not share Morgan's sunny outlook on what the State would provide in exchange for her testimony.

Ashley slowly backed out of Morgan's room and silently closed her door, turning back to the hallway where Deputy Zachary Brinks was standing guard. There was no place to sit. Which was a shame because Ashley could've used a rest. She'd had one hell of a day. The hallway was silent, and she tried to ignore the deputy, but she could feel the weight of his stare. She would have liked to go somewhere else, but she needed to be nearby when George arrived. So, she stood there, awkwardly rocking from her heels to her toes, then Deputy Brinks spoke.

"So, proffering, huh? You think she has some good information?"

Ashley looked over at him and scowled. "None of this is about what *I* think. If what I thought mattered, Morgan would keep her mouth shut. But you jackasses have somehow convinced criminal defendants that it's better to 'come clean' and 'cleanse their soul' than to keep quiet, when all the while you know that 'coming clean' results in a pair of shackles and a lifetime behind locked doors."

"I'm new here," Zachary said, a look of genuine surprise flashing in his eyes. "I'm not sure how I got lumped in with the 'jackasses.'"

"It's the uniform," Ashley said, nodding toward the brown star stitched above his heart. "It comes with a gun and an innate hatred of the defense bar. But it isn't personal, you know. It's the way things have to be." Ashley made it a general rule to treat all cops the same—like shit—but that wasn't for personal reasons. She didn't dislike any of them, really, aside from George, and that was only because of what he'd done to Katie. She had an image to uphold, one of complete solidarity with her clients.

"I guess I get it." He fell silent for a long moment. "Hey, you have some involvement with the Mental Health Response Team, right?"

"Me?" Ashley asked, placing a flat hand against her stomach. "No. At least not formally. I just get grouped with them because the four people creating it happen to be the only four people in town who actually like me."

"People like you."

Ashley snorted. "Don't lie to me."

Zachary shrugged.

"Why are you asking about it?"

Zachary looked left, then right, checking that both hallways were empty, then he lowered his voice. "Are there any extra spots? I mean, on the team."

*Now that is interesting*, Ashley thought, straightening her back and reevaluating the young deputy. "I don't know. Talk to Forest Parker. They just came into some money. They'll be up and running soon." *And subject to Stephanie Arkman's control, thanks to her cash*, Ashley thought to herself before continuing. "So, you should reach out to Forest sooner rather than later."

"Thanks," Zachary said, a wide grin spreading across his face.

On the surface, it seemed as though Ashley was being kind, but she wasn't completely altruistic in her motivation. Deep down, she hoped that Katie would change her mind about joining the team and remain as Ashley's investigator, even though Ashley knew the likelihood of that happening was practically none. Ashley had budget problems, and unless she had another significant donation, she could only afford to pay Katie for one more year, anyway.

They fell back into a silence awkward enough that Ashley was almost happy to see Detective Thomanson as he turned the corner and headed down the hallway toward her. He moved quickly, each long stride taking him closer and closer. His expression was one of grim determination, with his brow furrowed and his eyes narrowed.

"Good evening, Detective," Ashley said when George drew near.

"'Good evening, my ass,'" George said with a snort. "What the hell was that on the phone? I told you not to call me that."

"Georgie?" Ashley asked. As she said it, she turned toward Zachary and winked.

"Yeah. So stop it."

"Sure."

"Sure?" George said. He was wound up and ready for a

fight. He clearly didn't know what to do with her sudden concession.

"Yeah. Sure. I'll stop calling you that." *At least to your face*, she thought. "Now, can we get down to business?"

"Umm, yeah."

"Where's Chuckie?" That was Ashley's nickname for Charles Hanson, the elected county attorney and lead prosecutor in Brine County.

George gave her a hard look, and she batted her eyelashes innocently.

"He's busy at the moment, dealing with..." He stopped and cleared his throat. "Something else."

"The bodies buried on Frank's property." Ashley said it as a statement, not a question, and Deputy Brinks looked up the moment he heard that. No doubt frustrated that he got stuck on guard duty while DCI and other law enforcement were out there doing real work.

"Yeah, that." His gaze darted toward Zachary, then back to Ashley. "Anyway, I brought our standard proffer agreement." He held a piece of paper out to her, and Ashley snatched it.

She knew what it would say before she even read it. It was full of fancy legal jargon—all drafted by an attorney general, no doubt—but it could be summed up as this: *you tell us everything, we promise nothing*. And a thorough scan of this document proved that Ashley's assumptions were right.

"Seriously, George? You aren't giving Morgan anything. You aren't even agreeing to lower her bond or release her under pretrial supervision. What is her incentive to talk?"

George quirked an eyebrow. "Oh, I don't think she cares about that. We all know Morgan is going to talk no matter what. You couldn't shut her up if you wanted to, and I'm sure you tried. So, what incentive does that give *me* to promise anything?"

*None*, Ashley thought. And that was precisely the problem. Morgan was already up shit creek, and up until this point, she'd had a paddle. But thanks to her inability to keep her mouth shut, she'd also thrown out her only mode of transportation. Soon she'd be paddling, elbow deep in excrement, and there was nothing Ashley could do to stop it.

"So, shall we?" George said, gesturing toward Morgan's closed hospital door.

"Whatever," Ashley grumbled. There was no point in delaying the inevitable any further. Morgan was going to talk, but this way, at least Ashley was present. Ashley knocked two times on the door, then twisted the knob. "Morgan," she called. "Detective Thomanson is here."

"Come in." Morgan's voice was groggy, and she was pushing herself up in bed when Ashley and George stepped inside.

"Hello, Morgan," George said, striding past Ashley, his shoulder bumping hers. "It's nice to see you again. You are looking far healthier than when I last saw you a few days ago."

*That's what detox will do*, Ashley thought.

"I know you are eager to talk." George pulled up a chair beside Morgan's bed. "But first I need you to read through this document and have you sign it."

Morgan accepted the proffer agreement and a pen from George. She started reading through it, then looked up at Ashley, who was standing in a corner with her arms crossed.

"It promises nothing," Ashley said. "Everything you say can be held against you, and you might not get anything in exchange. Basically, you are agreeing to confess." Ashley's tone was matter-of-fact. It was her professional way of saying, *I don't agree with this, and you're making a huge mistake, but it's your choice.*

"Okay," Morgan said, but there was an edge of uncertainty in her tone.

Ashley kicked off the wall. "You don't have to do this. We can boot George out now, and it won't hurt your case. In other words, you can change your mind now, but you can't unring that bell once you start talking."

George turned and shot Ashley a nasty look, but she ignored him. He would be pissed if he drove all the way back to town during the height of that nonsense down at Frank's property just to find out that Morgan had changed her mind.

"No," Morgan said, shaking her head. "I'll sign."

Ashley's heart sank. This choice was placing them in sole reliance on the "goodness" of the prosecutor. But that was such a subjective term, *good*. What was right and honest to one person was the opposite to another. And Ashley knew for a fact that Charles Hanson's idea of right and wrong was vastly different from Ashley's and Morgan's.

George pointed to a line at the bottom of the page. "I just need your John Hancock there, and we'll get started."

The words *John Hancock* grated on Ashley's nerves. Morgan was a woman, not a man. Couldn't society think of another term for signatures that wasn't based on a time period when men held all the power and women were little more than property?

Morgan signed her name, then looked up at George, her eyes wide and expectant. "What now?"

"Now, we talk." He pulled a recording device out of his pocket and placed it on the table that came across Morgan's hospital bed. "I just want you to know that I'm going to record everything that is said. Just so there's no debate about what was said and when it was said."

Morgan looked up at Ashley.

"This is your thing. If you insist on doing it, it's best for everyone if it's recorded."

"Okay," Morgan said, biting her lower lip. "I don't know where to start."

"Let's start with your relationship with Frank," George said, his smile widening.

"No," Ashley said through gritted teeth, "let's start with the women buried in Frank's yard." It had been literally seconds into the interview, and George was trying to steer the conversation to Morgan and Frank. This proffer was supposed to be about those still unidentified women, finding justice for them. It wasn't to tie up loose ends in Morgan's prosecution for Frank's murder.

George issued an exasperated sigh, but he relented. "Fine," he grumbled to himself before looking up at Morgan and saying, "How did you know the bodies were all women?"

Morgan's eyes darted from George to Ashley, then she heaved a sigh. "Because I knew them. All of them."

## 35

### KATIE

The meeting was ending by the time Katie and Rachel made their way back to Stephanie Arkman's formal living room.

"Oh, good. You're back," Stephanie said, but her words sounded forced. "I thought you'd gotten yourselves lost. I was about to send a search party."

"It is pretty easy to get lost in a place like this." Katie gestured around her. "It's a lot for one person."

"Two people, Ms. Mickey," Stephanie corrected. "At least until recently when my husband moved out. And I would think that surroundings such as these would be right up your alley, considering your childhood."

It took Katie everything she had to keep her jaw from dropping, but not because the others in the room didn't know about Katie's father. On the contrary, she'd trusted Rachel, Forest, and Tom with her secret, and she had thought that they'd all kept it to themselves. But maybe one of them had let it slip. It wouldn't be the first time a trusted friend had betrayed her by using her father against her.

But then again, it was also possible that Michael Michello could have told Stephanie. Katie did see him leaving through a side entrance earlier that evening. He wanted back into Katie's life. What better way to do it than to out her secret, forcing her to claim him as kin?

"Right," Katie said.

She was at a loss for words, and her mind was warring with itself. So much had happened in the past thirty minutes. She was having difficulty processing it all. Part of her wanted to confront Stephanie about the girl upstairs, but she decided against it. Now was not the right time. Forest would be appalled by her snooping, and Katie still didn't quite understand how Stephanie fit in with Frank.

"It looks like this meeting is over," Katie said, clapping her hands together. "I trust you got everything worked out for your little party." She looked to Stephanie.

"Yes." Stephanie rose to her feet with the grace of a swan. They were approximately the same height—five foot four inches—but Stephanie stood erect, and it made her seem like she had an extra inch or two on Katie. "No thanks to you. Your little bathroom excursion took quite some time."

"I thought you didn't want to discuss my bodily functions," Katie said with a snort.

"True," Stephanie said. Then she escorted Tom, Katie, and Forest to the front door. Rachel would be staying overnight. A change of events that would probably bother Ashley—she and Stephanie were in this weird tug-of-war over Rachel's affections—until Katie told her about Maria and the potential for Rachel to discover more information. Katie would not normally leave Rachel alone with Stephanie, at least not until she got to the bottom of whatever was happening, but Stephanie posed no danger to the teenager. They were family, after all, and the Arkmans were one clan that stuck together.

On the drive home, Tom peppered Katie with questions. She told him the full story, including sighting her father on the way inside Stephanie's monstrosity of a mansion and the discovery of Maria upstairs. As expected, Tom was as baffled as Katie about the entire situation. They both assumed that Maria was a child of one of Stephanie's factory workers, but that didn't explain why she was inside Stephanie's home. Or her condition. And then there was Stephanie's connection to Frank. None of it made sense, and Katie found a little solace in the knowledge that Tom found it all as mystifying as she did.

When they arrived back at the Public Defender's Office, the lights were still on. Which was strange. Elena didn't work late, and Ashley kept the front lights off when she was burning the midnight oil. Tom pulled up out front and parked at the curb. It was two-hour parking during the day, but that changed after five o'clock.

"Is Ashley here?" Tom asked.

"I don't think so," Katie said uncertainly. "She's probably still at the hospital. I assume she'll stay there pretty late, especially since Rachel won't be coming home tonight."

"Then who do you think is here?"

"There's only one way to find out," Katie said, unbuckling her seat belt.

The clench in Tom's jaw betrayed his concern, but Katie wasn't bothered. She spent plenty of years as a police officer, and she was well trained with a firearm. She wasn't an officer of the law anymore, but she had applied for and received a permit to carry. If there was an intruder in their office—which wasn't likely because they had little of value in there—then she'd handle the situation.

"I'm going to come with you," Tom said, putting the truck in park.

They both hopped out and walked up to the front door in silence. Katie tried the door, and it was locked. She removed her key and unlocked it. The door creaked open, and Katie listened intently. There was no music or noise coming from within. Which was unusual. After hours were usually pretty loud in the office. Especially when someone was there working alone. Sound made the place feel a little less empty.

Katie motioned for Tom to stay behind her, and she crept inside the entryway. When they were both inside, she motioned for Tom to close the door as quietly as possible. Then she moved toward the reception desk, keeping low to the ground, and moving slowly. Tom did the same. When they both had their backs to the reception desk, Katie pointed to herself, then up, a gesture saying, "I'm going to look, you stay here." Or at least she hoped that's what she'd conveyed.

She slowly rose to her feet and peeked over the desk. There was a shriek and Katie jumped back, her nerves fraying. Katie unholstered her gun in one swift movement, pointing it in the direction of the noise.

"Is that you, Katie?" Elena said, her breath coming in heavy heaves.

Katie holstered her gun. "Yes."

"You scared the shit out of me."

"Sorry," Katie said. "I thought you were an intruder." She motioned for Tom to stand, and he popped up next to her.

"Hey, Elena," Tom said, a smile splitting across his face. "We didn't mean to scare you."

"You're never here this late," Katie said.

"Yeah. I had some stuff to catch up on since I've been missing work with my mom being sick and all," Elena said. "And I was waiting for you."

"For me?" Katie and Tom came around the reception desk and into the back area.

Elena was sitting at her desk, and she swiveled in her chair to face them. "Yeah. You asked me to talk to my parents about the possible disappearance of immigrant girls."

"Yeah," Katie said, a sudden surge of excitement bursting through her. "What did you learn?"

"There are five of them. All between the ages of eleven and fifteen." Elena grabbed a sheet of paper off the top of her desk and handed it to Katie. "Those are their names."

Katie looked at the list.

1. *Rosa Ortiz*
2. *Josefina Munoz*
3. *Adriana Lopez*
4. *Juana Martinez*
5. *Maria Garcia*

"Is this in order of when they went missing?"

Elena nodded. "My mother said Rosa disappeared five years ago."

"Did you know any of these girls?"

"No," Elena said. "They never even made it to the community of workers. Their parents, brothers, and younger sisters all did, but not these girls. They disappeared somewhere along the way."

"Do you have any idea where they disappeared?"

"All I know was that they made it here from Mexico. That's the most dangerous part of the trip, the crossing, but my mom insisted that these girls made it through. Then they vanished somewhere between the border and Iowa."

"That last one," Katie said, tapping the page with her index finger. "Maria Garcia. What do you know about her?"

"I actually remember when she disappeared. That was only a few months back. I didn't know it at the time—my parents wanted to shield me from all that, even though I'm an adult," Elena said with only the slightest hint of irritation. "But I do remember the Garcias arriving, mostly because they'd been so distraught. It struck me as strange, because most families are overjoyed when they finally reach their American destination. But not that family. I had asked my mom about it, but she said they were just missing their extended family that they had to leave back in Mexico, which made sense to me at the time. But then the crying and carrying on continued. I thought that was even stranger, but I didn't ask any more questions. It wasn't my business. But then you asked me to check on missing girls, and that's when my mother finally told me."

"Has anything changed with the Garcias in the past couple days?" Katie asked.

"Come to think of it," Elena said and tapped a slender finger against her chin. "Yes. I wouldn't say they are *happy* now, but they have seemed more hopeful."

That had to be the same Maria that Katie found inside Stephanie's mansion. She was the right age, and the return time would fit. But she still didn't understand the connection between Frank and Stephanie.

"I know you've met Frank Vinny here at the office. Ashley represented him enough times in the past. I'm sure he's come into the office a time or two."

"Yeah. He did."

"Do you know how Stephanie Arkman knows him?"

Elena shook her head, a look of genuine bafflement crossing her face. "No. I really don't. I know you and Ashley aren't Stephanie's biggest fans, but she wouldn't have anything to do with someone like Frank. She's a good person. She's good to her workers. She provides them safe housing at a fair price."

Elena was talking about the trailer park community that Stephanie had built near her meat-packing plant. The plant was way out in the middle of nowhere, so Katie didn't have much cause to go out there, but she had passed by it a time or two while heading out of the county. It was clearly visible from the highway. While the homes were technically trailers, they weren't junky. They were clean and spacious, lined up in neat rows with flower beds between them. There was even a small park at its center.

"Stephanie pays them fairly," Elena continued. "Which is not common. Most of the time employers rip off employees that don't have legitimate immigration paperwork. They pay them way less than their documented employees. Stephanie doesn't do that. And she provides them medical care. My mom could never afford her doctor visits without Stephanie's help."

The way Elena described her, Stephanie sounded like a saint, but Katie knew better. Stephanie never did anything for strictly altruistic reasons. She had found a financial benefit in treating her workers well, and that was the only reason for her kindness. All of this was helpful information—it connected Stephanie and Maria—but Katie still didn't understand the correlation between Frank and Stephanie.

"Do you know any reason why Maria would be inside Stephanie Arkman's home asking for Frank Vinny?"

Elena cocked her head and gave Katie a look of genuine confusion. "No."

"Do you have any idea why doctors would be treating Maria for methamphetamine addiction and sexual assault?"

"What?" Elena said with a gasp, placing a hand over her mouth. She was silent for a few moments, blinking away the shock. "No. But Stephanie doesn't have anything to do with drugs. She wouldn't. That's why she hires migrant workers so often. They don't get caught up in the meth scene like the townies here who are born with the benefit of a birth certificate."

Katie placed a close-up photograph of Stephanie's bangle on the table. "Do you recognize this?"

Elena studied it for a long moment, then nodded. "Yeah. Stephanie wears it."

"I found this in the woods around Frank's house. I, of course, don't know when it fell off Stephanie's wrist, but I am taking a leap and making the assumption that it was somewhere near the time that the fire started. Do you know why *this* bracelet would be *there*?"

"No," Elena said, and Katie believed her.

Elena had never lied to Katie before. And Katie was well trained in sorting between deception and truth. Elena genuinely had no idea how Stephanie and Frank were connected. But Katie did know one person that might have the answer. Michael Michello.

She was reluctant to make the call, but she was out of options. The upside to making the call was that it would give her the opportunity to confront him about his presence at Stephanie's home as well. It was all interconnected. She hadn't thought so when she initially saw him on Stephanie's property, but she'd since changed her mind. This was one big mess, and somehow Katie's father had a hand in it.

"You knew them," George repeated Morgan's words slowly. "The girls buried out in Frank's yard. Is that what you're saying?"

"Yeah. Some of them better than others, but I definitely crossed paths with them."

This version of Morgan's story was different from the one she'd told Ashley the day before. It wasn't a lie; it was more of an omission of information. Morgan had previously claimed that there was only one girl there with her when she was subjected to the card game, and that she'd only seen one other girl with Erica that day that they snuck onto Frank's property. Now, she was telling the whole story.

"Did Frank introduce you to them?" George had pulled a notepad out of his pocket, but he wasn't writing anything. Ashley suspected it was more of a prop. Something to occupy his hands. Because he didn't need it. He was recording Morgan's every word.

Morgan snorted. "Introduce? That's a bit fancy for Frank."

"Okay. Did you meet them through Frank?"

"Everything I do," she cleared her throat, "I mean, did, somehow involved Frank. So, yeah, it was through him."

"So, tell me about them," George said, leaning back in his seat, putting his hands behind his head.

"Okay. I would guess that there are fourteen of them. Bodies, that is. But I think the total count of Frank's girls was sixteen by the end."

"You're saying we are going to dig up two other bodies?" George said skeptically. "A cadaver dog was all over that property, and all we found was fourteen."

"One was in the barn *with* Frank when he died."

"Let's focus on her, then. The girl in the barn. Who is she? We can't get a DNA match on her."

"Yeah, well, you wouldn't."

"I don't follow."

"Her name is Juana Martinez. She's a border hopper."

Ashley stiffened at Morgan's characterization of immigrants, but she didn't interrupt. Most of her clients were not well educated, and they often harbored prejudices. It wasn't the time or the place to correct her client. There was little chance Ashley could do anything to change Morgan's opinion, anyway. Morgan sure as hell didn't listen to Ashley when it came to her case, and there would be little reason for her to listen to Ashley after this interview ended. Either Morgan would get what she wanted, and she'd be insufferable, or she'd be screwed and go to prison for life.

"You mean she's an illegal immigrant," George said.

"Uh, yeah."

"From Mexico?"

"I guess. I mean, I don't know. I never asked. All those countries down there are the same to me."

"How did she get here? To America?"

"I don't know the answer to that."

Morgan's eyes darted around the room, bouncing from one item to the other. It was a tell. She was lying. Morgan knew, or she strongly suspected that she knew, how Juana made her way to America.

"How old was she?"

"Thirteen or fourteen. Somewhere around there. Maybe a little younger."

"How did she and Frank get mixed up?"

Morgan shrugged. "Probably the same way everyone does. He offered her drugs, she took them. Sometimes he forces it the first time, but after that first high," she sighed, "well, there's no going back."

"You're saying that Frank *made* this Juana girl use drugs. How did that happen?"

"Umm, he held her down and put a needle in her arm. Sometimes he had one of us help him."

"Who is 'us'?"

"One of us other girls that happened to be hanging around. There were guys too. Lots of them. Most of the time he relied on them. They were stronger."

Ashley was disgusted, but she tried to keep her emotions from showing on her face. Morgan had left this little tidbit of information out of the story when she'd told it to Ashley a few hours earlier.

"Is that what happened with all fourteen of the other girls?" George asked, astonished. "Frank forced them to use until they were addicted?"

"Pretty much. I mean, I'm guessing on that because I wasn't there for most of them. I saw it happen to Juana, but she was the only one. I assume some started willingly. I did, and so did Erica and Aubrey, but we were all older and living in town, so he treated us differently."

"When you say 'Erica' and 'Aubrey,' do you mean Erica Elsberry and Aubrey Miller?"

"Yeah."

"They witnessed all the same things as you did?"

Ashley saw where this was going, and it wasn't good for Morgan. George was interested in the information. He'd probably like to hunt these other men down and prosecute them, but if Aubrey and Erica knew all the same things as Morgan, he could do it without Morgan's testimony. He could send Morgan to prison for life and still have the testimony he needed by talking to Aubrey or Erica.

"I don't know. You'll have to ask them."

"I will," George said with a smile.

"But I don't think so. I was around a whole lot more. Aubrey is newer to town, you know, and Erica, well, she hasn't been using for more than a year or two. Some of these girls date back to ten years ago."

*Wow.* Ashley couldn't believe how long this had been going on. It was right under their noses, and Morgan had kept silent for so many years. So, what had changed? Why would Morgan all the sudden decide to burn it all to the ground as the prosecution claimed?

"Okay," George said. "So, Frank forced them to ingest meth. That sucks, but that doesn't explain how they all ended up buried in his yard."

"Have you checked their dope levels? You can do that, right? Using their hair or something?"

Ashley remained impassive. She doubted that George would answer. But then he surprised her.

"Yes and no. The criminologists say that it isn't as reliable as blood in determining cause of death. But some of the bodies are too badly degraded to test blood. All that's left of some of them are bones, teeth, nails, and hair."

Morgan nodded.

"But you already said they were using meth, either voluntarily or involuntarily. I don't see how testing their meth levels would make any difference."

*It would verify that Morgan was at least telling the truth about usage, for one*, Ashley thought. And evidence would be needed to bolster Morgan's credibility. She was a heavy meth user, and a jury—if it ever came to that—would not like her. Especially if the prosecution ultimately cut her a deal in exchange for her testimony.

"Check their levels. They should be off the charts."

George was silent for a long moment, tapping his pen against the paper. "You're saying all fourteen of those girls died of an accidental overdose."

"I never said it was accidental."

## KATIE

Katie picked up her cell phone and dialed the same ten digits that she had used to contact her father throughout her young life. She was surprised when muscle memory kicked in, her fingers flying across the screen, pressing numbers as though they were moving of their own volition. The phone rang only once before Michael Michello picked up.

"Katie," he said, his tone bright, "I've been waiting—"

Katie cut him off before he could finish whatever nonsense he was about to spew. "You need to come to my office."

"What? Why?"

"Because I need to talk to you about a few things." Katie began tapping her toe against the floor. She could feel Tom's and Elena's curious gazes, heavy upon her, waiting to see the outcome of the phone call and find out whatever information her father had to add.

"We're talking now, aren't we?"

"In person."

"Oh, I see," Michael said with a heavy sigh. "You want to see my expression so you know if I'm lying to you."

Katie grunted noncommittally. She had always been able

to read Michael's features. It had been a long time since she'd last done it, but she hoped she could still see through his lies to the truth.

"Fine. That's fine," he said after a few beats of silence. "But mostly because I want to see you and I'll take any opportunity I can get."

"I'll see you in, what, thirty minutes?" Katie said, glancing at the clock hanging on the wall. "You know where I work, right?"

"It'll be more like five. I'm already in town."

Katie's instinct was to ask, *Why? Why are you in Brine when you are supposed to be living in Ames?* But she held her tongue. She would have the opportunity to ask all her questions once he arrived.

"Five it is," she said before hanging up.

Tom and Elena remained silent, waiting for Katie to speak. The room was unbearably quiet. She could hear the *tick, tick, ticking* of the second hand on the clock. It drove her nuts. "He's on his way," she finally said. "He'll be here in five minutes."

"Do you want us to stay?" Tom sounded hopeful, but Elena's closed demeanor said the opposite.

"It doesn't matter. I can tell Tom wants to stay."

Tom smiled, his dimple popping out from his cheek, and nodded.

"But your mom's been sick," Katie said to Elena. "You probably should go check on her and get some rest yourself."

Elena stood and stretched. "Thank you. I'll let you know if I hear anything new about the five missing girls."

"Thanks," Katie said, although she suspected it was really four girls that remained missing so long as she was right about Maria. But she kept that information to herself just in case she happened to be wrong. "I'd appreciate that."

"Okay," Elena said, dropping her cell phone into a maroon

backpack and slinging it over her shoulder. "I'll see you tomorrow."

Elena headed toward the back door. There were a few beats of silence followed by the heavy bang of the door closing. Not two seconds later, the front door opened, and Michael Michello, Katie's father, stepped inside.

He wore a pair of slacks and a light blue button-down shirt. A midnight blue tie hung loose around his neck, looking more than a little like a noose. He was no longer wearing the jacket he'd had on when he'd left Stephanie's house, but Katie assumed that was in his car. Or whoever's car he'd been driving.

"Katie," her father said with a false note of excitement.

He strode up to the empty reception desk but stopped there, knowing that the area beyond was only for employees and those who had been invited into the space. Katie had not yet extended that invitation to Michael, and she wasn't sure if she would. There was something nice about the separation of the desk. It created space and some semblance of safety.

"Michael."

Michael stood there for a moment, then turned to Tom. "Michael Michello," he said, extending his hand as though they were at a business meeting.

Tom took it, as both Katie and her father had expected.

"Tom Archie. I'm a friend of Katie's."

"A friend, huh?" Michael's eyes darted from Katie to Tom in a way that irked her.

"Not *that* kind of friend," Tom said, flushing. "I, uhh, used to date her best friend."

"Ohhh, I see," Michael said, winking at Tom.

Katie bristled. "My personal life is none of your damn business, but since the topic of relationships has come up, let's get right to it. Are you screwing Stephanie Arkman?"

Michael sucked in a sharp breath, and he took a step back, shocked by Katie's bluntness.

"No," he said, once he regained his composure. "I'm not sure why you'd say that."

"Then why did I see you leaving from a side entrance of her house earlier today? You must have some kind of relationship. If it isn't sexual, then what?"

The silence stretched, but Katie refused to fill it. Yes, it was uncomfortable, but she was not going to do anything to relieve his level of discomfort, even if it meant she had to endure more.

"Professional. I'm doing some work for her."

"What kind of work?"

His job prior to imprisonment had been in the financial world. He had been a financial planner. Unfortunately, he'd taken the money of his clients and never actually invested it as he had claimed, and instead used it to run a Ponzi scheme. Unless Stephanie had an interest in earning herself a long stint in prison, Katie guessed that she had no desire to entangle herself in his previous profession.

"A little of this and a little of that."

"What kind of *this* and *thats*? Be more specific."

Michael sighed with exasperation. "I'm trying, Katie, really, I am. But I can't tell you some of this stuff."

"Because it's a crime?"

"No, because my job depends on it."

"How about this," Katie said, her nostrils flaring. "Your relationship with me depends on you answering. And you know I'm a stone's throw away from permanently cutting you out of my life anyway. So, which are you going to choose? Stephanie or me?"

"Fine, fine. But you have to promise not to tell anyone. And I need him to leave." He nodded toward Tom.

Tom started moving toward the door, but Katie grabbed his arm. "Tom stays, and you talk. That, or I walk."

"Okay, okay, but this has to stay quiet."

Both Tom and Katie agreed to keep his secrets, but Katie's promise was hollow. There was a good chance that Tom's was, too. She was going to tell Ashley no matter what, and she expected Tom would do the same, especially since they were working on a new, tentative friendship. Depending on the content of the information, Katie might also end up going to the proper authorities. She was not going to allow her father to victimize anyone else.

"You know I go way back with Stephanie's father, Arch, right?"

Katie nodded. "I remember him."

He'd been like a mentor to her father, introducing him to all the right people and sponsoring his entry into all the coveted country clubs across Iowa. But he'd retired several years earlier and tapped Stephanie as the child to take the reins of the business. Not that it was any real prize. All of the family members were set for life with fat trust funds. Stephanie didn't need the money, but perhaps it was the power that had attracted her to the position.

"Well, they've got an underground thing going. Where they bring up illegal immigrants from the Mexican border and hire them as employees."

"Okay." She didn't find this particular fact surprising. The Arkmans had two large businesses that needed manual work-ers: farms and meat-packing plants. It made sense that they would want reliable, cheap labor.

"How long?"

"Probably twenty years."

"I don't see what that has to do with you," Katie said, crossing her arms.

"Nothing. At least not before my imprisonment. I just knew about it. One day when I was in jail waiting for trial, the feds showed up. They told me they could convince the State to offer me a sweet deal if I'd agree to testify against the Arkman family about what the agent called 'human trafficking.' Of course, I refused. So, I ended up in prison with the Arkman family owing me a big favor."

"But why would you stand up for them when you could have gotten out and been with me?"

Michael shook his head slowly. "It wasn't an easy decision, but you were a teenager. You would be graduating from high school soon, and I reasoned that you had your mother."

"Well, I didn't have her. She left shortly after you were taken away."

"I found that out later. But even if I'd known before, I don't think it would have changed anything."

"Why not?"

"Because," he said with a note of exasperation, "what was I going to do to make money? How could I provide for you? Nobody would hire me."

Katie snorted. "I see. You decided it would be better to leave me to fend for myself so that you'd have a job and a powerful family owing you a favor once you got out."

"Something like that." He looked down. "I'm not proud of my decision, but that's what happened. If I'd been released back then, I would have been penniless. I knew the Arkmans would reward me if I kept their secret. And they did. Stephanie is giving me plenty of money to meet my needs."

"I've noticed the car."

"That's part of it."

"Did she pay for your cell phone for all these years?"

"Yes. Although, I didn't have it. An employee was using it

while I was imprisoned. So, that wasn't exactly an altruistic kindness. Stephanie benefitted, too."

"That sounds like her." Katie had already discovered that bit of information about Stephanie. She never did anything strictly for others. There was always something in it for her.

"Well, now, don't be too harsh on her. Stephanie really is good to her immigrant employees. Pays them well, provides medical treatment and even nice housing. She is basically running a charity for refugees."

"Charity, my ass," Katie growled.

"What?" Michael's bushy eyebrows shot up.

Katie turned and grabbed a print-off of the picture she'd taken of Stephanie's bracelet, slapping it on the top of the reception desk.

Michael glanced at it, knowing instantly who it belonged to. Katie could see it in the slight twitch of his jaw.

"That's Stephanie's, right?"

"Looks like it." His answer was reluctant, which annoyed Katie, but at least he wasn't lying to her.

"I took this photograph on Frank Vinny's property." She paused for effect. "While firefighters were working to put the fire out.

Michael's mouth formed into an *O*, but he didn't say anything.

"So, tell me, is burning people to death part of her 'charity' operations? Or did Frank and that other young lady just get lucky?"

Michael's shoulders slumped forward in such a look of defeat that Katie wished she had been recording their meeting. If for no other reason than to rewind and rewatch this unshakable man break down before her.

"That's not exactly how it happened."

"Then how did it happen?"

## 38

### ASHLEY

"Are you saying that Frank Vinney forced all fourteen of those girls to overdose?" George asked.

He'd set his pen and notepad aside, giving Morgan his whole, undivided attention. On its face, it seemed like a good thing for Morgan. That maybe she would get what she wanted —an offer of immunity—but Ashley knew better than to think so optimistically.

"Yes."

"Why?" George leaned back in his chair, crossing his legs at the ankles. "Why would Frank go through the trouble of getting these girls addicted—against their will, might I add— and then killing them? I know you aren't much of a logical thinker, Morgan, but I can't wrap my head around it. I mean, if his goal was more customers, then what incentive did he have to kill them?"

It was a good question, and it also meant that George had no intention of taking Morgan's words at face value. Not that Ashley ever believed that he would.

"He didn't want the girls as customers," Morgan said,

crossing her arms indignantly. "He used them as a perk for his customers."

"I don't follow."

"Frank has a card game that he plays with his male customers. He does it during those parties that he used to have a couple times a month out on his property."

"I know of the parties." George dropped his feet back on to the ground and sat up straighter, his interest piqued. "What happens at them?"

Morgan launched into the full story about the card game and the sexual assaults, and by the end of the story, George was on the edge of his seat. As shocked as Ashley had been when she'd originally heard the story.

"Okay, let's say everything you are telling me is true."

"It is true," Morgan insisted.

"For argument's sake, let's presume that I believe you. I still don't understand why Frank would then *kill* these girls. If it had been going on for ten years, he was getting away with it. Making a lot of money from each girl. Which means there are some holes in this story." He put emphasis on the word *story* like he believed it to be a fairy tale rather than an eyewitness account.

"I'm not lying. He killed them because they got difficult. Some tried to run, others tried to contact family members. Aubrey's sister, Maxine, he killed her because he found out that Aubrey had moved to town in search of her."

Ashley's breath caught at the mention of Aubrey's sister. Morgan didn't know that Aubrey had told Ashley that her sister was her reason for coming to town. It lent credence to Morgan's version of events. But it also meant that Morgan had been lying to Aubrey for over a year. They weren't friends, exactly, but it was pretty coldhearted for her to keep that kind of information back. Despite the odds, Aubrey had probably spent all that time hoping her sister was still alive. She didn't know for sure that her sister was dead, let alone buried in the backyard of the man who was selling her methamphetamine.

"Aubrey Miller?"

It was a clarification question, not a challenge, but Morgan did not react well to it. "Yes, Aubrey Miller. Who the hell else? Do you even know another Aubrey?"

George put his hands up in a sign of surrender. "Okay, so you're saying one of the bodies out there is Aubrey's sister, Maxine Miller. We should be able to figure that out easy enough. And you said the girl inside the barn was an illegal immigrant named," he leaned over and glanced at his notebook, "Juana Martinez. It might be harder to get a positive ID on her. But what about the other girls, the other thirteen?"

"Three of them were like Juana. They barely spoke English. But the other ten, those were runaways like Maxine."

"Huh," George huffed, his chest rising and lowering. "Where was Frank finding all these illegal immigrants? Iowa is a long way from the border."

"I don't know for sure, but I overheard him on the phone one day with someone. I don't normally pay attention to his phone conversations because he's usually selling the services of one girl or another—sometimes even me—and I'd rather be surprised than to be forced to sit there, waiting and knowing what was going to happen. But this phone call, he was polite to the person. Called her ma'am."

"Okay. And what was the content of the call?"

"He was arranging the transportation of people from the border back to Iowa. To work or something. I think that's how he found the Mexican girls. They 'fell off the truck,' is what I once heard him say about them. He also said they were his favorites because he didn't have to worry about anyone looking for them. Their families couldn't call the cops because they weren't supposed to be here anyway."

Ashley shook her head in disgust. Frank had thought of those people as items rather than humans. It was revolting. She'd always thought of Frank as unnerving, but she could hardly believe the depths of that man's behavior. And to think she'd represented him. Kept him out of jail so he could continue doing these horrible, unforgivable acts.

"Who was Frank talking to when he arranged to get the immigrants from the border?"

Ashley suspected she knew the answer, but she wasn't about to volunteer that information to law enforcement.

"I don't know. Like I said, I wasn't meant to hear it. I couldn't go up to Frank and say, 'I was eavesdropping, and I want to know who you were talking to.' Frank would have beat my face in. Or, worse, he would have forced one of those over-loaded needles into my arm and I'd be pushing up daisies like the rest of those girls."

"Okay," George said. He glanced at his notepad again. "You said there were a total of sixteen girls. You've told me about fifteen of them. The fourteen bodies and then the girl that was burned in the barn. But what about the last, that sixteenth girl?"

Morgan shrugged. "I don't know what happened to her. She must have gotten away."

"Do you know her name?"

"Yeah. Maria Garcia."

George grabbed his notepad. "Maria Garcia, you say? Where can I find her?"

"Hell if I know."

But Ashley knew of one person who might have the answer. And that was Katie. She'd been at Stephanie's house earlier that evening, snooping around. Maybe she'd come across something that linked Frank, Stephanie, and even this Maria girl. Katie was an excellent investigator, so Ashley presumed that she had discovered *something.* Which meant that she needed to talk to Katie before this interview progressed any further. George didn't seem inclined to offer Morgan anything yet. But maybe, just maybe, Katie had the information that would change his mind.

"Let's take a short break," Ashley said, pushing off the wall. "Give Morgan a chance to rest. We can reconvene in," she glanced at her watch, "ten minutes. That sound good?"

George issued a sigh of annoyance and muttered something that sounded a lot like *attorneys* under his breath, but he begrudgingly agreed.

## 39

### KATIE

The Public Defender's Office was quiet. Most of the lights had been shut off. The only illumination was from the bulbs above the reception area. Katie's father remained on one side of the desk—on the outside—while Tom and Katie were on the other.

Michael had begged Katie to send Tom away so he could discuss his business relationship with Stephanie in privacy, to "keep it within the family," but Katie had refused. Tom's presence was comforting to her. She didn't want to be alone with Michael. There might be one day that she'd forgive him for his betrayals, but not yet. His honesty here could be a huge step in the right direction, but that was out of her control.

"So, tell me, why is it that this bangle," Katie said, tapping a photograph of the bracelet with her index finger, "ended up in Frank's forest? And don't even bother to sell me some bullshit lie about Stephanie being there for some legitimate reason. I knew Frank from my law enforcement days, and he's not interested in legitimacy."

"Right." Michael swallowed hard. "Stephanie wasn't ever there."

Katie crossed her arms. She couldn't believe this. Or maybe she could. He was going to lie straight to her face. Which seemed shocking, but hadn't he done that to her his entire life? Lying to her about his "successful" business, when all the while he'd been stealing from his clients.

"Then how did that bangle, the one she never takes off, find its way into the forest?"

"This is a long story," Michael said, running a hand through his hair, mussing it.

"I've got plenty of time."

"Okay, well, the truth is that Stephanie and Frank have had an arrangement. It dated back to before Frank was an adult when his father was still around."

"Brad Vinny." That was Frank's father's name. Katie knew of Brad, but she hadn't ever met the man. He wasn't a problem for law enforcement, not like his son, but George had told Katie that Brad wasn't always so straitlaced. He'd had his brushes with the law when he was young. He'd just grown out of it. Frank, unfortunately, never did. "Didn't he die of a heart attack several years ago?"

"Yeah. Five years ago. But before that, he had an arrangement with the Arkman family. Once every couple of months, when the family made the request, he'd drive down south in his Winnebago and pick up a group of immigrants. Usually, it was one family or two. The Arkmans had learned a long time ago that migrant workers were loyal, they worked harder than most employees, and they stayed away from drugs. The family paid Brad well, and everyone was happy. It was a partnership beneficial to everyone."

Katie considered the information. It sounded truthful, and it fit with what she knew about the Arkman family and their hiring of immigrant workers. Someone had to bring them to Iowa, and Brad Vinny was as good an option as any. He did have an old beat-up Winnebago. She remembered because he had kept it next to his house downtown, and the neighbors used to call and report it all the time. It was technically a violation of city policy to store a mobile home in a driveway, but Katie still felt like the complaints were a little petty. Yes, it was an eyesore, but it wasn't hurting anybody.

"When Frank got old enough, Brad introduced him to the family business," Michael continued. "Brad would take him along for the rides. The idea was that Frank would take over once Brad retired, which was sooner than anyone had planned, thanks to those blockages in his arteries. But everything was in place when Brad passed. It was supposed to be a seamless transfer, and it was at first, but then there were issues."

"What kind of issues?"

"Now, I was in prison when this all happened, so I'm going off what I've heard. I don't know anything firsthand."

"And you heard it from Stephanie, I assume."

"Yes. This part, at least."

Katie nodded and made a *go on* gesture with her hand.

"Well, that's when Stephanie started getting complaints about girls disappearing. The first few times, she didn't know what to think. There were so many things that could go wrong along the drive, and Frank wasn't the most likable person. He claimed they ran away, or they disappeared overnight or whatever, and Stephanie believed him. But that changed with the disappearances of the fourth and fifth girls."

"What were their names? The girls that disappeared?"

"I don't know about the earlier ones, but the two Stephanie was primarily concerned about were named Juana and Maria. They disappeared more recently."

That also fit with the information Katie had received from

Elena. Five girls, the last two being Juana and Maria. "How recently?"

"Juana was several months ago. Stephanie was in the process of figuring out what had happened to her. She'd hired a private investigator, but that person couldn't get onto Frank's property to see what was going on. Then Maria disappeared, and Stephanie decided she couldn't wait any longer. She needed someone who could get onto the property without suspicion and report back to her."

"And that was..."

"Aubrey Miller."

Katie was taken aback. "Aubrey? I thought you were going to say Morgan Stanman."

"No. Morgan was too far into the drugs. She wasn't reliable. Although, Aubrey did say that Frank was playing games with Morgan. Telling her he wouldn't give her any more dope. I don't know how true that is or if he even meant it, but Aubrey said Morgan was pretty bothered by it."

If that was true, it could have been the motive behind Morgan setting the fire. He had her so addicted, she might have done about anything to get the drugs. Maybe she'd been trying to get him to hand some over, but things didn't go the way she had planned.

"Aubrey found both Juana and Maria. They were locked in the shed outside. Both were dirty and coming off serious meth highs. She left them there, though, and reported back to Stephanie. And that's where I came in. Stephanie hired me to drive Aubrey back out there to let the girls out. She was scared. She said Frank would kill her if he ever found out. Stephanie promised her a big payout, so she agreed, but she wanted to take something for leverage. To make Stephanie show that she was serious about the money. Stephanie offered to pay half before and half after, but that wasn't good enough for Aubrey. She wanted Stephanie's bracelet. Stephanie didn't have anyone else who was somewhat reliable and who could get onto the property without raising alarms, so she agreed."

"And Aubrey dropped it in the forest."

Michael nodded. "I don't know if it was intentional or not, but Stephanie was pretty pissed. Aubrey claimed that she didn't know where she dropped it. I'm sure Stephanie would appreciate it if you would tell her where it is."

Katie grunted noncommittally. That all depended on the next part of the story.

"Okay, so Aubrey went back and released the girls."

"Well, not *girls*. She could only find Maria."

"Then she lit the fire and burned Frank intentionally and Juana by accident."

Michael shook his head. "I don't think so. She put Maria in the car and said she had to go back and do something. I left with Maria because that was the plan. I don't know how Aubrey made her way back to town, but she did."

"So, why did you say that you don't think Aubrey set the fire? It sounds like she easily could have done it."

"Because I never saw any smoke. Not the whole drive back to Brine or past that and onto Stephanie's property. That kind of fire, I would have been able to see something. I didn't even hear any emergency sirens. The fire alarm must have come through far after I had left with Maria."

"Maybe she waited to light the fire."

"That's possible, but I don't know why she would do that."

"There's only one way to find out," Katie said. "I'll have to talk to Aubrey."

Aubrey was still in jail, serving a sentence for possession of methamphetamine. It was getting late, nearing ten o'clock, but the jail staff would let Katie in. Or so she hoped.

# 40

---

## ASHLEY

Ashley paced back and forth along the long hospital corridor, her ballerina flats tapping against the linoleum flooring. She dialed Katie's number. When there was no answer, she tried again. But she wasn't answering.

*What is going on?* she wondered. This wasn't like Katie. She hadn't heard from Katie since before she left with Tom to go to Stephanie Arkman's house. Had something happened to her? Should Ashley be worried?

She paced several long loops, passing by Morgan's door and her guard, Deputy Zachary Brinks, several times. His eyes followed her, but he didn't say anything. George had disappeared, which brought her some solace. At least he wasn't present to see her deteriorate into a ball of worry and frustration. She ignored Zachary and pressed the redial button, bringing the phone to her ear. But as she did, something—or rather someone—caught her attention.

It was Tom. He was coming down the hallway toward her, moving in long, familiar strides. Yet there was something hesitant in his gait, like he was eager but unsure.

*Tom*, Ashley thought with relief. *Tom is here, and everything will be okay.* It was an automatic reaction. A residual response. One left over from the time that they'd spent together as a couple. Or perhaps it had started earlier than that, back when they had only been friends. And if that was the case, she didn't have to stifle the emotion. They were friends now. It was okay to rely on him. Wasn't it?

He came to a stop in front of her, his clear blue eyes searching her face for something, but Ashley didn't know what it was. Maybe a sign. She wanted to give whatever it was to him. To bury all the hurt in their past. Perhaps she could. She wanted to try, but she didn't know what to say. In the end, all she could manage was, "Where's Katie?"

Tom's gaze dropped to his shoes. "She's at the jail, talking to Aubrey."

"Aubrey?" Ashley said, surprised. "Why?" Aubrey's case was resolved. All that was left for her was to serve a thirty-day sentence and then she'd be cut loose. It seemed odd for Katie to suddenly take an interest in her, especially when there was so much more to do with Morgan's case.

"So much has happened," Tom said with a heavy sigh. "Let me fill you in."

Tom took her by the hand, and to her astonishment, she didn't resist. A small part of her wanted to, but the larger portion screamed for her to not only allow the contact but to accept this beautiful man's attention with open arms. He led her down the hallway in silence and to a cafeteria. It was nearing ten thirty at night, so the lights had been lowered, the kitchen closed. They were the only people there, which afforded them some semblance of privacy. Tom released her hand, and they both sat down.

"What's going on?" Ashley asked.

"So much."

"I don't mean to rush you," Ashley glanced at her watch,

"but I've got about five minutes before George starts the meeting with my client without me."

Their friendship was still tentative, and it showed in the way that they spoke to one another. A year ago, Ashley would not have been so polite. She would have looked at her watch and said, *Hurry it up, Tom, I'm running out of time.* It was a distinction that wasn't lost on Tom. She could see it in the momentary sag of his shoulders.

"We, well, Katie, found something at Stephanie's house. Actually someone. We found someone."

He was rambling, and it was her fault. She'd made things weird between them. She'd refused to provide forgiveness once it was due. Sure, he deserved punishment for lying to her about his roommate all those months ago, but hadn't she done that when she'd broken up with him? She'd been too furious back then to realize that she was going overboard, allowing her anger to consume her. But all that resentment had dissipated over the past few days, and she could see things more clearly now.

"Who did you find?" Ashley said, reaching across and placing a hand over Tom's.

"Her name is Maria."

A burst of excitement shot through Ashley. "Maria Garcia?" she said excitedly. "Where? How? I have so many questions."

Tom smiled. "It wouldn't be like you if you didn't." Then he launched into a story about Katie's adventures snooping around Stephanie's house and finished with the meeting at the Public Defender's Office with Katie's father.

"Holy shit." It was all Ashley could think to say.

This turn of events could be so good for Morgan. Especially if Aubrey confessed. There was an eyewitness that could place Aubrey at the scene of the crime shortly before the fire started. Sure, Michael Michello claimed that he hadn't heard any sirens or seen any smoke, but he also wouldn't have been looking for it. His focus would have been getting Maria back to Stephanie's house for medical treatment. Which led to Ashley's next question.

"Why would Michael Michello take Maria to Stephanie's house instead of the hospital?"

Tom shrugged. "Maybe because she's not legally in the country. Stephanie might have been afraid of deportation."

It was just like Tom to believe the best in everyone. But Ashley didn't think Stephanie's intent was that altruistic. If Maria and her family were caught, Stephanie could be in trouble, too. She was the one arranging for immigrant labor without using the proper channels. Not that Ashley was opposed to it, but it was still illegal.

"Do you believe him?" Ashley asked.

"Katie's father?"

"Yeah."

"I don't know," Tom said, shaking his head. "Katie would be a better person to ask. This was my first time meeting him. He seemed honest, but I don't have any background to base that assumption on. It's little more than a guess."

"Well, Katie must have found something believable about the story if she rushed over to the jail." Ashley could barely contain her excitement. This could be the breakthrough they needed in Morgan's case.

"Yeah, but he's a felon. And his crime is one of dishonesty..."

Tom had a point. Michael Michello had been convicted of a felony that was a theft-related offense. If he was called to the stand to testify, opposing counsel could, and would, point those two things out to the jury, as well as note the connection between Michael and Katie. Any one of those things was a problem, but all three could prove devastating to their defense.

It meant that Ashley could not take Michael's statement at face value. It would fall apart in court, and Ashley would look like a fool for putting on such shaky evidence. They would need some heavy corroboration, but perhaps that was the reason Katie had rushed over to see Aubrey.

Ashley wished that she could be there with Katie, to hear Aubrey's words straight from her mouth and gauge her expression. But she couldn't. Morgan was in the middle of an ill-advised proffer, and there was no talking her out of it. Ashley had already tried on more than one occasion, and this new information about Aubrey would not be enough to change Morgan's mind.

"Thanks for letting me know," Ashley said, patting Tom on the hand before pushing her chair back and standing up. "I've got to get back to that train wreck of a meeting between my client and King George."

"Okay." Tom looked uncertain. Like he wanted to help, but he didn't know how.

"Can you let Katie know where I am and ask her to stop by when she's done with Aubrey?"

Tom nodded and smiled. It was the first time that Ashley had asked him for anything since they'd severed ties. Ashley could have sent a text to Katie herself, but she knew she needed to give him a way in. It was a small request, but it carried significant implications, at least to them. Because to these two former lovers, there was no mistaking what it meant. A start of something more.

# 41

## KATIE

Katie sat across from Aubrey. They were in the attorney-client room at the jail, a first for Katie without having Ashley at her side.

Aubrey yawned and stretched. "So, what's this all about? I was almost asleep. Do you know how hard it is to sleep in a place like this?" She gestured to the solid steel walls around her.

"No, but I can imagine."

"The banging doors, buzzing lights, and constant chattering. It's enough to drive anyone insane."

"Is that what happened to Morgan?"

"No. Morgan was crazy before she got here. This place didn't help."

"You gave her the toothbrush, didn't you?"

"Morgan and I are cordial, but we aren't friends."

"You didn't answer my question."

"Did I give it to her? No. Might she have found it? Yeah."

"Did she find it as a shank or a toothbrush?"

Aubrey shrugged.

"Why?"

Aubrey shrugged again and leaned back in her chair, relaxed.

"You want to know what I think?"

"Does it matter?"

Katie huffed out a superficial laugh. "I think you wanted Morgan to kill herself. It would solve a lot of problems for you."

"You have no idea what you are talking about."

"I know about your arrangement with Stephanie Arkman and Michael Michello."

Aubrey was picking at her nails, and she froze when she heard that. With what looked like a tremendous amount of effort, she went back to her nails and said, "What arrangement?"

"This is going to come as a surprise to you, but Michael is my father."

Aubrey looked up, her mouth dropping open.

"We don't look much alike, do we?" Katie said with a half-hearted smile. "It's why I've been able to slip into a new identity in a new location and few people connected the dots."

Aubrey worked her jaw, clenching and unclenching her teeth. Agitated, but holding her silence.

"I can tell that you don't want to talk, so I'll do the talking for you. I know you were out at Frank's property shortly before the fire. I know you were there looking for some children of Stephanie's employees that had gone missing. I know that you were keeping Stephanie's bangle as leverage, and you dropped it by accident. I also know that you found and rescued a girl named Maria. That was the girl that my father drove back to Stephanie's home."

Aubrey slipped lower in her seat, trying to make herself smaller.

"Am I right?" When no answer followed, Katie said, "I am, aren't I?"

"Not about all of it."

"Okay. Where am I wrong?"

"I wasn't looking for Stephanie's employees' children. At least not specifically. I was looking for my sister. I thought he was keeping her alive somewhere off the property. I told Ashley Maxine had left with Frank when she ran away. When I heard about immigrant girls, I thought he'd have them all together somewhere. It turned out that he only had the one. Or, actually, two, but I didn't know the other girl was in the barn."

"You didn't know when you set the barn on fire?"

"No." Aubrey shot Katie a narrow-eyed glare. "I didn't know when I locked the barn door. You see, he wouldn't tell me where I could find the girls. I had to lock him inside before he would answer. We spoke for a little while through the door, but I never heard a girl in there. It sounded like it was only him."

"Okay. Then what happened?"

"I locked him inside and told him that I wouldn't let him out until he told me where I could find the girls. Then he said to look in the shed. I did, and I found Maria there. She was a complete mess, but she was the only one. I brought her up the path to Michael, er, your father, and she got in the car. I was supposed to leave with them, but I turned around and went back."

*This is it*, Katie thought. Aubrey was going to confess, and it would save Morgan's case. "Did you go back to set the fire?"

"No." Aubrey shook her head vehemently. "I already told you that I didn't set the fire. I went back to ask more questions about my sister. I didn't know then that it would be a waste of time. She had been gone and buried as soon as I got to town.

But I didn't know that at the time. I didn't know until Morgan started running her mouth in here." Aubrey gestured to the concrete walls surrounding them. "The bitch knew the whole time that Maxine was dead. She could have told me, but she didn't."

"Is that why you left your toothbrush out?"

"Damn straight. She was losing it. I had tried to help her. You know I did. I kept warning Ashley that she was going to try to hurt herself. But then, one day, she starts telling a story about a girl that ran from Frank. She was talking to Erica, but I was their cell mate. I heard it all. Morgan said he'd caught the girl and injected her with a lethal amount of dope. She described how the girl died. It was disgusting, but also fascinating. Until she described a tattoo on the girl's ankle. How Frank had cut it off and thrown it into the fire. Two little doves with a circle around them. It was supposed to symbolize my family. Me and Maxine. That bitch didn't even know she was talking about my sister. Or maybe she did. She was just too far off the deep end to put two and two together."

"I see," Katie said, but it wasn't in a judgmental way.

She was starting to see Aubrey in a different light. If she'd been in Aubrey's shoes, she might have followed the same course of action. To hear about the death of a sibling in such a horrible way, well, it was unforgivable. Morgan should have been thankful that Aubrey gave her a decision at all. She could have taken the shank and plunged it into Morgan's neck.

"If you didn't start the fire, who did?"

"Honestly, it could have been anyone. There were so many people on and off that property, looking for a fix. But my best guess is that the cops are right on this one."

"You're saying Morgan did it?"

"Yeah."

"How did you come to that conclusion?"

"Because she was there, too."

"Okay." Katie was skeptical, but she was willing to hear Aubrey out.

"I went back down to ask Frank about Maxine, but I was too late. Morgan was standing right where I had been a few minutes earlier, talking to Frank through the barn door."

"What was she saying?"

"I don't know, but I didn't stick around to find out. I thought Morgan was going to let him out. I figured she was there to buy dope, and she couldn't do that unless she opened the door. Which would have been a real problem for me. Frank's a psycho when it comes to revenge. If she let him out and I was still there, he was going to kill me. I felt it deep in my bones. Even before I knew about what he'd done to Maxine and all those other girls."

"So, Morgan killed Frank?"

"She's the one with gasoline on her hands. It's too late to test mine, but I'm being truthful. I didn't start that fire. Now that I know about Maxine, I wish I would have. It would have been nice to be the one to avenge my sister, but that wasn't the case. I didn't know then what I know now."

Katie believed Aubrey. It fit with what her father had told her, and it also matched all the facts that she had learned about the case. That meant that George Thomanson had been right all along. Morgan had been the one who struck the final, fatal match.

Katie picked up her phone and texted Ashley. *Are you still at the hospital?*

*Yeah. Detective Dickbag is here, and Morgan is proffering.*

"Shit," Katie said aloud.

"What?" Aubrey asked.

"I've got to go."

She stood and typed out a message to Ashley while she

waited for the jailers to let her out. *Take a break. I'm on my way. I have something to tell you.*

Then she rushed out of the jail and down the stairs, desperate to get to the hospital. If Ashley couldn't put a stop to the proffer meeting, Morgan was going to screw herself. While Katie had little sympathy for most murderers, Frank was a special kind of evil. He did deserve to die. If she'd been where Morgan was at the time, knowing what she knew, she would have lit the match herself and stood back to watch the whole place burn.

# 42

## ASHLEY

Ashley read through Katie's text message. Katie was on the way with some important information. Otherwise, she wouldn't have interrupted Ashley while she was at the hospital, and she wouldn't have insisted on Ashley stalling the proffer.

"We need to take another break," Ashley said, tucking her phone into her back pocket.

"Another one? Seriously?" George said, dropping his pen on top of his notepad with a *thwump*. "We're never going to get through this tonight at this rate."

Ashley shrugged. "I need to go to the bathroom."

"Why didn't you go when we took the last break?" He sounded like he was speaking to a petulant child.

Ashley bristled. "Are you really going to question why a woman of my age might need to use the restroom? *Really*? Because if you don't already know, it isn't my place to explain to you what happens with a woman's body once a month, unless, of course, she's pregnant, which I'm not."

George's eyes widened, and his face turned beet red. "Sorry."

"Sorry, my ass," Ashley muttered as she shoved up from her chair, grabbing her computer bag and stalking toward the door. Before leaving the room, she turned back to Morgan. "Do not breathe a word to that man until after I return. Are we clear?"

Morgan nodded, but Ashley didn't trust her, or George for that matter. When she stepped out into the hallway, she found Tom chatting amiably with Deputy Brinks.

"Tom," she said with a relieved sigh. "I need your help."

"Sure, anything," he said, then turned back to Zachary. "Send me your résumé, okay? I'll make sure it gets to Forest. The funds are there, so the formation of the MEHR team should be a done deal, and we're going to need one or two more members."

"Thanks," Zachary said.

Tom patted him on the shoulder, then walked over to Ashley, his smile widening. "What do you need me to do?"

"Stand here," she motioned to the area just outside Morgan's door, "and make sure Georgie and Morgan don't strike up a conversation while I'm gone."

"I can do that."

"Thanks," Ashley said before turning and jogging down the hallway toward the waiting area.

A few moments later, Katie came through the front door. She scanned the room. When her eyes fell on Ashley, she swiftly walked toward her.

"What is it? What did Aubrey have to say?"

Katie filled Ashley in on her visit with Aubrey. It was a shock to hear that Aubrey had known that Morgan was guilty from the start and that she'd kept it a secret, but the surprise wore off quickly. They were part of a different kind of society. One where everyone minded their own business and kept far away from law enforcement. In that vein, it made perfect sense that Aubrey wouldn't say anything. But would that change now that Aubrey knew that Morgan had known about her sister and never spoke up?

"Shit," Ashley said, hissing through her teeth. "I can't think of a way that Morgan isn't screwed."

"What? Why?" Katie said, furrowing her brow.

"Aubrey's going to go to the cops once she finds out that Morgan survived her suicide attempt. Or whatever you'd call her wrist cutting." Ashley still didn't believe that Morgan had ever intended any lasting damage. She wanted out of jail, and she'd gotten it. Now that she was in the hospital rather than a jail cell, she seemed perfectly happy and normal.

Katie nodded. "Probably."

They were both silent for a long moment, Ashley chewing on her lip and Katie tapping her toe.

"So," Katie said. "What do we do?"

Ashley sighed heavily. These kinds of decisions were tough, and they weighed on Ashley. If she made the wrong choice, her client could end up in prison serving a life sentence. "I guess we finish with the proffer. It's the only chance Morgan has."

"Okay," Katie said dejectedly. She, too, understood that there was no great solution to Morgan's problem.

"We better head back before Sir George loses his mind," Ashley said, glancing at her watch. "It's been ten minutes, and he isn't one for waiting."

Katie gestured with an open palm as if to say, *After you*, and Ashley started making her way back down the hallway, Katie following close behind. They were halfway back when Tom came rushing toward them.

At first Ashley felt a surge of irritation working its way into her chest, but then she saw the look on Tom's face. He was practically radiating excitement.

"What's got you all sunshine and daisies? It can't be the surroundings," Katie said, nodding at the drab hospital walls.

"No. No." He shook his head. "You aren't going to believe this." He grabbed them both by the wrist, one in each hand, and pulled them to the side of the wide hallway. "George left Morgan's room to take a phone call. He must not have seen me standing there, because I overheard the whole thing. Whoever he was talking to was speaking pretty loudly, so I heard every word."

"Stop with the suspense, Tom," Ashley said, "and spit it out already."

His smile widened at her sharp response. They were getting back to normal, slowly but surely. "He was talking to the medical examiner. Toxicology came back for the girl that burned in Frank's barn."

"Juana Martinez," Ashley said.

"I'm not sure that they've identified the girl yet, but—"

"It's Juana," Katie said.

"Anyway," Tom said, his even, white smile flashing in the florescent lighting. "She had an astronomical amount of meth in her system. The ME said that she was likely dead or almost dead at the time of the fire."

That was good news. Juana was the only sympathetic victim of the two. Frank's name was going to be dragged through the coals soon, considering the number of bodies buried out there on his property. By Ashley's count, there were a total of fifteen bodies, counting Juana's, and one survivor, Maria.

"All right," Ashley said, clapping her hands together. "Let's get back in there and put an end to Morgan's proffer agreement. The State's case has just taken a nose dive."

Ashley, Katie, and Tom entered the hospital room, Tom closing the door behind them. Ashley spoke first, telling her client all the information that they'd gathered over the past couple of days, including what they learned from Aubrey. By the end, Morgan looked dejected.

"What do I do?" she asked, her eyes as wide as a newborn fawn's. "I'm screwed."

"Maybe, maybe not. But you've got a lot better shot now. And finishing this proffer will only make things worse."

"It will?" Morgan's eyes darted from Ashley to Tom, as though asking for confirmation. It annoyed the shit out of Ashley—how so many people seemed to need a man's approval before they even considered a piece of advice—but she kept that thought to herself.

"Fine," Morgan said after a long pause. "Let's end it."

# EPILOGUE
## ASHLEY

Two Months Later

Butterflies flitted through Ashley's chest as she sat there next to Morgan at counsel table. Charles Hanson was seated at a table nearly identical to theirs, except his was closer to the jury box. The room was full, every seat taken, but not by onlookers. These were potential jury members empaneled for State of Iowa versus Morgan Stanman. The trial for Frank Vinny's murder and arson for burning his barn. The State had dismissed the second murder charge after they found out Juana was already dead when the fire had started.

Court administration had chosen to call in more than one hundred potential jurors. The panel had been expanded due to the vast amount of media coverage. Ashley could have asked for a change of venue and had the trial moved to another location that had less of an interest in the goings-on in Brine County, but she had decided against it. She wanted Frank's trial to be here in front of his neighbors, the same ones who now knew all about his sordid sex games, including the rape and murder of innocent young girls. She couldn't think of a better place to try a case.

"All rise," the bailiff shouted.

Ashley hopped to her feet, giddy with excitement. Trials were her favorite part of her job. The hard work of preparation was already done, and all that was left to do was to present their side of the story. And what a story Morgan had to tell.

"The Honorable Judge Ahrenson presiding," the bailiff said as the tall, wiry frame of the familiar judge swept into the courtroom.

"Are the parties ready to proceed?" the judge asked, and both Ashley and Charles answered affirmatively.

Ashley's gaze cut to her client. She was in a white, long-sleeved sweater that belonged to Ashley, the furry cashmere contrasting nicely with her dishwater-blond hair. Color had returned to Morgan's cheeks, and she'd put on some weight since her term in the hospital. Judge Ahrenson had reconsidered her bond after her suicide attempt and allowed her to remain home on strict house arrest pending trial.

The judge started out by introducing himself and all the parties to the jury, before motioning for Charles Hanson to start his portion of jury selection. In the legal community, it was called voir dire, and it allowed both attorneys a chance to personally address the jurors. The first set of proposed jurors were already seated in the jury box, and Charles Hanson stood and began his questioning.

Like many prosecutors, he took forever to get through his set of questions. He spoke for a full four hours, and the jury was half asleep by the time it was Ashley's turn. But she didn't mind. She didn't have a lot to ask. She already knew that these people were on her side. They were from Brine, after all, and they didn't take well to unsympathetic victims. And that was precisely what Frank Vinny was.

Ashley rose from her seat and approached the jury box, clasping her hands in front of her before addressing the potential jurors. "By a show of hands, who here knows the legend of Robin Hood?"

Several hands shot up, but most people hesitated, looking to their neighbors for guidance. This was expected. Those that answered right away were the leaders of the group, the likely candidates for foreperson if they were chosen to serve on the jury.

Ashley waited in silence, and within a few moments, all hands were in the air.

"That's what I thought," Ashley said with a chuckle.

She glanced down at her map of names. It was something that every trial attorney did, arranging the names of jurors onto a seating chart. They did it so they could call upon jurors as though they were in a classroom, partially to create rapport, but also so the court reporter could take down who in the jury had spoken.

"Mr. Davis," she said. He had been the first to raise his hand to the Robin Hood question. "You were quick to raise your hand. I take it you like the story."

"My mum used to read it to me at bedtime when I was just a lad."

Ashley smiled. "Mine too." She moved closer to Mr. Davis, who was in the middle of the jury group. "You know that Mr. Hood was a criminal, right?"

"Yeah. But the good kind of criminal."

This was precisely the answer that Ashley had hoped for. "What makes him the *good* kind of criminal?"

"He helped his community."

"Would you consider preventing the future rape of chil-dren to be helpful to a community?"

"Objection," Charles Hanson said, jumping to his feet. But the question was already out there, and Mr. Davis was more than willing to answer.

"Yes, I would. And that Vinny guy can rot in hell, if you ask me," Mr. Davis said, his gaze cutting to Morgan. "Your client did us a favor."

And that was the beginning of the end of the prosecution's case against Morgan.

## UNSOLICITED CONTACT
## ASHLEY MONTGOMERY LEGAL THRILLER Book 4

**When her client is charged with his girlfriend's brutal murder, defense attorney Ashley Montgomery will fight to clear his name in this gripping legal thriller.**

Public defender Ashley Montgomery is shocked when a well-known Brine local is found in a lake at the outskirts of Brine County, dead and locked inside a large toolbox. Ashley has represented the victim and her boyfriend, Noah, for many years.

The Brine County sheriff's department goes after Noah as their main suspect, but Ashley is intent on his innocence, and she injects herself into the investigation to protect him. A search of his house turns up a series of letters addressed to Erica. The letters prove that someone else was in contact with the victim before her death, but a deputy sheriff takes them away before Ashley can get a closer look.

The stakes rise even higher when other women in town start receiving similar letters, including Rachel, Ashley's close friend and long-term houseguest. Now, Ashley must race against the clock to discover the identity of the killer...before he adds another victim to his list.

**Get your copy today at SevernRiverPublishing.com/Laura-Snider**

# JOIN THE READER LIST

Never miss a new release! Sign up to receive exclusive updates from author Laura Snider.

**Join today at**
**SevernRiverPublishing.com/Laura-Snider**

# YOU MIGHT ALSO ENJOY...

**Ashley Montgomery Legal Thrillers**

Unsympathetic Victims

Undetermined Death

Unforgivable Acts

Unsolicited Contact

Never miss a new release! Sign up to receive exclusive updates from author Laura Snider

**SevernRiverPublishing.com/Laura-Snider**

# ACKNOWLEDGMENTS

Although none of this book was on true people or true events, so much of life makes its way into writing fiction. My career as an attorney has helped me form many of my ideas. My everyday interactions with other attorneys, clients, court reporters, and judges created that fodder of inspiration needed to bring these characters and their stories to life. For that, I want to thank all those involved in the criminal justice system that I have worked with over my many years in practice, especially Paul Rounds and Michelle Wolf, both public defenders and true inspirations when it comes to defense work.

Of course, I wouldn't be writing this acknowledgement at all if it weren't for the continued and constant support that I receive from my family. From my parents, Madonna Mergenmeier, Dennis Mergenmeier, Alan Barnaby and Tammy Barnaby who have supported me all my life, giving me the fortitude and opportunities to complete many years of higher education. To my husband who has supported by writing career from the start, and my children, H.S., M.S., and W.S., who are an abundant source of everyday joy.

A special thanks to my agent, Stephanie Hansen, of Metamorphosis Literary Agency. She gave me a chance when there were so many other authors begging for her representation. Her constant determination and encouragement created the gateway for my books to see publication. Without her, this book and this series would not exist. She literally makes dreams come true.

Thank you to all members of the Severn River Publishing Team. You saw potential in my books and in me. Your professionalism, organization, and attention to detail transformed a good book into a fantastic series. Every day I continued to be impressed by your devotion to your authors.

# ABOUT THE AUTHOR

Laura Snider is a practicing lawyer in Iowa. She graduated from Drake Law School in 2009 and spent most of her career as a Public Defender. Throughout her legal career, she has been involved in all levels of crimes from petty thefts to murders. These days she is working part-time as a prosecutor and spends the remainder of her time writing stories and creating characters.

Laura lives in Iowa with her husband, three children, two dogs, and two very mischievous cats.

CPSIA information can be obtained
at www.ICGtesting.com
Printed in the USA
BVHW062131010322
630318BV00007B/505

9 781648 751776